I0760961

SMART MOUTH

WORK FOR IT BOOK #4

EMMA LEE JAYNE

WWW.SMARTYPANTSROMANCE.COM

COPYRIGHT

This book is a work of fiction. Names, characters, places, rants, facts, contrivances, and incidents are either the product of the author's questionable imagination or are used factitiously. Any resemblance to actual persons, living or dead or undead, events, locales is entirely coincidental if not somewhat disturbing/concerning.

Print Edition
ISBN: 978-1-959097-49-5

CHAPTER 1

TOM

The first time I saw Gwen, she was hanging upside down over the edge of my childhood bunk bed.

I was fifteen and hadn't been home to Austin in over four months. Boys of Summer was still in "rehearsals," but hadn't released anything yet. Dad and I had been living north of Dallas in the huge, soulless mansion that Clark, the band's manager, had rented for all of us.

For the first time since I'd been hired to be the fifth member in Boys of Summer, Clark gave us the weekend off. Because he was a manipulative bastard who liked to torment all of us, he only gave us twelve hours' notice. Which meant James, Bex, and Mom weren't there by the time Dad and I made it home to Austin.

This was back when James was still doing his competitive piano thing and they were in Houston for the weekend. Mom wanted to pull James from the competition and come straight home, but I begged her not to. Instead, Dad basically dropped me on Mom's doorstep and went to "catch up with friends." Which was code for hang out in a bar and try to get laid. Which was basically what he did in Dallas, too.

So there I was, alone in the house. *Alone* alone, in a way I hadn't been in months. So, I went into the bedroom I used to share with James, climbed into the bottom bunk, and slept.

I guess Gwen let herself in while I slept, because when I woke up, there she was, dangling upside down from the top bunk. Her hair was a mass of red curls that seemed to encompass my entire field of vision. The afternoon light streaming in from the bedroom hit her curls and lit them up.

"Oh, you're awake!" she said, as she awkwardly flipped over and landed in a lump of curls and denim overalls, before popping back to her feet. "I thought you were in Houston for the weekend."

I had no idea who she was or what she was doing in my house, but before I could respond, she looked me over and gasped.

"Oh my god! Were you masturbating?"

"What? No!" I responded automatically, sitting up and hitting my head on the top bunk.

"You had your hand down your pants," she pointed out.

I jerked my hand out of my pants. "I'm a guy. That's how we sleep sometimes. Who are you?"

"What is wrong with you? How hard did you hit your head?" She laughed.

I climbed out the bottom bunk, rubbing the spot on my forehead, praying it wouldn't leave a mark because that was the last thing I needed to catch shit about from Clark. "Not hard enough that I don't care that there's a strange girl in my room."

She gave me a weird look. Then, slowly, her smile faded and she gaped at me. "Oh my God. You're him, aren't you?" She tipped her head to the side, studying me like I was a bug. "You're the twin. The one in a band."

"Wait, you thought I was James?"

"Well, duh. You're in his room. In his bed."

"It's my room, too." Though, when I look around, I barely see any reminders I once shared this room. "And that's my bed."

She looked doubtful. As if I'm the crazy one here.

"Who are you?" I ask again.

"Oh! Right." She thrusts out her hand. "I'm Wendy. No. Wait. Gwen. James's best friend."

After a second, she jerks her hand back.

Clearly, she just realized that I'd have to shake her hand with the hand that was just down my pants. Not masturbating. Not even touching my dick.

But still, she jerks her hand back and slams it into the pocket of her overalls.

"Hi, Wendy-no-wait-Gwen. I'm Tom."

She narrows her eyes in a way that's mischievous and suspicious. "It's not Wendy-no-wait-Gwen. It's just Gwen. They're both nicknames for Gwendolyn. I was always Wendy at my old school, but when we moved here, I thought I needed an upgrade. When you're Wendy, people just expect you to spend all your time sewing people's shadows back on."

She pauses, giving me a look like she expects me to respond.

When I don't, she waggles her hand in a catch-up kind of way. "You know... Wendy. Peter Pan. He loses his shadow? No?" After a second, she shakes her head, shrugs, and changes the topic before I can admit I've never seen Peter Pan. "Sorry about the whole accusing you of masturbating thing." She gives an exaggerated wince. "Obviously I would not have said that if I knew you weren't James. But if you had been James—oh my God—I would have had so much fun teasing him about that."

I had no idea how to respond to that. Frankly, I was still confused by the idea that James had some new best friend, who was a girl, and who he'd never mentioned to me.

She tipped her head to the side and considered me. "So if they're all in Houston for the weekend, why are you here?"

"I didn't know I would have the weekend off. By the time I arrived, they'd already left. But they're going to drive home tonight instead of Sunday," I explained. And then countered with a question of my own. "If they're in Houston, why are you here? And how did you get in?"

She laughs. "Duh, I snuck in through the back. What kind of friend would I be if I didn't know how to break into my best friend's house? You know, that window into the living room that doesn't lock, right?"

"So you just broke in? When you thought they were out of town?"

"No. Obviously, I saw James… well, not James. You, it turns out. But I thought you were James. I knew James was supposed to be in Houston. So I thought maybe he'd played badly and gotten cut from the competition early."

"So that's why you broke in?"

She gives me that look again. Like I'm the crazy one here. "I'm his best friend. Obviously, if he's upset, it's my job to check on him. I texted him, but didn't hear back. So yes, I broke in to make sure he was okay. And if he's bummed out or beating himself up about how he did, then it's my job to make stupid jokes to cheer him up. That's what friends do."

She says this so easily it makes something ache inside of me. I didn't know until this minute how much I missed having friends.

Yeah, theoretically, I'm friends with the guys in Boys of Summer. Clark keeps stressing that we are selling our friendship as much as we're selling our music. We have to look like we're best friends. We have to make people want to be part of our friendship. It's the reason he's basically held us hostage for the past four months, all living in the same house and spending twenty-four hours a day together. It's the reason he's limited our contact with the world beyond rehearsals and practice.

And, yeah, I guess we are friends. And they're good guys, even if they haven't entirely accepted me yet, since I was the last one who joined. But that friendship still feels forced and hesitant.

I've had plenty of shit days performing and none of them have broken into my room to make stupid jokes until it cheers me up.

Suddenly, inexplicably, I wish Gwen was my friend as well as James's. I don't know if it's that crazy red hair of hers that gleams like pennies in the sun or those goofy overalls that are, hands down, the least flattering clothes I've ever seen on a girl. They make her look like an over-grown toddler. Whatever it is about her, I want in on it.

"What else would you do to cheer him up? If he was having a shit day?"

She gives me a hard look. "Why? Are you having a shit day?"

"I'm having a great day," I say automatically. Four months in and Clark has already programmed bad days out of my vocabulary. "I'm just asking for research purposes."

"Hmmm…" She eyes me suspiciously, clearly not convinced. "Obviously he would need popcorn and Reese's Cups and Dr. Pepper floats. To be consumed during some kind of movie marathon. I'm thinking Monty Python or Spinal Tap."

"Spinal Tap?" I ask.

"This Is Spinal Tap."

"What is spinal tap?"

"This Is Spinal Tap. The genius mockumentary." She pulls a face of mock horror. "Please tell me you've seen This Is Spinal Tap."

I shrug. "Never heard of it."

She gives me an assessing look. I can't tell for sure, but I think she's trying to figure out if I'm teasing her. For the record, I'm not.

After a long moment, she nods, and loops her arm through mine to lead me out of the bedroom and into the living room.

"Do you know what time your mom, James, and Bex will be home?"

"After midnight I think, since they're driving back tonight."

"Okay, then. We will need pizza also."

We spend the rest of day on the sofa, eating enough crap food to give my personal trainer an aneurysm. Popcorn with so much butter it's actually soggy. Dr. Pepper floats with Reddi Whip sprayed right on top. She even climbs the fence between our houses to "borrow" cash from her parents to pay for the pizza and to retrieve "her personal emergency stash of Reese's Cups."

We watch This Is Spinal Tap and we both laugh so much during the Stone Henge concert that she rolls off the sofa. Halfway through Monty Python and the Holy Grail, she breaks out the Reese's Cups.

I've never seen anyway eat them the way she does, carefully nibbling all the chocolate from the outside rim, so that she's left with just a disc of peanut butter filling between two thin layers of chocolate.

It is somehow cute and sexy all at the same time.

That's when it occurs to me that maybe she isn't just James's friend. Maybe she is the girl he wishes was his girlfriend. The idea makes my heart pound like it's trying to escape my chest. Frankly, if she's not, then he's an idiot.

And if she is, then I'm the idiot.

She leaves just before midnight, only a few minutes before my family makes it home from Houston, sneaking out the back. By the time she leaves, I'm a goner.

I spend the next two months subtly trying to dig for more information about Gwen from James or Bex or anyone who might know more about their relationship.

I never figure out what's actually going on between them, even though I make a real effort to make it home more often. But every time I visit Mom, James, and Bex, Gwen is nowhere to be found. That spring, we have our first concert in Texas, opening for a popular female artist. Obviously I get tickets and backstage passes for my mom, James, and Bex.

When I text James and ask if Gwen wants to come, too, he tells me she doesn't listen to Boys of Summer. The same thing happens a year later when we headline our first concert. And the following year when I offer to fly everyone out when we play at Coachella.

By then, even I'm smart enough to take the hint. Turning down a trip to Coachella is about more than not liking our music. It's about not liking me.

CHAPTER 2

GWEN

Twelve Years Later

There are two types of people in the world:

A) the kind of people who carefully mix the foods onto their fork to create a bite that's the perfect blend of all the right flavors, and

B) the kind who won't even let their foods touch on the plate.

I am a perfect-blend-of-flavors person, through and through.

Derek, a PhD candidate in the physics department at one of the universities in Austin and my date this evening, is a foods-can't-touch person.

That was my first sign that this date would crash and burn.

Actually, my first sign should have been when he told the hostess we wanted separate checks as she was handing us the menus. Or maybe when he asked the waitress if they had gluten-free balsamic vinegar.

Don't get me wrong, I am a strong and financially independent woman who can pay for her own dinner. Also, I eat mostly vegetarian, so I fully support people wanting to know what's in their food. It wasn't the fact that he asked. It was the way he asked, like he was looking for a reason to be unhappy with the restaurant I'd chosen.

Yes, I ignored all the red flags. Only because it was my first date in months and my sister, Jackie, swore her friend had the perfect match for me.

After all, Derek and I have a lot in common. On paper.

We're both doctoral students. Both scientists. Both… I don't know… human? I guess.

I mean, I'm human. And I'm pretty sure robots aren't quite this realistic yet. So, sure. We have that in common, too.

Unfortunately, that is where our similarities end.

I feel like the balsamic vinegar was a low bar. Once he couldn't clear that one, it went downhill from there.

Twice he implied that microbiology wasn't real science.

"Sure, it's not like political science or anything," he explained. "But it's not exactly a hard science. Not like physics."

When I tried to explain that by every measurable standard, microbiology was a hard science, he said, "Isn't it mostly mucking around with microscopes?"

I should have left then. I hadn't even ordered yet. I could have dropped a twenty on the table for the waitstaff and gotten the hell out of Dodge.

But, no, in the spirit of trying new things, I decided to tough it out. I'm putting myself out there. My life is currently in a very Schrödinger's-cat-esque state of flux.

I don't defend my dissertation until late May, which means I won't officially be Dr. Mathews until I walk the stage at graduation in August. But I am currently ABD—all but dissertation. I'm done with my course work and, as of two weeks ago, I'm even done with my research. Technically, I still have my job as a research assistant in the lab of the amazing Dr. Ramsey, but even that feels tenuous right now, because I know it's ending soon. I've known my next step in life since I was twelve. Now, suddenly, I don't know what's next.

When I do start my job search, I'm going to start here in Austin since it's pretty much the tech and educational Mecca of Texas. Even if Derek doesn't immediately seem like my perfect future romantic partner, surely we could be friends.

Until he puked all over me. Fled the restaurant. Stuck me with the bill. And left me stranded, in Central Austin, on the Thursday night before the South by Southwest Festival. When every rideshare in the city is charging outrageous surge fees.

"Are you sure I can't get you..." The petite hostess gives me a horrified once-over. Again. "...anything?"

"I'm fine," I say, praying for patience as I tap refresh on the ride share app.

She eyes the remains of my date's vegan paprikash. "A towel?"

"I'm fine."

"A wet wipe?"

"I'm fine." I cleaned up what I could in the bathroom, but my shirt is undoubtedly ruined. This is—was—my favorite date shirt. My only date shirt, if I'm honest. All the wet wipes in the world won't save it now.

"A cab?" she offers with a tight-lipped smile and wrinkle of her nose.

Yeah. I get it. I'm stinking up the restaurant's foyer and probably offending the clientele.

I don't blame her. I wouldn't want me standing here either. I just really don't want to brave the crowds outside, but it's not like I can hide in here all night.

With a sigh, my bile-paprika-scented shirt and I leave.

Technically, my shirt can't sigh, but I sigh dramatically for the both of us.

Every spring, Austin hosts South by Southwest. It started out as a music festival, then they added movies and technology and who knows what else. I was absolutely not cool enough to get tickets to go when I was in high school, or even when I was in college, so I don't know how much it's grown in the years I've been away.

Based on how crowded the restaurant is, not to mention the streets outside the restaurant, I'm guessing a lot.

The place I picked for the date is north of campus, in a trendy new shopping center. It's one of those perfectly planned communities of residential housing mixed with bars, restaurants, and small businesses. It's exactly the kind of place I'd love to live if I could afford it. I picked it because a) it's far enough from downtown that there shouldn't be too much traffic from South By, and b) it's comparatively close to my parents' house just off Far West.

Yes, as if getting puked on isn't humiliating enough, I'm a twenty-six-year old woman who got dropped off for a date by my dad since my aging Kia is currently in the shop, no doubt giving a death rattle at this very moment. Nothing says cool like having your dad shout, "Have fun, sweetie!" when he drops you off outside a restaurant.

And if that isn't bad enough, my parents are at a South By panel—yes, they are cooler than me, that's not the point here—so they can't pick me up.

Which leaves me two options. I can:

A) suck it up and pay the outrageous surge fare, or

B) I can walk home.

I route the path on my phone. Six and a half miles?

Holy shit! I haven't walked over six miles since… ever. That's like, a fourth of a marathon.

Fuck.

I pull up the rideshare app, ready to suck it up and pay the extra money, but in the time I've been stalling, the surge has gone from three times the normal fee to five times the normal fee, which means it will cost me close to two hundred dollars to get home.

People in the shopping center are starting to give me odd looks since I'm pretty much just standing in the middle of the walkway. Loud music pours out of the bars on either end of the pedestrian street. At the far end of the block is a park with a mostly empty children's playscape. I head in that direction, because at least I'll be out of the way.

I find a bench, pull out my phone, and consider my options. According to the app, walking would take over two hours. And I'm pretty sure the app is overestimating my walking speed. Not only that, but a two-hour-walk through north-central Austin on a Friday night during South By is practically begging to be kidnapped. Sure, Austin is pretty safe, but it's not so safe I can afford to be stupid.

Calling my parents is a last resort. I don't think my ego could take the blow of interrupting their South By panel because my date puked on me.

That leaves calling a friend and begging for a ride.

I grew up here.

True, I haven't lived here in eight years, but I do have friends here.

I open my messages app and scroll until I find the name I'm looking for. James Mendoza.

James lived in the house behind mine when we were teens and he and I were inseparable all through high school. We remained close in college, since we both went to UT, even though we were in different departments. I was a groomswoman in his wedding. I stepped in to fill the space when his brother, Tom, dropped at the last minute.

Tom was supposed to be the best man. When he couldn't make it, their sister Bex stepped in. And then I filled in for her. With thirty-six hours' notice, I found a dress that matched the bride's color scheme—pink, no less—and had it tailored to fit me. It was short and tight and unflattering. And, did I mention pink?

I know, I'm making kind of a big deal out of that, but I'm a redhead, so pink is not a good fit with the freckles. I'm pretty sure I looked like Miss Piggy. No… scratch that, Miss Piggy has way more style than I do. She could have pulled off that dress with panache to spare. I, on the other hand, was and will always be completely panache-less. I don't know which muppet I looked like. Probably Beeker.

The point is, I was there when James needed me. If I need him, he'll come get me. Even though we drifted apart after he got married, James is the most stand-up guy I know. And besides, back in January, he texted me that his marriage is officially over, so it doesn't matter that Maggie never liked me.

Maybe my big mistake tonight was that I shouldn't have been forcing myself to make new friends. Maybe I just needed to reconnect with the friends I already have.

CHAPTER 3

TOM

Every kid with an identical twin switches places with their twin.

It's an inevitable, immutable law, like Newtonian physics. It just happens.

As a kid, having an identical twin is like having a soul mate, a best friend, and a nemesis all rolled into one.

You've been gifted by Loki, the trickster god, with power beyond that of mere mortals. But at some point, you learn the awful truth. Loki gifts no mortals. He simply toys with all of us. There's nothing he loves more than the trouble twins cause when they switch places. While we're down here on earth, suffering the consequences, he's up in Valhalla—or wherever the fuck Loki lives—laughing his ass off.

I learned my lesson when I was eighteen.

I swore then that I'd never again switch places with my twin, James.

Here I am, twelve years later, and I still haven't broken that promise I made to myself.

But—there's always a but, right?—switching phones with James isn't the same thing as switching places with him, right?

I have my reasons for this bit of chicanery.

James and his wife, Maggie, are on the brink of divorce. He let his dedication to his career and his political ambitions get in the way of his relationship, and six months ago, she got tired of his bullshit and walked out on him. Dinner tonight is his last chance to show her their marriage is worth saving.

So, yeah, I switched phones with him. Because the last thing he needs is getting some call from a client he "can't ignore." Our phones are the same model. We both have facial recognition set up on them. It was just a matter of switching the cases. Since there are only about a dozen people in the world who have my number, I know he won't be getting any calls.

Sneaky? Yes. But my intentions are good.

He still has a phone in case of emergency—after all, I'm not a barbarian. With any luck, he and Maggie will have a nice dinner and remember why they were so great together, and he won't even notice it's not his phone until… well, at least halfway through appetizers, right?

If it seems like I'm a little (or a lot) too emotionally invested in the success or failure of my brother's marriage, yeah, I know. My therapist agrees. She says it's a sign of my unresolved guilt over the success of my music career and my feeling that it should have been his career. She's probably not wrong.

After all, my relationship with James hasn't been the same since our dad took James to an audition for a boy band when we were fourteen. James had been playing the piano since he was four and taking lessons since he was five. Music was his life and his passion.

I only tagged along to the audition because Mom needed to take Bex, our sister, shopping and I didn't want to go. Since I was there, Dad put both our names on the audition sign-up sheet.

A month later, I was the fifth member of the manufactured boy band, Boys of Summer. I later learned that Clark, the band's manager, didn't need "another musical phenom" because he'd already filled that slot in the band dynamic. No, he was looking for "the energetic goof-ball."

Does it matter that my serious, focused twin was never going to be hired as "the energetic goof-ball"?

It probably should matter. That should alleviate my guilt, right?

But it doesn't. Because he's my brother. My twin. We are supposed to be closer than this.

And, yeah, everything about this situation is made so much worse by the fact that we're Latino.

Sometimes, I feel inundated by the myth of the big Latino family.

For us—for me—family is supposed to be everything. I should be surrounded by siblings and cousins and aunts and uncles. Instead, my mom was an only child. My dad's family all live in west Texas and we weren't close to them even before the divorce. Bex, Mom, and I are close, but James barely talks to me.

If I can just help fix this, then maybe I'll be one step closer to earning his forgiveness for all the other shit I messed up years ago.

And, at the very least, he deserves to be happy. He was happy with Maggie, even if he doesn't remember that right now.

So, I locked myself in the studio, determined to ignore the incessant buzzing from his phone and get some editing done. James will be pissed when he figures out what I'd done, but I'm hoping he'll be short-term pissed. Besides, James is pissed at someone half the time anyway, so it might as well be me.

My plan to save my brother's marriage was going great until about eight-thirty when his phone buzzed repeatedly with a ringtone I didn't recognize. It wasn't the normal, efficient bleep of his business associates.

Every time I—or our sister Bex—have possession of his phone for more than a few minutes, we change all the family numbers to ring with the Addam's Family theme song. It's not that either.

This ringtone sounds suspiciously like TLC's "Waterfalls."

Which is Gwen's favorite song.

I sit there, glaring at James's phone, which now buzzes with texts, Gwen's name popping up on the screen, and I try to tap down my emotions.

Gwen. Fucking. Mathews.

What are the chances?

First off, it's Gwen. Seeing her, thinking about her… whatever… always makes me… grumpy. Yeah. Grumpy. We'll go with that.

Secondly, James has one last shot with Maggie, so the last thing he fucking needs right now is to get texts from his back-up.

No, James and Gwen have never been a thing, but I know damn well back in high school they made one of those if-neither-of-us-are-married-by pacts.

Tonight, James needs to remember that his wife is fucking amazing. He does not need to feel like a man with options.

And, yeah, it's also true that I need to not spend my time thinking about Gwen. Ever, really. So, I flip over the phone and try to ignore it… ignore her.

But Gwen is the one woman I've never been able to ignore or forget. Not since that first day we met and spent the whole day hanging out. Hell, if I'm honest with myself, probably not since that first moment I saw her, hanging upside down from the top bunk, all that outrageous red hair blocking everything else from view. I thought about her, I obsessed about her, for months, even though James told me, over and over, that she wasn't interested in me and didn't even want to be my friend.

When he told me to back off, I did. Until we were eighteen and Bex told me that he was planning on ditching her for their Halloween plans. I grabbed my chance to see her again, and made a total fucking ass out of myself to impress her. I hadn't been able to help myself.

Because my feelings for Gwen made me do stupid things.

After several incessant buzzing texts, I cave and flip over the phone and open the messages. Because, apparently, I'm a glutton for punishment… and stupid.

Yeah, yeah, I know.

Reading my brother's texts is a horrible invasion of his privacy, blah, blah, blah…

Whatever.

It's not like I fucking want to text with Gwen.

I just want to make damn sure that whenever James gets his phone back, there aren't messages from her on it.

Gwen: Hey, long time no text. Lol…

Gwen: How are things going? I know you said you and Maggie are divorced.

Gwen: I'm so sorry to hear that. She was great.

Gwen: I mean, she hated me, but I'm an acquired taste, right? Lol.

I toss the phone down on the desk, stand, and pace away from it.

Who the fuck goes from "lol" to "sorry about your divorce"? Also, who punctuates "lol"?

Gwen Mathews, that's who.

Gwen has the face of a pre-Raphaelite model, the body of a runway model, the brain of a Nobel Prize winner, and the emotional intelligence of a thirteen-year-old boy. Is it any wonder I fell so hard for her when I was fifteen?

Two more texts come in in rapid succession. Against my better judgement, I pick up the phone and read the next batch of messages.

Gwen: I know this is awkward, but I need a favor.

Gwen: Okay, a big favor.

Gwen: Like, huge.

Gwen: Okay, I'll just blurt it out and pray you're getting these.

Gwen: I'm trapped outside a restaurant over in the Buchanan Center and I need a ride.

Gwen: I'm not trapped trapped. I'm not like, locked in a box or something. I just don't have a ride. And it's South By. The next available rideshare isn't for two hours and it's crazy expensive. Please, please, please come get me.

Gwen: I'm begging you.

Gwen: I wore pink for you.

Fuck.

Jesus.

She's laying it on a bit thick, isn't she?

Never mind that she didn't actually wear pink for James. She wore it because I couldn't make it to his wedding. It's been years and I still feel guilty about that shit.

I'm pacing the studio like I'm hopped up on heroin when another text comes through.

Gwen: I know I'm asking a lot because you probably don't want to drive across town this late. But I don't want to walk.

I stare at the phone in shock for a minute. She doesn't want to walk? Why the hell is that even an option? This isn't fucking New York City or London. Austin isn't a "walking" kind of city. Not only is she currently miles away from our old neighborhood, but she's on the other side of the highway. Walking home from Buchanan Park would be dangerous. Borderline suicidal. The fact that Gwen is even considering it is a sign of… I blow out a breath and pray for strength… it's a sign of her Gwenness. Her dewey-eyed, total belief in the inherent goodness of people, mixed with her clueless, careless, and total disregard for the real world that exists outside her head.

The real world, in which she will undoubtedly get kidnapped, raped, mugged, or stabbed if she tries to walk home from Buchanan Park at this time of night.

Jesus, this woman is going to give me a stroke. Once again praying for strength, I punch in a response.

James: Don't walk. I can come get you.

Gwen: Really? Thankyouthankyouthankyou!

Gwen: <gif of a chimpanzee throwing confetti>

Gwen: You've saved my life.

James: Just send me a pin where you are. I'll be there in ten minutes.

Gwen: I don't know how to send a pin.

Gwen: <woman shrugging emoji>

Gwen: I'm in Buchanan Park. By the pink dinosaur and the playscape.

James: I'm on my way.

Gwen: You're my hero!

Gwen: <gif of a cat licking its paw>

Gwen: Ignore that. I suck at gifs.

I save the audio file I've been doing post-production work on and practically run across the lawn from the recording studio to the main house. I pause just long enough to change into a long sleeve shirt.

Dallas, one of the guys from BoS, is staying with me for South By, but he's out, listening to music.

Despite Gwen's fear that it's "this late," it's barely after nine.

I'm in the car and backing out of my garage before I realize the irony of Gwen's statement.

I'm her "hero"?

Not fucking likely.

Gwen and James were best friends all through high school, but, other than that first time we met, she never liked me. According to James, she didn't like our music and she thought I was a show-boating asshole.

When she finds out she's been texting me and that I'm the one picking her up?

She'll probably be pissed. But what's she going to do? She begged me.

CHAPTER 4

GWEN

When you have a sister whose life is perfect in every way, it's easy to fall into the habit of blaming her for everything wrong in your own life.

When she's eighteen months younger than you, petite, curvy and gorgeous, it's even easier.

And yeah, I can already hear you asking, "How is she both petite and curvy?" Just trust me on this. She is.

She's five-four and has the body of a Golden Age Hollywood starlet, while I am five-nine with the body of a two-by-four.

We're opposites in every way. She was always delicate and prissy and doing things like ballet. I was nerdy and bookish and clumsy. I hit my big growth spurt in 5th grade while she still weighed less than a bag of dog food. I could literally carry her around on my hip.

I felt like the King Kong to her Ann Darrow.

By the time we were in high school, she was a cheerleader and insanely popular. I was competing in science competitions. Don't laugh. They're a real thing.

When I turned seventeen, I spent the summer transplanting dandelions from all over the neighborhood to our backyard, because I'd heard butterflies needed them and I was obsessed about the declining butterfly population. That same summer, Jackie was sixteen, went to all the cool parties, and lost her virginity to a football player over the Fourth of July at his parents' lake house.

That's us in a nutshell.

If it's dorky and uncool, I'm fascinated.

If it belongs in an Instagram post with the hashtag "Blessed" and gets ten thousand likes, Jackie is all in.

You would think, given how different we are, that Jackie would just give up on me and find cooler people to hang out with. But no. Apparently, her own life has reached its maximum capacity of blessings, because in the past three months, she's become obsessed with helping me "set realistic and attainable life goals," so that I can live my very best life. I didn't bother to argue that I might already have goals of my own. She knows me too well for that. Instead, I let her take over. After all, she's a tiny, beautiful, heat-seeking missile of inspirational aspiration.

Her laser-focused determination is one of the reasons I didn't bail on the date with Derek the moment it started to go south. She was so sure we would be perfect together, who was I to say we might not?

While I wait for James to pick me up, I work on the story I'll tell my sister to explain how the date went.

I'm sitting on the swing in the playscape, having abandoned the bench to a group of college-age club-going types. I'm crafting an excuse with the perfect mix of mutual disinterest and lack of chemistry when my phone buzzes with a text.

I open it automatically, hoping it's from James saying he's already here. I'm not that lucky.

Jackie: How is the date going?

With a sigh, I flick the phone back asleep and ignore the text. But another comes in a second later.

Jackie: Don't ignore me.

Jackie: I know you saw the text.

I glare at my phone. How? How does she know?

Jackie: My app marked it as delivered and read.

Jackie: You know, for a nerd, you should really learn how to maximize the functionality of your phone.

I give my phone the finger before texting her back.

Gwen: The date is going great. I wasn't ignoring you. I was trying to enjoy the moment. Like you suggested.

Jackie: <gif of a hot man laughing>

Gwen: What is that even supposed to mean?

Jackie: I know you're lying

Jackie: It's funny you think you can fool me

Gwen: How do you know I'm lying? And how was I supposed to get that from some random man laughing?

Jackie: A) not some random man. Chris Evans

Jackie: B) I know you're lying because Gracie texted me and said you scared him off

Gwen: Who is Chris Evans? Do I know him?

Jackie: <face palm emoji>

Jackie: Chris Evans the actor

Gwen: ???

Jackie: who plays Captain America

Jackie: <gif of a man holding a shield>

Gwen: Okay. Whatever.

Jackie: Also stop trying to distract me

Jackie: What did you do to scare off Derek?

Gwen: Why do you assume I'm the one to blame? Maybe he just scares easily.

Jackie: You talked about maggots, didn't you?

Gwen: They're not maggots. They're black soldier fly larvae.

Gwen: He's a scientist. He should have a stronger stomach.

Jackie: God. Damn. It.

Jackie: How many times do I have to tell you?

Jackie: Don't tell people about your maggots. No one likes maggots.

Jackie: No one

Jackie: They're gross

Gwen: Okay. Gotta go. My ride is here.

I close the messaging app and give my phone the finger again before putting it to sleep.

My ride—James—is, in fact, not here yet, but trying to defend myself to Jackie is exhausting in person when I can't flip her off—in both the shooting her the bird sense of the phrase and in the turning my phone off sense.

When I have the option of ignoring her, I might as well take it.

Besides, they really aren't maggots. And lots of people like them.

I can feel my phone continuing to buzz.

I glance down only long enough to see Jackie's messages flickering across the screen without actually opening the app. I really need to figure out how to turn that feature off, so she won't know when I'm ignoring her.

She's moved away from criticizing my maggots to worrying about my ride. She's worried that unscrupulous people are pretending to work for ride share apps to take advantage of tourists during South By. I just can't handle her right now. I know she's trying to be helpful, but most of the time I feel like she and I are two different sub-species of humans. All of the people-ing part of being human has always come so easy to her. The opposite is true for me. It never really occurred to me that romance and love and happily ever after might be a thing I could have.

Then, last year, my boss—the brilliant scientist Dr. Max Ramsey—fell in love with Holly Dolinsky. And I had a front row seat to the most unlikely romance ever. Before they met and fell in love, I was satisfied having my life compartmentalized. I was content believing that big romance and deep love weren't for people like Max and me, people who are a little—or in Max's case, a lot—emotionally clueless. Nerds with our brains so focused on scientific minutiae we are more likely to annoy the opposite sex than attract them.

But then Max met Holly, and fell head first in love with her, and now they're married and in the process of adopting four kids from the foster care system.

While I couldn't be happier for him, I'm woman enough to admit I'm a little jealous. Not because I ever had feelings for Max, but because it made me realize that I want that. Or rather, something like it.

Do I really think I'm going to find someone brilliant and loving who fills in all my awkward angles and completes me… well, completely? No. That would be asking too much. But if Max can find someone who loves him, flaws and all, shouldn't I be able to find someone?

I don't expect the perfect guy to sweep me off my feet. I'm far too practical for that. If there's one thing I've learned volunteering to walk dogs at the no-kill shelter—other than the value of daily cardio—it's that you can't expect to just luck into a pure-bred show dog in perfect health. Westminster-worthy dogs are rare. But there are lots of perfectly acceptable, healthy (or healthy-ish), friendly dogs who just need the right person to see past their poor training and mange long enough to give them a chance.

Surely, somewhere out there, there's a perfect acceptable, intelligent man who would make an acceptable life partner. I don't need a pure-bred show dog. I just want a life companion who isn't rabid. And who can listen to my work without puking.

Though, it's become increasingly obvious that charting a vomit-free future for myself will be a bigger undertaking than I hoped. Since James still isn't here, I push aside that depressing thought, and open the web browser on my phone to Google Chris Evans.

And he is… wow. He is really hot.

Then I Google his complete filmography and make a list of titles that sound appealing so I can watch some of them while I'm staying with my parents since they have all manner of streaming services I can't afford until I've graduated and have a real job.

By the time I've opened my notes app and have no fewer than ten movies listed, my phone rings. I check to make sure it's not my sister before I answer.

"Hey, James," I say into the phone. "You almost here?"

"I am here," he says in a voice that sounds low, growly, and bit angry. "Where the hell are you? I'm at the bench by the playscape and you aren't here. There's a bunch of drunk college students."

"Oh! Sorry!" I jump up and hurry off toward the road. "They wanted the bench, so I wandered off and—" Then I realize I left my purse by the playscape so I turn around. "Shit." I find my purse, but when I bend down to get it, my glasses slide off and land on the ground. "Fuck."

"Are you okay? What's wrong?" His voice comes through the phone sharp and worried.

"Gah. Give me a minute. I just—" I trail off as I squat to look for my glasses in the dark. I drop my phone to pat at the ground.

I can hear James yelling at me through the phone.

I pick it back up. "Sorry, I dropped my phone while I was looking for my glasses."

"What the fuck, Gwen? Where are you?"

"Hold on." I put him on speakerphone. "I'm here. Just give me one…"

I find the glasses and slide them back on my nose. Then I pick up the phone, bringing it to my ear as I grab my purse and walk to the edge of the park.

"Sorry about that."

"Are you okay?" he asks, unexpectedly loud and… almost… desperate?

That's weird.

"I'm fine. Hang on, let me take you off speakerphone." I pause, switch the phone off speakerphone then raise it back to my ear as I head back to the road. "Sorry. I just… there was a crowd. You know I don't like crowds."

The crowd of drunk students is still clustered around the bench, now singing loudly. The tune is familiar, but I don't place it right away.

I give the crowd a wide berth and when I navigate around them, it's to see a crossover SUV parked at the curb. James is standing next to it, one hand holding his phone, the other waving at the crowd of drunken students, like he's trying to shoo them out of his field of vision as he scans the park.

"Oh, there you are," I say into the phone, even though I'm almost close enough he could hear me.

He whirls around and spots me. His gaze narrows as he slowly lowers his phone and punches the button to end the call. He is practically simmering with annoyance.

As I reach the door to the car, I finally recognize the tune the crowd is bellowing in his direction.

"Tonight's a good night!" they chant. "And I'm too young to act this old! I'm not gonna worry. I'm not gonna think. I'm gonna act my age."

I stop in front of the passenger side door and offer a toothy smile that's only a little bit of a wince.

"I'm sorry," I say again. For like the fifth time.

"Just get in the car," he grumbles.

It takes a second for me to figure out how to operate the handle, because his car is way fancier than mine. By the time I've got the door open and am sliding in, one of the drunken revelers has stumbled over.

The guy isn't menacing. He's clearly trying to help me with the door, which seems very weird to me until he uses the opportunity to lean into the car just enough to tell James, "Dude, I love that song. It's epic!"

James gives a polite nod, managing a smile that almost seems genuine. "Thanks, man. Means a lot."

"You performing this year? I didn't see you on the line up?"

I try to send James a look that says, "OMG-I'm-so-sorry-how-do-you-put-up-with-this."

But James just smiles at the guy and shakes his head. "Not this year. Too much on my plate."

"Right." He gives a sage nod. "Self-care, man. I respect that." Then, like he's just thought of it, he adds, "Dude! You want to hang out?"

"I'm good," James says.

"He's good," I blurt, wrestling to get the door away from Mr. Dude. "We're good. But thanks!"

"Okay. Another time. Right. Awesome."

Mr. Dude finally lets go of the door and steps back. I pull it closed, just as James shifts into drive and pulls away from the curb.

"Oh my God. Does that happen often? That must be so annoying."

"What?" James asks dryly. "Strangers asking me to hang out? Or driving across town to pick up a friend, only to realize she's not where she said she'd be. And then have her not answer her texts. And panicking thinking maybe she got accosted or something."

"Oh." I cringe, biting down on my lip as I realize he is white-knuckling his steering wheel, even though there's enough pedestrian traffic and traffic traffic that we're barely creeping through the shopping center. "About that… I'm really sorry?"

"Is that a question? Are you asking me if you're sorry?"

"No. Wait. Let me say that again. I'm really sorry. And I'm sorry about the sorry thing. I'm trying to get better about that. My friend Holly says it's linguistically confusing when I use upspeak, but I'm more sorry about making you worry. My sister was texting me a bunch and she was mad at me about the date not going well. I was ignoring her texts and researching Captain America and I lost track of time."

Even though it's pretty dark in the car, I can see James begin to relax as we drive past the occasional streetlight.

Even though the look he shoots me is still one of annoyed confusion, his shoulders look less tense and rage-y.

"Anyway, my point is, I'm sorry. And I'm sorry you had to deal with Mr. Dude."

"Who?"

"Mr. 'Dude!'" I draw out the word *dude* the way the guy did, pointing my thumb over my shoulder for emphasis. "I bet that gets really annoying, having people sing your brother's hit song at you."

"It's not the worst." James shrugs, glancing in my direction. "Where do you need to go?"

"Oh, I'm staying at my parents'. Isn't that embarrassing? Twenty-six years old and living in my childhood bedroom. Not permanently. At least I hope not. But still, I'm a mess." I sigh, glancing over at the guy who's been my friend since I was thirteen.

We're not close anymore. Not like we once were. We drifted apart when he started dating Maggie in college. I don't think we've even been in the same room since his wedding, but we still text and exchange messages via social media. He's known me longer than anyone I'm not related to by blood, but somehow, right now, he feels like a stranger to me. I hate that feeling. Suddenly, I feel this desperate need to reconnect with him. To reclaim our friendship.

CHAPTER 5

TOM

I try not to take it personally that Gwen adores James and can't seem to stand me. After all, he's allowed to have friends who aren't me.

Obviously, he's allowed to have other friends.

Everyone always assumes that your twin is supposed to be your best friend, just like everyone assumes if you're Latino, you have a huge, amazing, supportive family. That's not the way it is with James and me. Yeah, we were inseparable for the first decade or so of our lives. Then he auditioned for Boys of Summer, I got "discovered," and our parents got divorced.

Everything—and by *everything*, I mean everything in our family—went to shit after that.

In the four years since BoS broke up, Bex and I have gotten close again. I've worked my ass off trying to create that big supportive family everyone assumed I had growing up.

I try to be for other people the support system I didn't have. All of which is to say, I'm not going to let my brother's friend walk home during South By, even if she does think I'm a self-centered, lazy slacker.

Still, I'm annoyed.

Of course I'm annoyed.

First off, who the hell assumes she'll be able to get a rideshare during South By?

She grew up in Austin. She knows what it's like. She's an actual fucking genius. She should know better.

Am I happy to give her a ride? Yes. But she should have fucking planned better.

Secondly, I told her to stay where she was. But did she? Nope. Because Gwen is… well, Gwen. She doesn't march to the beat of her own drum. She wanders around on the football field, barely aware the rest of the band is even there. I guess I should just be thankful she didn't end up drugged and on a bus to Canada.

And third—because this is Gwen and there are always at least three things about her that irritate me—she needs to stop apologizing about the damn song.

"Look, it's no big deal," I say. For what's got to be the hundredth time, because —Jesus!—she will not let go of how horrible it must be for "me" to be mistaken for Tom.

Clearly I just need to tell her I am Tom.

But I know she's going to be all pissed off and judgy about the phone-stealing thing. And I was kind of hoping I could just drop her off without her ever knowing. That's why I grabbed a long sleeve shirt on the way out the door, because I have tats on my wrists that James doesn't.

Tomorrow, I can explain what happened to James. If things go well with Maggie, he probably won't care. If they don't, he'll be too pissed off with me about the phone thing to care. Either way, all I needed to do was get Gwen safely home and keep my mouth shut.

Except she won't stop talking.

Because apparently being related to me is such a big fucking chore.

"All I'm saying is, it's got to be frustrating when people think you're him."

Okay, time to bite the bullet. "Yeah, about that—"

But, classic Gwen, she just keeps talking. "So what? He has a couple of catchy songs."

A couple of catchy songs? Try four number-one hits.

I blow out a breath, praying for patience. I know she wouldn't irritate me so much if I didn't have other—more complicated—feelings for her. I know my annoyance is "rooted in her perceived rejection of my adolescent romantic overtures," blah, blah, blah. I can have my therapist send you her notes about it. My point is: Gwen is annoying.

And she's at her most annoying when she won't let me finish a sentence. "What I was saying was—"

This time she doesn't cut me off, but from the corner of my eye, I see a flash of yellow fabric and a blur of movement. Christ. What is she doing now?

I take my eyes off the road for a second to see her sitting there, shirtless in only a bra.

"What the hell?" I ask.

"What?" she shrieks.

"Why is your shirt off?" I have to force my eyes away from the sight of Gwen half-naked. "What the hell are you doing?"

"What?" she asks, less panicked, but still sounding squeaky.

"Your shirt," I enunciate, desperately trying to look anywhere other than over at Gwen. "Why is it off?"

"Oh. That."

I'm still not looking at her, but I see the movement of fabric as she shakes the shirt in her fist.

"That asshole threw up on it! On my favorite shirt. And now it's ruined. It's sticky, and gross, and I couldn't stand to wear it for another minute. You know how weird I am about wet clothes."

"He threw up on you?" I ask, glancing over briefly and seeing the bright orange smudged on the yellow fabric. "Shit, that's a lot of vomit."

I try not to look at her tits.

I swear to God, I try not to.

But that's a lot of pale, creamy, freckled skin to not be looking at.

She's wearing a sexy as hell, golden-yellow, push-up bra. Her breasts are small but perfect, and in that bra, it's like they're displayed on a platter.

"Jesus," I mutter, then quickly add, "Do you need me to pull over and find you a shirt or something?"

She laughs, a low, husky sound of pure amusement that immediately makes my cock twitch. As if her sitting shirtless in my car wasn't bad enough.

"Oh, my God. Stop being weird!" Still laughing, she reaches across the console and punches my arm. "It's not like you haven't seen me like this before."

Wait. What?

James has seen her shirtless before?

How the fuck did I not know this?

Why has James seen her shirtless?

Have they slept together?

Desperate to stop my spinning thoughts, I repeat her words. "Right. I've seen you like this."

"Exactly. I think this covers more of me than that bikini I used to wear."

Okay. I exhale, feeling a wash of what feels suspiciously like relief.

Not that it's any of my damn business if James has seen her shirtless. Nope. Not my business. No reason to be relieved about that.

She's right. It's just like a bikini. And I've seen a lot of women in bikinis. Hell, I've seen a lot of women fully naked. It's just that I've never seen Gwen in a bikini. And that the idea of James seeing her fully naked makes me uncomfortable in ways I do not want to think about. Because it's not my business.

And if I keep repeating that long enough, maybe I'll even believe it.

Fuck my life.

How the hell did I end up in this situation?

I blow out a breath and keep my eyes on the road.

All I have to do is just keep driving. Get her home. Get her out of my car. Without checking her out.

But she punches me lightly on the arm again. "You're still being weird."

"Respectful," I grind out. "I'm trying to be respectful."

"We-ird!" she volleys back, drawing out the word.

"I just didn't think you'd be this comfortable… you know…" I try to gesture in the general direction of her torso without glancing at her.

"Only because it's you." She shrugs. "You're my best friend. If I can't take off a puke-covered shirt with you, who can I?"

Right. Because she thinks I'm my brother.

She would never in a million years take off a puke-covered shirt if she knew she was in the car with me. She'd probably wear it to the grave before taking off her shirt in front of me.

Which means now I can't tell her I'm not James. Not only would she be pissed off at me, she'd also be embarrassed.

So now I'm stuck pretending to be James until I can get her out of my car. Which is fine.

It's all fine.

I can absolutely do this. Just keep my eyes on the road. Not a problem.

Hoping to steer the conversation away from our supposed years of friendship, I clear my throat and ask, "Was it food poisoning?"

"What?" Then she holds up the shirt and sighs. "Oh, the puke? No. Derek barely got through his vegan, gluten-free paprikash."

She says *Derek* and *vegan paprikash* with a sneer of derision.

"Not a fan of Derek?" I ask. "Or of paprikash?"

"Oh, I love paprikash. But why order vegan, gluten-free paprikash? To me, it's all about the sour cream and the spaetzle. And this place had so many great gluten-free and vegan options! Okay, he's got to eat gluten-free. I respect that! But this place makes homemade spaetzle so tender it'll make you want to cry.

Subbing those out for gluten-free noodles is an insult to spaetzle everywhere!" She sighs. "I sound like an insensitive bitch, don't I? I guess I should be grateful for my dairy- and wheat-tolerant Scottish genes."

I chuckle despite myself.

"Please don't tell anyone I made fun of his dietary requirements."

I can't help myself. I glance over at her—keeping my eyes pointedly at her face.

She's giving me begging-puppy eyes.

"Your secret is safe with me."

"I would be less annoyed with him if he hadn't ordered the paprikash." She holds the shirt up again, the bright orange practically glowing in the passing streetlight. "If he had gotten the roasted vegetable platter, maybe I could have saved my shirt."

Now that we're away from some of the trendier parts of town, the traffic isn't as bad, but this is the week when even the out of the way places are packed, so it still takes longer than normal to get from the Buchanan Park area to Gwen's parents' mid-century ranch style house off of Far West.

I know the neighborhood because the house I grew up in is one block away and one door down, so that our backyards were catty-corner.

That's still where my mom lives, despite my offers to buy her something bigger or nicer. She swears she likes where she is and that with the housing market in Austin so out of control, that even I couldn't afford to move her anywhere else.

Which I take as a sign that Dad really screwed her in the divorce, if she doesn't know I made enough money back in my Boys of Summer days that I could afford any house she'd want to live in.

"So if it wasn't food poisoning, then what?" I ask as I steer the car through the small residential neighborhood.

"Me. It was me."

"He was allergic to you? Like your perfume or something?"

"No, my conversation apparently. He asked what my dissertation was about, so, I told him. It's not my fault some people are entirely too squeamish about rotting food."

I resist the temptation to ask her what her doctorate in microbiology has to do with rotting food, because James undoubtedly knows that shit.

She twists in her seat, partially facing me, she gesturing as she talks. "You know what? I'm not even sorry I made him puke. If you ask me, a grown-ass man who is a scientist should be able to discuss fly larvae over dinner."

I pull onto her street and slow the car to a crawl. I can't keep myself from glancing over at her again. Her hair, that crazy red hair of hers, bounces around her head while she berates her date's weak stomach.

"You know, maybe I think all his talk about the Big Bang was gross. But did he ever consider that? No. Not at all."

"I don't think anyone thinks the Big Bang is gross," I point out as I park in front of her house. "Except maybe the fundamentalists. Even then, I think it's more that they don't believe the science behind it, not that they think it's gross."

Showing no signs of getting out of my car, she counters, "Think about it. Every atom in our bodies was present at the Big Bang. They've traveled through space to get to our planet and become the building blocks of life. If he's such a damn germaphobe, why isn't he worried about his carbon molecules being contaminated?"

Again, I can't help but chuckle. She's so unguarded. So animated. So genuinely offended by the idea that her research repulsed that idiot. It's adorable.

She's adorable.

Oh, fuck.

I don't want her to be adorable. I want her to be irritating and annoying. I want her to piss me off. Because if I can't maintain my annoyance…

I am so fucked.

CHAPTER 6

GWEN

Somehow, despite the disaster this evening started out as, I'm having a good time.

Even though I'm sitting here in my bra—which is grossly damp—I'm more comfortable than I am with anyone else. More relaxed than I've been in weeks. Sure, when I first got in the car and he was acting all grumpy, he seemed more like a stranger than my friend, but now it feels comfortable to be with him. It feels right.

We're in front of my parents' house, and even though it's night, the familiar streetlight on the corner casts the right amount of light—just enough to see without blinding us. He's put the car in park, but I'm not quite ready to get out.

"Do you ever think it's weird," I ask him, "the way we can not talk for a year and then still be this comfortable around one another?"

He's got one hand still on the steering wheel, tapping out a beat. His knee is bopping along to whatever frantic beat is in his head. He scrubs his free hand down his face, then drops it onto his thigh, shifting only slightly to glance at me.

In that instant, I realize he's not quite as comfortable with me as I have been with him.

He's tense. Fidgety. And he's barely been meeting my gaze, but when he does look at me, it's like he's really looking at me.

Like he's really seeing me for the first time in years.

Okay, true. It is actually the first time we've been physically in the same space in at least a year. We've lived in different towns for the past three years. And even though Hillsdale, where I did my graduate work, is only an hour and a half away from Austin, I didn't see him when I came home.

His brief, tumultuous marriage to Maggie changed things between us. Once he and Maggie split, it didn't feel right to see him, but I could tell he needed a friend because he started texting me again, for the first time in years. And then, just after Christmas, I got a text from him saying it was officially over. I know how much he loved her and how heartbroken he must have been. I certainly wasn't glad they broke up, but I did wonder if our relationship would go back to the easy, comfortable way things have always been.

Given the way he's looking at me now, I guess maybe I was wrong.

"You're like a hoodie," he blurts.

"What?"

"You know. That favorite hoodie everyone has. It's comfortable. Easy. Sometimes you almost forget you even have it. Then you find it in the back of the car, slip it on, and it just feels…" He trails off, looking out the front windshield.

I think he's not going to finish his sentence, so I try to finish it for him and we both speak at the same time.

"Right," I say.

"Perfect," he says, his gaze moving back to roam over my face. Then dropping slowly, inexorably down my torso.

His gaze stops at my bra and I suck in a breath. I can practically feel him looking at my boobs.

I did not have high hopes for tonight and I almost wore one of my plain, practical bras. Instead, I wore my demi-cup, push-up bra. The one that matches my now ruined date shirt. The one that makes my boobs almost look like they're a respectable size.

The one that—apparently—makes my breasts look good enough that James is noticing they actually exist. If I had to guess, I'd say it's the first time he's even considered the possibility.

I didn't know until this precise moment that I wanted James to know my boobs existed, but suddenly, I am grateful I did wear the good bra. And I may have to go buy twenty more of this exact same bra.

Only because he's actually looking at me in this way—this maybe-you're-not-a-hoodie-but-a-sexy-bra-wearing-woman way—I look right back at him. Really look at him, in a way I haven't in years.

Back in high school, James was one of those boys who was so good looking he was almost feminine. Almost pretty. And he was shorter than me by several inches. Because I'm like King Kong and he didn't get his last growth spurt until college.

As I study him tonight, he almost looks like an entirely different person than the guy I was friends with back then. In a lot of ways, he is a different person. I feel like the same person I've always been, maybe because I'm still student. But it feels like he's a real adult. Like a real man.

He's been taller than me since college, but now he's filled out even more. His shoulders are broader, his arms muscular.

He's in jeans and a button-down shirt with a funky retro pattern on it. His hair is thick and unkempt, like he's been running his hands through it all night. It's messier than I'm used to seeing it. Back in college, he was meticulous about styling it. He's got a close-trimmed beard, which I know from his ex's social media posts he's had for a couple of years. It's very scruffy and… sexy.

"You look like a Chris Evans," I say awkwardly.

"What?" His gaze darts back to mine.

"He's an actor. He plays Captain America." Oh, God. Why do I sound out of breath? "He's very popular apparently."

"I know who Chris Evans is," James says, his lips curving into a faint smile. "And I'm pretty sure he's not Hispanic."

"Oh. Yes. Obviously. I didn't mean you look exactly like him. More just that you look similar to him in a lantern-jawed, heroic kind of way."

Forget sounding out of breath. Why do I feel out of breath?

Am I having a heart attack?

That seems statistically very unlikely, since I'm only twenty-six and my last blood work showed cholesterol levels well within normal range. Maybe I'm having a panic attack. After all, I've had a very stressful night. And my best friend is looking at me in a way that is intensely unsettling.

I'm excruciatingly aware that I took my shirt off in front of him.

"I should go inside!" I exclaim.

Like it's some sort of emergency.

Before I can bolt, James shifts, angling his body slightly toward mine, reaching out his hand, then dropping it back down.

Suddenly, it's not just that I can't breathe. It's that every part of me seems frozen in time. I can't breathe, but I can't move either. I can't bolt, like I know I should.

I can't even seem to think.

And, then, before I can stop myself, I ask, "Do you ever wonder what it would be like?"

He must know what I mean by "it," because he's shaking his head, even as his gaze drops again. Not to my boobs this time, but to my lips.

"If we hadn't been best friends forever," I continue, sounding as breathless as I feel. "If I wasn't just some comfortable old hoodie."

"Gwen, don't," he pleads, pulling his gaze from my mouth to my eyes. "Don't do this."

And he's right.

I know he's right.

He's my best friend.

Flirting, kissing, sex… it's all part of this line we've never crossed. Not when we were drunk. Not when we were horny teenagers. Not when we were in college and I slept in his apartment almost every weekend—usually in his bed, with him—because his apartment was so much nicer than my dorm and I've always had shit luck with roommates. I've actually woken up with his morning wood jammed against my thigh and we both laughed it off, because we were best friends.

It didn't feel right to think about him that way. Because he was my buddy.

I knew he didn't think of me that way, but I didn't think of him like that either. If I was his hoodie, it was okay, because he was my hoodie, too.

But now, all of sudden, everything feels different.

I don't know if it's because of that officially-over text I got a couple of months ago. Or because I haven't seen him in person for so long. Or because I took off that stupid puke shirt.

Or maybe it's because something in the back of my head has been screaming at me for the past year that it's time to actually do something with my personal life or I'll be left behind forever.

Or maybe it's because he's actually looking at me. And I'm looking at him.

And… Shit… He might be hotter than Chris Evans. And he must smell better than Chris Evans. I'm sure of it, because there's no way anyone else in the universe smells this good.

"The thing is," I say, shifting in my seat, almost up onto my knees so that I'm leaning across the console, "I haven't really thought about it. Until now."

My breath catches in my throat as I realize that I want him to make a move. I want something I've never wanted from him before. I want him to lean across the console and kiss me.

But he doesn't.

In fact, he's leaning back against the driver-side door. He couldn't be farther away from me without fleeing the car.

"Okay, then." I bite down on my lip to hide the unexpected prickling of tears against the backs of my eyes. "Question answered, I guess." I force a laugh as I hold up the ruined shirt. "I guess maybe I shouldn't have asked the question when I already have tangible evidence that men find me repulsive, huh?"

"Gwen," he says my name again, in that low, growly voice of his. The one I've almost never heard him use.

“No, it’s okay.” I chuckle in a way I pray sounds genuinely amused and not at all like I’m wallowing in resignation.

This time he does close the distance between us, leaning across the console to cup my cheek. “It’s not you,” he murmurs, running his thumb across my mouth, gently tugging my lip free from my teeth. “It really isn’t. Some other time. Maybe.”

“No.” God, now I have to swallow actual tears. What is wrong with me? “I get it. I’m just not who you want. I—”

“Fuck it,” he mutters before I can finish the sentence. And then his mouth meets mine.

CHAPTER 7

TOM

I've done a lot of stupid things in my life, but kissing Gwen is the best stupid thing I've ever done.

I know it's a mistake. I know James will probably kill me if he ever finds out—and he will find out.

Hell, Gwen will kill me herself, if she ever finds out. Plus, she's smart enough to get away with it—and to make it painful.

Despite all of that, I can't sit here and let her think that I don't want her. I can't let her believe she's repulsive or any other ridiculous idea. I can't fucking watch her cry over it.

I've never really understood James and Gwen's relationship. I've never understood how he's been friends with this gorgeous, smart, awkward, frustrating woman without hitting on her. I don't know how he made it through high school and college without kissing her, because, fuck it, I couldn't make it through a thirty-minute car ride without wanting to kiss her.

I sure as fuck am not going to let her climb out of this car thinking she repulses men.

I don't have a plan when I lean across the console and pull her to me. At least not beyond ridding her of this notion that I don't want her.

But the second my mouth touches hers, I'm a goner.

I'm lost in the feel of her lush lips under mine. In the taste of her. My hands get lost in those glorious curls of hers that somehow smell like mint and strawberries. In the feel of her tongue sliding against mine.

Then, her hands are on my shirt, fumbling with the buttons. I groan when she touches the skin of my chest. Her hands are cool, despite the warmth of the night, and her touch is light, almost hesitant. I want her to touch me everywhere. It's all I can do not to take her hand in mine and bring her palm down to my aching cock.

I don't do that, because, first off, I'm a fucking gentleman. And secondly, I know that I want that. I know the thousand dirty, filthy things I want to do with this woman. Just like I know she's not ready for any of that. I want her so badly I can barely think, but somehow I know if I rush her, she'll freak out.

But I can be patient.

Patience is my middle name. My mantra. My fucking superpower.

Until, that is, I feel those hands of hers pushing my shirt off my shoulders and hear her gasp out my name.

Except it isn't my name at all.

"James," she moans.

Fuck me.

I still, pulling back a millimeter.

Hands still in her hair, the taste of her still on my mouth, I suck in breath after breath, trying to calm my raging hard-on. Trying to figure out how I forgot—even for a second—that Gwen doesn't know what she's doing here. She thinks she's making out in the car with her best friend. With my brother.

"What's wrong?" she asks. "What did I do wrong?"

Her voice is husky and sounds as breathless as I feel.

"Nothing," I murmur with my eyes still closed, trying to reassure her and figure out how the hell I'm going to peel her off of me, get her out of my car, and somehow fix this mess. I pull her hands from my skin and bring them up to my mouth to rub a kiss on her knuckles. "Just give me a minute."

Except before I get that minute, she stills, jerks her hands from mine, and scrambles to the other side of the car.

I open my eyes to see her pressing her body against the door, knees pulled tight on the seat, eyes wide with horror, looking at my chest. She's pointing at me with one hand, her mouth opening and closing like she's trying to form words she doesn't have. She rips her gaze up to meet mine.

I follow the line of her finger to see she's pointing to my tattoo. My Boys of Summer tattoo that I, and all the guys in the band, got when our first album went platinum.

My Boys of Summer tattoo, that James definitely does not have.

I meet her gaze to see abject and absolute horror in her eyes. And rage. Yeah, there's a healthy dose of rage there, too.

"Tom?"

Shit.

I reach out a hand, but before I can say anything, she fumbles the car door open and flees.

Fuck. Fuckfuckfuckfuckfuck!

I sit there for several long minutes, sucking in one deep breath after another, trying to slow my suddenly racing heart, while I debate what to do.

And, yeah, trying to get my raging hard-on under control, because, shit, if I'm going to go after her and try to explain, sporting wood won't help my case.

Eventually, I leave the car and walk up the path to the front door. I don't bother knocking, because I know she won't open to me. Instead, I pull out my phone—shit, James's phone—and call her.

She doesn't answer, so I shoot her a text.

James. Answer the phone or I'm coming in anyway.

Ellipses appear in response and then disappear.

A second later, the phone rings to the tune of "Waterfalls."

"What?" she snaps when I pick up.

"Let me in so we can talk."

"Um… no. Not just no. Hell, no. Like, never in a million years no."

"Gwen, let me explain."

"No. I think we just covered that."

"I'm not leaving until you let me explain."

She hangs up.

Okay, that's fair. She's pissed. And probably freaked out. I'm sure from her point of view, what I did was reprehensible.

But I wasn't lying when I said I wasn't leaving until we talked.

James: I'm serious

Gwen: fuck off

James: Fine. We'll do this your way.

Five minutes later, I've circled the block and I'm parked in front of my mom's house. I don't text her to let her know I'm coming, because of the I-have-James's phone issue. Instead, I call Bex.

"Hey, I thought tonight was your big date with Maggie. Why are you calling me?"

"It's Tom, not James. I have his phone. It's a long story."

"Let me guess, you stole his phone so he wouldn't take work calls during his date?"

"I guess it's not that long."

"Hey, it's what I would have done. What do you need?"

"Are you home?" I ask my sister.

She's still in college and lives at home with Mom. To save money. Again… does no one care how much money I have? Or do they not let me pay for shit as a way of twisting the knife?

"Yeah, I'm home. What do you need?"

"Is Mom up?"

"Watching *Law and Order* in bed, last I saw. Probably asleep by now."

"I'm outside the house. Can you come let me in? I need access to the backyard, but don't want to answer a lot of questions."

"Okay…" She trails off to indicate her confusion, but I can hear her footsteps on the stairs through her end of the phone.

A moment later, she answers the door. She's dressed in yoga pants and a cropped T-shirt, her dark hair clipped on top of her head. It's nine-ish on a Friday night, the first weekend of spring break, and this is what my college-age sister is doing?

I guess I really am the rebellious one.

She gives me a quick hug. "Do I even want to know why you need to sneak into the backyard?"

"Do I even want to know why you're at home studying when it's spring break?"

"Duh. South By. You think I want to go out in that traffic?"

Shaking her head like I'm crazy, she heads back upstairs without asking any more questions. I head to the backyard through the sliding glass door. I skirt the patio, with its wrought-iron furniture and fire pit and head to the north corner of the yard. Technically, the privacy fence along the back belongs to the neighbors, so the support slats face my mom's side. That and the big oak tree in Gwen's parents' yard makes getting down on her side as easy as pie.

Getting into her house is equally easy, mostly because I remember James describing how he used to do it. There's a dog door onto the sunroom big enough for the German Shepherd they used to have, and they never lock the door from the sunroom into the house. Simple.

Except nothing is ever simple when it comes to Gwen, is it?

About ten seconds after I open the door from the sunroom to the living room, I notice the beeping.

Shit, that sounds like an alarm system. There's no control panel by this door. By the time I find the panel by the front door, the beeps are faster.

"What the hell?" Gwen yells at me.

I glance up to see her at the top of the stairs. Fuck me, she's still shirtless. "Do you have the code?"

"Why are you here?"

"You refused to talk to me and I needed to make sure you were okay."

"So you just broke in?"

"Yeah. When your friend is upset and you're worried about them, you check on them. Even if you have to break into their house." Her gaze narrows to a glare as I talk. Still I drive the point home. "That's what friends do. You taught me that."

"Fuck off." She crosses her arms over her chest and glares at me. "I should just let the police come and arrest you."

"Really, Gwen?"

"Yeah, really. You broke into my house. I should have you arrested."

I study her, trying to gauge just how serious—and how upset—she is because I'm still haunted by the look on her face when she fled my car.

"Fine. You do what you need to do. You want the police to come arrest me? Fine. At least I'll know you're okay."

She smirks. "Right. You're one-fifth of the most popular band to ever come out of Austin. You're a goddamn hometown hero. If the police come, you'll be able to talk your way out of it."

"Nah." I cross my arms over my chest and lean against the wall beside the alarm panel. "In my experience, grown men don't listen to Boys of Summer, but maybe I'll get lucky and the cops will be women."

She narrows her gaze at me. "You really want to get arrested over this?"

"No. What I really want is to talk this over and make sure you're okay, but if having the police here will make you more comfortable, we'll do it your way."

I'm both bluffing and I'm not. I sure as hell don't want the police to come, but I'm also not leaving until I know she's okay. Hopefully, the worst case scenario is the police come and they call her parents. At least then she won't be alone.

The beeps merge into one long buzz.

"Fine." She stomps down the stairs. "It's zero, four, one, two, one, nine, nine, eight."

I type in the numbers. The buzz doesn't stop.

"Hit 'Enter.'"

I do and the noise finally stops.

A moment later, the phone on the wall starts ringing.

She stomps over to the phone and picks it up.

"Hi, this is Gwen Mathews," she says in a voice sweet enough to build a bomb out of it. "Yeah. Sorry about that. I tripped the alarm on my way into the house." She pauses. "No, that's my mom. Yeah, of course."

She rattles off the series of numbers again.

This time, hearing them, I realize they must be a birthday. Not hers, because she was born in ninety-six. So it must be her sister's.

Into the phone, she says, "Yes. Of course. The backup word is George Milton."

Then she laughs, a beguiling little chuckle. "Yeah, my parents are Steinbeck fans. No, no. I'm fine, I promise. I just got home and before I could enter the code, I noticed there was a rat in the living room."

She turns to glare at me.

"A really big, nasty one."

The person on the other end of the line says something, to which Gwen replies, her tone still light, "Oh, don't worry. I've got it trapped under a shoe box. As soon as we get off the phone, I'm going to beat it to death with a shovel."

I take it back. She's not beguiling. She's terrifying.

Like, Robert Patrick in Terminator 2 terrifying.

She hangs up the phone and turns back to me. “Are you going to leave on your own or do I have to get a shovel?”

I’d laugh, but I’m afraid she might be serious.

Instead, I hold my hands up, palms out. I don’t know if I’m trying to seem harmless or if I’m begging.

“Look, I’m not leaving while you’re this upset. I just want to make sure you’re okay.”

“I’m fine,” she says glibly.

She’s almost even believable—God knows I want to believe her—but she seemed genuinely upset in the car, first when she thought James found her repulsive and then a moment later when she realized she’d kissed me, not him. Under the circumstances, I want more than a glib *fine*.

“At least let me explain,” I beg.

“Okay, fine. Explain.”

But she doesn’t actually give me a chance to explain. Instead, she marches across the room and jabs me in the chest with her finger.

“No, wait. Let me guess. You swapped phones with James for some reason that seemed like a good idea at the time. Then when you came to pick me up, you didn’t bother to tell me who you really were, because”—she breaks off, throwing up her hands in the air in obvious frustration—“I don’t know. Why didn’t you just tell me? ‘Hey, Gwen, I’m Tom, not James,’” she rattles off in a mock deep voice, before switching back to her normal voice. “It doesn’t seem that hard.”

“I don’t know why I didn’t tell you,” I admit. “Maybe I thought it would be easier not to tell you. Maybe I thought you wouldn’t notice. I really don’t know.”

Even as I say it, I wonder if I’m lying, if maybe I didn’t tell her who I was because as soon as she got in the car, she was treating me the way she’s always treated him. She was relaxed and fun, and it was easy. She wasn’t annoyed with me. She didn’t look down her nose at me. She was just… Gwen. That fun, amazing Gwen she was the first time we met.

Yeah, if I say that shit out loud, she’s definitely going to beat me with a shovel.

"Look, I'm sorry. I fucked up. What do you want me to do to make this right?"

"I want you to travel back in time and not do it!" Her voice continues to rise. "But time travel is only theoretically possible and that would be a very irresponsible use of time travel even if it was possible."

I can't help it. I laugh at that. I know it's the wrong response in the moment, but I still can't help it. Because only Gwen could bring this conversation around to the ethical use of time travel.

Her glare ratchets up several more notches. "I'm serious!"

"I know you are." I hold out my palms again. "That doesn't make it any less funny."

"Fuck you," she snarls, but this time she's not yelling it at me. And maybe even her lips are twitching.

"Again, I'm sorry. I fucked up. But can we at least talk about it?"

Her gaze twitches and I can tell she's trying to assess my intentions. Eventually, she says, "Well, I'm not getting a shovel yet, so start talking."

"Can you put a shirt on for the conversation?"

"No," she says defiantly. "Because this is my house, damn it. My parent's house. Whatever. You know what I mean. And if you don't want to be here, then you can leave. And this whole situation is just so weird and uncomfortable, I'm just going to lean into it."

Okay. Her being shirtless is less than ideal. It's going to make this entire conversation harder. And possibly some other things as well. Which is definitely not going to help.

I'll just have to work really hard to maintain eye contact. Really, really hard.

"Okay, whatever you need. I just—"

"You know what," she interrupts me. "This bra still has puke juice on it. It's wet and uncomfortable. I couldn't find anything else to change into. So I'm going to take it off, too."

And before I can stop her, she's got her hands twisted around her back and she's yanking off her bra. I whirl around, turning my back on the temptation I know I won't be able to resist.

"Jesus, Gwen, will you please put a fucking shirt on?"

"No, I can't, because I was looking for a clean shirt to change into when the alarm started going off because you were breaking into my house. So now you're just stuck with me shirtless and braless. I'm sure these are the least spectacular tits you've ever seen, but you'll survive."

Even though my back is to her, I squeeze my eyes closed. Like that's gonna help.

Christ, she has no idea. No fucking idea.

When I open my eyes, I see a bright green throw draped over the back of the sofa. I grab it.

"Just please have something on." Head tipped up, practically staring at the ceiling, I turn back to her and wrap it around her shoulders like it's a shawl.

She must not be as comfortable naked as she's pretending to be, because she lets me cover her up, even going so far as to clench the ends together in one her fists. Her tits are covered, but it still leaves a very tempting triangle of bare skin above and below the fabric.

She glares at me indignantly. "I'm only wearing this because it's cold in here."

I nearly groan, because now I'm picturing her nipples pebbled and hard.

Fuck my life.

CHAPTER 8

GWEN

"Can I please go get a shirt for you?" Tom asks again, sounding rather desperate.

"No. I just arrived today, and the first thing I did was put all my laundry in the wash. Everything I brought is in the dryer right now. I moved it over when I came in, but it'll be at least another hour before it's done."

He gives a wry chuckle. "I guess my lie of omission didn't traumatize you that much if you ran inside and started doing laundry."

"Oh, I was very traumatized."

I keep my tone light, mostly to hide the jumbled swirl of emotions I don't yet know how to process. Traumatized is such a dramatic word. A very not-Gwen kind of word. I'm not, by nature, an overly-emotional person. The scientist in me is far too practical to be traumatized by something as mundane as kissing the wrong guy. Was I surprised to find out that I wasn't kissing an old friend, but instead was kissing a super-hot pop star? Yes. Surprised, but not traumatized. Maybe… disconcerted. Unnerved.

Yes, those are all much more appropriate words to describe my emotional state. I was expecting a gentle, exploratory kiss from an old friend and instead got a panty-melting, soul-searing make out session with the hottest guy I've ever met in person. Of course I was disconcerted! And unnerved!

Tom may interpret my immediate need to do laundry as a lack of emotion on my part, but I know the truth. After I ran into the house, the most logic course of action would have been to find a shirt. Instead, I moved laundry. Any time I eschew the logical course of action in favor of a mindless task, it's a sign of inner emotional turmoil. I don't tell Tom that. I *can't* tell Tom that, because then he would know that I found his kiss… very turmoil-ing.

So instead, I sink to the sofa, prepared to bluff my way through the conversation. Which I just might be able to get away with if I pretend that Tom isn't Tomás Mendoza. And didn't kiss me tonight. And isn't Chris Evans levels of hot.

Which now that I know it was Tom in the car earlier and not James, it seems exponentially absurd that I told him he looks like Chris Evans. Who am I kidding? Tomás Mendoza isn't Chris Evans level of hot. Chris Evans is Tomás Mendoza levels of hot. None of which makes me feel less turmoil-y.

"I'm just also practical enough to want to have actual clothes on when my parents get home," I say, pretending this is all perfectly logical. "My night has been pathetic enough without having to explain the puke shirt to my parents. Who, by the way, are out attending a South By panel. When did my parents get cooler than me?"

Tom opens his mouth and then closes it again, like he doesn't know how to answer that.

I wave the question aside. "Don't answer that. We better not try to calibrate our internal yardsticks for what is cool."

Tom, again, looks like he's so baffled by me he can no longer form sentences, which isn't a good sign for a songwriter. He bobs up and down on his toes. "Can I get you another shirt? Maybe from your mom's closet?"

"Have you seen my mom? No, thank you," I say with an eye roll. Then, I realize he probably hasn't seen her, so I explain, "She's as tiny as my sister. If I try to wear her clothes, I'll look like the Hulk."

Still, Tom seems to be trying very hard not to look at me from the neck down. Like he's afraid my hand might slip and he'll catch a glimpse of my obviously subpar boobs. And then maybe the image will be seared onto his retinas and he'll never again be able to appreciate the beauty of a pair of double Ds.

Plus, my hand is starting to cramp from clenching the throw so tightly, because, despite my earlier bravado, I do not excel at "leaning in" to my near-nakedness. Instead, I'm weirdly aware of the fact that I've been nearly naked with Tom for longer than I have with any other man that I haven't slept with.

Disconcerted by that thought, I try to adjust the throw so it covers more of me, knotting the two corners together and slipping it up so the knot sits on my shoulder. In my mind it looks like one of those cool one-shoulder halters.

In the interest of not driving myself crazy, I'm going to pretend I pull it off.

I look up to find Tom pacing the length of the living room, one hand buried in his hair like he's trapped in an escape room too hard for him to puzzle his way out of.

I don't know what to think about how agitated he seems or about how insistent he was that he come in to check on me and make sure I was okay. If I'm honest, I don't know what to think about anything related to Tom. He's been a mystery to me since the day we met. No amount of stewing over his motives and actions right now will help. Instead, I summon my deepest reserves of emotional detachment and practicality. Which I might even be able to do if I pretend he's not really Tomás Mendoza, famous pop star.

"Apology accepted," I announce. "You didn't mean to hurt my feelings or whatever. You can leave, guilt free, and get on with your night."

He stops, turning slowly to face me, his gaze searching my face in that way of his that is so disconcerting. "Did I?"

"Did you what?"

"Hurt your feelings?"

"Oh." I grimace. Why had I said it like that? As if my feelings were involved? I don't have any feelings when it comes to Tom. "No. I mean. I don't…" I stand up, suddenly unable to sit still. "Look, if you're going to stay, sit down. If you're going to go, go. But it's awkward for me to just sit there watching you pace like a…."

"Caged tiger?" he supplies.

"Tiger?" I quirk an eyebrow. "Well, you think highly of yourself. No surprise. I was going to say a perpetual motion machine."

He gives another one of those wry chuckles.

I should have realized as soon as he chuckled back in the car that he was Tom and not James. James isn't a wry chuckler. He's much more serious, like I am. He's not like Tom, who apparently can find amusement in any situation. Even ones that are deeply awkward and embarrassing. But his amusement is never cruel or harsh, and instead leans toward self-depreciating.

"Why do you do that?" I ask.

"Why do I pace?" He shrugs. "I'm just a pacer, I guess. Too much energy."

I don't tell him that's not what I was asking about. Instead, I say, "James isn't a pacer."

Which is a pretty stupid comment, since they're brothers and Tom probably knows that. But, hey, I'm known for my scientific mind, not my pithy conversation.

Tom makes a rueful clucking noise. "I am the twin with ADHD."

"Hmm." I murmur, because I don't know what to do with that information.

I never knew Tom had ADHD. I know James doesn't. Or, at least, I assume he doesn't, because it's never come up.

Then, I say, "Oh, my friend Holly has ADHD." Tom just frowns and I feel compelled to add, "Not that I expect you know her or anything. It's not like y'all have a club and all hang out together."

His lips twitch. "Oh, we totally have a club. We have secret meet-ups all over the country. I hang out with Tony Hawk all the time there. It's how I know Simone Biles."

"Oh my God, you know—"

"No. I don't. I was joking."

"Oh. Sorry."

I resist the urge to bury my face in my hands to hide my embarrassment.

This is one of the reasons Tom and I have never gotten along. I'm gullible and take everything seriously. He takes nothing seriously and is… arrogant isn't quite the right word. Self-possessed, maybe? He's always seemed like he knows exactly who he is and where he's going. No doubts. No questions. No fumbling around.

All I do is fumble. Everything, really.

Which isn't to say I didn't want to be his friend. When we first met, I'd been sure we would be friends. It wasn't until much later that I learned the truth, that he hadn't had fun with me, he just hadn't known how to get me to leave. I'd been mortified when James explained it to me. But I was practical enough to understand. I was too dorky for my own sister to hang out with. Why would a pop star—someone who could hang out with anyone—want to spend time with me?

"Why are you still here?" I ask abruptly. "I mean, you apologized. I accepted it. You can leave now. I'm sure you have better things to do on the first Friday night of South By than to wait around for my laundry to dry."

He gives me an assessing look. An unexpectedly serious, assessing look, considering how I was just thinking that he doesn't take anything seriously.

"I need to make sure you're okay. In the car on the drive home, you seemed a little…" He trails off like he doesn't know the most polite word to use. Like he's afraid of offending me.

"Crazed?" I supply. "Frantic? Weird and ramble-y."

"I was going to say lost."

"Oh. I wasn't. I have a maps app."

"I meant emotionally."

"Oh. Then, yes. I was definitely that. Or, rather, I am that."

I sink to the sofa, leaning back to stare up at the vaulted ceiling of my childhood home. Part of me knows I should let Tom off the hook and send him on his way. Despite that, there is something oddly freeing about being emotionally vulnerable with someone who already thinks you're a loser. It's not like anything I admit to Tom will make him think I'm more of a dork.

"It just feels like everyone else knows who they are and where they're going," I admit. "Like everyone else is on track for something. And I'm not."

I feel the sofa shift as he finally sits down. Not directly next to me, but close enough that I get another hit of his yummy scent. It's something woodsy and fresh that makes me think of log cabins and campfires—expensive log cabins and campfires. The kind on magazine covers. I bet cologne companies send him samples in hopes he'll be their spokesperson because he's a celebrity.

I lift my head to find him studying me.

He meets my gaze, his lips twisting in a crooked smile. "How could you think your life's not on track? You have your doctorate."

"Not for another two months. I defend in April. I won't be official until August."

He quirks his eyebrow, like this somehow proves his point.

I sit up, rearranging myself so I'm sitting cross-legged and can face him better. Plus, it puts a little more space between us. "But that's just it. Until now, the road ahead was clear. High school, college, graduate school. Sure, I had to pick the schools and the program, but I also knew the direction I was headed. I knew what I wanted to study when I was nine."

He surprises me by asking, "You knew you wanted to study fly larvae and rotting food when you were nine?"

"Hey, you remembered!"

He shrugs, like it's no big deal.

Which it kind of is, because even my sister—who I talk to at least once a week—describes my research as "something to do with maggots."

"Not exactly that," I say, answering his question, because it's easier to do that than to consider the possibility that Tom might have actually been paying attention to the things I said tonight. "But I remember standing outside a restaurant watching them throw away all that extra food. I wanted to do something with it other than just dump it in the landfill. We recycle glass and cardboard and car batteries. Why can't we recycle food, too? And then I thought—" I cut myself off. "Damn it."

"What?" Tom asks.

"I'm doing it again! For the second time tonight, I'm sitting across from an attractive member of the opposite sex and I'm talking about larvae. It's like I'm broken! Like whatever part of my brain is responsible for flirting is either not there at all or permanently damaged. I wonder if I was dropped on my head as a baby."

Tom chuckles again. I glare at him.

"Are you laughing because I just admitted you're attractive or because you're thinking that I've actually talked about larvae three times tonight?"

"Maybe I'm laughing because you're funny."

I roll my eyes. "Not likely. But go ahead and laugh. All this stuff is easy for you, because you're gorgeous and a celebrity. And weren't dropped on your head as a baby."

"I'm not entirely sure what you mean by 'all this stuff' that supposedly comes so easily to me."

"You know, all the stuff. The sex stuff." When his eyebrows shoot up, I add, "I don't mean that kind of sex stuff."

I can feel my cheeks heating, because—hello!—this is Tomás Mendoza I'm talking to. He is, as I stated earlier—one-fifth of the most popular band to ever come out of Austin. I'm pretty sure he's got "that kind of sex stuff" handled.

"I meant the dealing-with-members-of-the-opposite-sex stuff. Not professionally or friendship-wise. I work with men. I've always had friends who were men. But romantically? I'm a fucking disaster at that. No pun intended."

Oh, God. I'm still talking? Why am I even allowed to speak out loud?

"No puns, huh?" he asks, lips twitching. "That's rough."

"Very funny." I narrow my gaze at him. Yeah, Tom, I see what you did there, implying my lack of puns equates a lack of sex.

Of course, it would be funnier if it wasn't so damn true.

Since he's already seen me shirtless and knows men puke on me—I'm pretending the whole kissing-in-his-car-thing didn't actually happen—I continue my new leaning-in policy.

"But totally on the nose. No puns at all. It is officially a pun drought. A veritable pun desert."

Tom clears his throat. “Just to be clear, are we talking all puns across the board? Or just puns given to you by others?”

I narrow my eyes, considering my answer for a hot second before replying, “I’m going to plead the fifth on that one. In the interest of maintaining some shred of dignity while talking to the most famous person I’ve ever met.”

“Don’t do that,” he says, his tone suddenly serious and intense.

“Don’t do what? Maintain my dignity? Yeah, that ship might have already sailed anyway.”

“Don’t make a thing out of the fame. It’s not real. It’s just a thing that happened to me.”

“Oh, please. I hear your music everywhere. You weren’t exactly a one-hit wonder. Everyone knows your songs.” Then it hits me. I sit bolt upright. Then bury my face in my hands. “Oh my God. Everyone knows your songs! That guy at the park—Mr. Dude—even he recognized you and realized you weren’t James. And I kept trying to apologize that he was singing Tom’s song to you. And you’re Tom!” I pull my hands down just enough to peer at him over my fingertips. “Mr. Dude is more observant than I am. And I’m a scientist. Observant is supposed to be my thing.”

“In your defense, Mr. Dude probably doesn’t even know I have a twin brother.”

“That’s not much of a defense, because Mr. Dude also hasn’t known you and James since you were fifteen. Also, I clearly should have known you weren’t James because James would never wear a shirt with…” I lean closer to squint at Tom’s shirt. “What are those? Roller-skating penguins?”

“Hey, what’s wrong with my roller-skating penguins?”

He actually sounds offended, so I look up at him as I answer.

“Absolutely nothing,” I say seriously.

Except now, I realize that, for the second time tonight, I am sitting very close to him. Too close. Maybe closer than I’ve been to him in years—ignoring the fact that earlier tonight, I had my tongue down his throat and my hands all over his chest, because I’m still pretending that’s a thing that didn’t actually happen.

So I clear my throat and lean back. "No, the penguins are great. I mean, who doesn't love penguins? And roller skating! Roller skating is an excellent form of exercise."

"Gwen," Tom says softly.

I close my eyes then tip my head up to stare at the ceiling. "Yes?"

"Now can we talk about what happened tonight? Now that we've covered everything from rat extermination to my musical career to roller-skating penguins?"

"No." I force myself to straighten my neck and meet his gaze, because the last thing I need on top of everything else is neck strain. "I think we should just consider it a non-thing."

"A non-thing?"

"Yeah. Like a dream sequence in a TV show. It didn't really happen. It doesn't affect the plot or the characters. It doesn't mean anything."

Some emotion I can't quite read flickers across Tom's face, and for a moment, I wish that I knew Tom as well as I know James, because then maybe I could tell what he's thinking.

I don't know why, but right now, I really, really wish I knew what he was thinking.

After a second, Tom pushes to his feet, and then he's pacing again, hands plowing through his hair, that frenetic tension in his muscles.

How did I ever mistake this man for James? They even move differently. Tom has an easy athletic grace to his movements, even when he's frustrated and pacing. Probably from all those dance lessons, and all the choreography they had to learn for the music videos.

The fact that I did mistake Tom for James makes me wonder if I really know James as well as I thought I did. And why I still think of him as my best friend when we really haven't seen each other in years. What is wrong with me that I've been through five years of grad school and still don't have a friend I think of as my best friend?

I'm stewing on this grim thought when Tom stops and turns to face me. "But it did happen. We—"

I jump to my feet. "That doesn't mean we have to talk about it. Or think about it. Like, ever again."

"It does if you're planning on kissing James."

"I'm not—" I cut myself off, because what I am supposed to say here? That I'm not planning on kissing James? That argument doesn't really make sense, since when I kissed Tom, I thought he was James.

Or did I?

On some level, wasn't I aware of that tonight in the car? Didn't I know I felt an attraction to "James" that was different than anything I'd ever felt before?

Oh no.

No, no, no, no. Nonononononononono!

I am not going down this rabbit hole, because what if it leads to the upside down, wonderland world where I might be attracted to Tom?

I can't be attracted to him. I can't let myself be attracted to him, because there's no way my relatively punless body—let alone my relatively loveless heart—could survive the likes of Tomás Mendoza.

CHAPTER 9

TOM

I like to think of myself as a fairly open-minded guy. A civilized guy.

I meditate. I recycle and do yoga.

I go to therapy. Okay, so for me, therapy wasn't so much a choice as a necessity, but I'm still proud of myself for going, because a lot of musicians just self-medicate. My point is this: I'm evolved. Or at least try to be.

Typically, I don't get jealous.

It's just not my style.

If I'm with a woman who would rather be with someone else, what would be the point of trying to hold on to her? If I'm not making her happy, doesn't she have the right to be with someone who can?

My attitude isn't something all my past girlfriends have loved. I don't cheat, but I also don't fight for someone who has doubts about me. Given that, my current emotional state is a bit of a mystery.

Gwen and I aren't together.

We've never been together.

In fact, this is the longest conversation we've had since we were teenagers, and we've covered a lot of territory.

Despite that, I shouldn't be jealous of the idea that she might want to kiss my brother.

I shouldn't be, but I am.

I'll chalk it up to the fact that she was my first serious crush, the first girl I wanted who was not at all interested in me in return.

The first girl I ever moped over and fucking pined for. And no, James doesn't know I felt that way about her. What would have been the point?

She was his best friend. As far as I was concerned, that put her officially in the no-fly zone. Also, other than one perfect day we spent together on the day we met, she's always acted like I'm not worth her time.

Obviously, I've moved on. I was fifteen when I crushed on Gwen. I've put a lot of miles on the metaphorical tires since then. I've fallen in love—sort of. I've dated. I've dumped. I've been dumped. I've gotten over it.

But you know the one life lesson you learn when you join a boy band at fifteen?

There's nothing like your first love.

That's the whole reason boy bands exist. It's the reason I still get fan mail from twelve-year-old girls (and boys). It's the reason I sometimes see fifty-year-old women bopping along to one of the BoS songs at the grocery store. It's why Taylor Swift is popular and why "Mr. Brightside" by The Killers was the first song from the 2000's to have over a billion streams on Spotify. And it's why, standing here in Gwen's living room, with the taste of her still on my lips, I can admit that I'm jealous of my brother.

Jealous in a way I've never been before, about anything.

Not when we were kids and he always got the first slice of birthday cake because he was born three minutes and twenty-three seconds before me. Not when we were in school and our parents lavished him with praise for his good grades and punished me for getting notes from our teachers like, "Tom would live up to his potential if he could just sit still in class."

Not even when, after our parents got divorced, James got to live at home with Mom and Bex, while Dad "managed my career," which was code for, "spent my money and banged the groupies." Not even when I had to learn how to hide my anxiety and my panic attacks because as Clark used to say, "Boy bands are all about the fantasy. You think anyone fantasizes about a guy who throws up before going on stage?"

Even then, I'd been able to rationalize around any stirrings of jealousy, because I love my brother. I'm proud of him. And even if sometimes I missed Bex and Mom and the life I left behind when I joined BoS, it wasn't like I wanted James dealing with all that pressure instead of me.

So this feeling of jealousy that I'm wrestling with now? Yeah, this is entirely new to me.

I don't really understand it. I definitely don't like it. But I have to admit that it's there.

Trust me when I tell you I would love to turn tail and run. To bury this shit deep and forget I ever cracked open this dark closet in my soul.

I can't do that for two reasons.

First off, Gwen may want to pretend she didn't kiss me, but she refused to say she wouldn't kiss James. If I boil down her earlier rambling about puns and fucking, I think she meant she doesn't have much experience with men and dating and she wishes she had more. I can't pretend to understand what's going on in that brilliant mind of hers, but as far as I'm concerned, that means she's planning on doing it.

Secondly, James has enough on his plate right now. I can't fix his relationship with Maggie. That's on the two of them. But I do genuinely believe she's the best thing that ever happened to him. If Gwen does put the moves on James, it will ruin everything.

Are my motives for cock-blocking Gwen and James entirely pure? Probably not.

Okay, definitely not. The idea of them getting together makes my blood pressure skyrocket.

Despite that, my motives aren't purely selfish either. I'm cock-blocking for the greater good.

I stop pacing—I wasn't really aware that I was pacing until I stop—and turn back to Gwen.

"You can't kiss James again."

"Obviously." She rolls her eyes in a well-duh gesture, but her nervous laugh tells me she's not being entirely honest.

"I mean it. I don't know what he told you, but he and Maggie aren't divorced yet."

She wrinkles her nose, and I try not to notice how adorable it is.

"Eww. I kissed a married man?"

"No, you kissed me."

"No, that's a dream sequence." Then she frowns and I can practically see her thoughts churning. After a second, she gives a beleaguered sigh. "I see your point about the dream sequence thing getting confusing. I guess I have to own that I kissed you."

I don't point out that technically I kissed her. And I knew who she was when I did it. I also don't point out that we didn't just kiss. She was unbuttoning my shirt, a clear indication it wasn't a benign peck on the cheek that wouldn't go any further. Nor do I admit that if she hadn't seen my tattoo, we would have done a lot more. That I wanted a lot more of her. That if I let myself think too much about kissing her or about the fact that she's barely wearing a shirt, I wouldn't be able to stand up without embarrassing myself. That it's taking a hell of a lot of self-control from me not to pull her against me and lay all of that on the line right now.

The only reason I don't do any of that is because of how horrified she was when she realized she was kissing me instead of James. The way I see it, when a woman throws herself out of a car to get away from you, that's a pretty firm no.

So I don't try to kiss her again. And I don't look at her from the neck down, because how someone can look sexy wrapped in a sofa throw, I don't know, but Gwen pulls it off.

I stand up and start pacing again, because at least if I'm moving I won't be tempted to touch her again. "My point is, their divorce isn't a done deal."

"But he texted me back in January and said it was officially over."

"That was probably about the time he moved out." My annoyance with James ratchets up and I can feel my jaw tightening. What the hell was he thinking? Texting Gwen like that as soon as he moved out? I don't know what's worse, the fact that he did it so soon after moving out or that his text was ambiguous. Either way, it was a dick move. "Just don't kiss him."

Gwen visibly recoils. "Again, eww. And also, obviously I'm not going to kiss him again."

Even as gratifying as her revulsion is, I feel compelled to add, "And please don't remind him about that pact y'all made back in high school."

"Wait. What pact?"

I stop and look at her, unable to avoid seeing the creamy skin of her exposed shoulders and the furrow of confusion between her eyebrows. "I thought y'all made a pact to get married if neither of you were married by the time you were thirty."

The furrow deepens as she tilts her head to the side. "Huh. I guess we did." She shrugs and the throw shifts, tempting to reveal the crest of her breast, and I'm back to staring at the top of her head. "But he also promised that he would never eat a Reese's Cup without saving the other one for me, and I'm pretty sure we've both forgotten about that."

"What are you saying? You forgot he was your backup?"

"Yeah, I guess I did." She gives another shrug, then seems to realize the effect of that action on her bare-skin-to-covered-skin ratio and adjusts the throw. "I mean, sure, we said that back when we were in school, but I've never thought of him like that until—" She breaks off, her mouth pinching into a little bow of annoyance. "Yes. I had forgotten he was supposed to be my backup."

"So that's not why you kissed me? When you thought I was him. That whole conversation about whether or not he ever thought about having sex with you? That wasn't you trying to pin him down because you thought he was single again?"

"No! God, no. It was just a…" She flutters her hands around her head. And then she stands up and starts pacing. "Just a spur of the moment impulse. It didn't have anything to do with James being my backup. It's not like that's legally binding. Or even very practical. In six months, I'll have my doctorate. I'll be living somewhere else. Either teaching or doing post-doc work or working in the public sector or whatever. And this felt like my only chance to—"

She stops, cutting herself off. Frowning and looking deeply perturbed, she pushes her glasses up onto the top of her head. Then she runs her hands over her crazy mass of curls, as if she might somehow tame them with that small gesture.

Because she seems so discomforted, I supply the end of the sentence she seems unwilling to say out loud, "To be with James."

"Well, yes, but not necessarily in that way. Because like I said, it isn't about him. It's about me and how I'm moving into the next stage of my life, but I'm totally unprepared for it. In this next stage, this is when I'm supposed to find my person, right? But how am I supposed to do that when I barely know how to talk to men? At least, not without making them puke on me. I don't know how to date. I don't know how to flirt. Hell, I don't even know how to swipe right. Or is left the direction you're supposed to swipe? If you like that guy, I mean."

"Stop right there," I say, interrupting her. "Stay away from Tinder." Just the thought of her on Tinder chills me to the fucking core. It'd be like pushing a newly hatched bird out of a nest and off a cliff. "You aren't ready for that."

"That's what I'm saying! I know I'm not ready for that! The problem is, I don't have anyone to help me get ready for it. And you know what sucks? Before James married Maggie, he was my best friend! He was—" She snaps her fingers and then points at me. "He was my hoodie!"

I wince, suddenly wishing I'd never brought up the hoodie analogy. "I'm not sure the hoodie analogy really works here."

"No, but it does. Don't you see? A great hoodie is practical and comforting."

When I used that term, I wasn't thinking practical and comforting. I was thinking more of that single, perfect hoodie. The one you can't live without. The one that makes you feel safe and at home no matter where you are.

Shit. I need to just stop. I need to stop romanticizing Gwen and what she might have been to me if things had been different. I need to stop thinking about her all together.

Gwen is still talking, totally unaware of my internal bargaining.

"I told him everything," she says. "And he always knew how to give me advice about how to handle awkward social situations, and how to pick out clothes that don't make me look like a corpse. He's the one I went to for advice when my college boyfriend asked me to fill out a customer satisfaction survey instead of just asking me if I was faking my orgasms."

I don't know whether to laugh or cry at that. "Were you?"

"That's not the point. The point is, I miss having that person in my life. The one I can tell anything to. The one who will always give me good advice. These next couple of weeks might be the last time I'll be living in the same city with a friend I trust like that. Without James, who am I left with? My sister, that's who. And she's not so much a hoodie as a really uncomfortable pair of Spanx. And who knows what kind of weak-stomached physicist she's going to throw at me next?"

"I'll do it," I surprise myself by saying.

"What?"

"I'll do it. For the next couple of weeks, I'll be a stand in for James. I'll be your hoodie. If you need advice about anything, you can come to me. Advice about dating or flirting or post-sex customer satisfaction surveys. By the way, that last one is not a thing. I hope James told you to dump the guy."

"Yeah, he said he was a douche canoe. But are you sure?"

"Am I sure that the guy who needed a survey to figure out you weren't climaxing is a douche canoe? Yeah. I'm sure."

I don't know who this moron was, but if I took Gwen to bed, I'd make damn sure she came before I did, and I wouldn't need a survey to prove it to me.

"I meant, are you sure you want to be my hoodie?"

No. Not at all. The last thing I want is to be a stand-in for Gwen's comfortable confidant. But what's the alternative? She goes to James for advice? Or worse, jumps on Tinder on her own?

No way.

"Yeah, of course I'm sure." I flash a smile that feels fake to me, but I'm hoping she's too distracted to notice.

She gives me a cautious side-eye look. "Are you sure? I mean, it's the week of South By. Isn't this a super busy time for you, since you're in the music industry?"

I'm not performing this week—BoS hasn't toured in years and we aren't officially a band anymore—but there are a shit ton of industry professionals in town right now, so I have meetings all week, but most of them are largely social. And there's only one band who has booked studio time, and it's only because they wanted me to work on a specific song.

Besides, one of the benefits of having ADHD is I can hyper-focus and miss sleep to get things done.

"Nah," I say with a shrug. "I've got a couple of things scheduled." I force a smile. "Nothing I can't miss for my favorite hoodie."

Clearly she buys it, because she gives an adorable little hop up and down, clapping her hands. It's the kind of thing that would probably make her tits look amazing if I wasn't focusing all my attention on the top third of her head. But, by God, if she can forget or ignore the fact that she's half naked, then I can, too.

"Yay!" she squeals. "This is so exciting!"

"That's a lot of enthusiasm for someone who was threatening to have me arrested earlier tonight," I can't help but point out.

"Yes, I suppose." She tips her head to the side. "But you're a different person than you were then."

"I'm a different person than I was forty minutes ago?"

"No." She waves her hand as if she can physically clear away my confusion. "Forty minutes ago, I thought you were the same person you were back in high school, but obviously you're not that person anymore. You're more mature. More trustworthy." She meets my eyes, holding my gaze for a long moment, studying me in a way that makes me feel exposed. "So, yes, I'm excited for you to be my friend again." Then a blush floods her cheeks and chuckles nervously. "You know, temporarily. It's not like I expect us to be best friends forever or anything. And it's probably less exciting for you."

"You have no idea," I say dryly.

And that's the truly pathetic thing. She truly doesn't seem to realize how appealing I find her or that I don't want to be her friend, temporarily or otherwise.

With that grim realization, I give her my real phone number, to the phone James still has, and make her promise not to text it until after she hears from me. We agree to meet up sometime in the next couple of days to… I don't know what, because I'm still not entirely sure what I've signed up to do.

I'm just grateful that I'll be doing it instead of James.

Not only because I'm sure that James and Maggie belong together, but also because part of me is afraid that if James and Gwen start spending a lot of time together, James will remember how great she is.

Sure, Maggie is great, too, but Gwen is spectacular in ways Maggie just isn't.

Besides, maybe this will finally cure me of this unhealthy obsession I have with Gwen. If tonight's taught me anything, it's that I'm still not entirely over her. That doesn't mean I can't get over her, though.

But you want to know what's even more pathetic than me pining after the same girl for over a decade? It's that I've never quite had a friend like that, a slipping-into-your-favorite-hoodie kind of friend.

It sure as hell isn't James. Things have been somewhere on the spectrum between tense and outright weird since I got hired for BoS and he didn't. Bex and I are pretty close, but I wasn't around for most of her formative years.

I'm still friends with the other guys from BoS, but those friendships were formed in the weird pressure cooker of fame, proximity, and a pact that we would never share women, no matter how many of them offered. For years, we spent three-hundred and sixty-two days a year together. And, no, I'm not exaggerating. We're still tight, and I know they'll be there if I need them, but those friendships are more complicated. More like a compression gear than a hoodie.

I leave Gwen's with the promise to call her tomorrow and by the time I make it back to my place in South Austin, it's late and I'm on edge. I have wristbands to South By, and there are probably dozens of places I could go out and listen to music. Or I could go back into the studio and tweak on my current project.

Instead, I pull up "Mr. Brightside" by The Killers. I blast it on repeat in my backyard and swim laps in my pool until my neighbor, a grumpy old guy named Mr. Rodgers—and no, I'm not making that up—throws an eggplant over the fence and yells at me to turn it down.

By then, I'm almost physically tired enough to fall asleep, so I do.

And for the first time in a decade, I have a wet dream and come all over myself like a damn teenager. What was the dream about, you ask?

I dreamed I was masturbating into a hoodie.

CHAPTER 10

GWEN

For the first time in weeks, I wake up excited to face my day instead of filled with dread.

Yeah, I'm still terrified that my train is running out of the track that's been laid down for me. I still don't know what the future holds. But for the first time in a long time, I'm excited to find out.

I don't know what to think about Tom's reappearance in my life. I never have known what to think or feel about him. He's been a mystery to me, dating all the way back to that first time we met, during my freshman year of high school, before Boys of Summer hit it big. We had that single day together. One fun, amazing day. I'd left that night sure I had a new, second, best friend. And then I didn't hear from him for years, not until he showed up at the Halloween party my senior year as part of some kind of joke or dare or something.

When you're a dorky science nerd, having a pop star pretend to be your friend as a practical joke is pretty much the worst thing that can happen. It was borderline cruel. But I got over it. Whatever. That Halloween eight years ago was the last contact I'd had with Tom until tonight.

So what I am supposed to think about the fact that he's the one who came to my rescue? It's South By, for Christ's sake! I can only imagine the parties and shows and… whatever it is pop stars do during South By… that he's missing out on to be here. The fact that he came to pick me up means my fundamental understanding of his personality is somehow wrong. The fact that he broke into my parents' house and risked getting arrested to check on me is baffling. Add to that the way he practically quoted what I had said to him all those years ago, about how it's okay for friends to break into one another's houses to check on each other…

I just don't know how to splice this new knowledge about Tom into the matrix of my understanding of him. I can only assume he's changed. That he feels bad about how he treated me and that this is his attempt to make amends.

My parents are still asleep when I make myself coffee in their French press. Normally, I never take the time to make French-press coffee, even though it's my favorite. Plus, since I'm a "starving grad student," the beans I can afford are way crappier than theirs, so it's a double treat.

I even make a second cup, then pour them both into one of the ceramic travel mugs my parents keep handy. It's still early, so I go online to check my email. After I blow through those, I dig up a few medical articles and read about ADHD. A lot of what I learn is familiar from my conversations with Holly. I learn that, contrary to popular believe, most people with ADHD can't treat it with changes in diet or eliminating sugar. That it results in scientifically documented differences in brain scans and hormonal uptake. That people with ADHD tend to be more sensitive to the emotions of others, but also impulsive. Which might explain why he was (impulsively) cruel to me all those years ago with what he thought was a joke and is now working so hard to make it up to me.

I can feel myself getting too sucked into the research, too intent on creating a narrative around his motives that excuses all the time he spurned my efforts to be his friend. I can't let myself do that, so I close up my laptop and resolve to take his offer for help at face value. Whether or not he feels guilty is irrelevant.

I close all the open tabs about ADHD and change tracks, searching for information on how to date. I skim past the articles about the various apps available now. Too bad none of them are designed for a scientist. I also ignore the articles that seem less about dating and more about getting your partner off. I have several degrees in biology. I know how the human body works. Eventually I get sucked into an article that's a reprint of an article from the nineteen fifties about how to find a husband. It's as horrible as I imagined. How would standing in the corner at a party and crying silently help? Or learning how to make toupees so I can meet bald men?

On the other hand, what do I know? Maybe bald men who take advantage of emotionally distraught women are perfect life partners. I stop short of googling tips about toupee-making. Clearly I need help. If Tom is willing to give it, I'll take it.

I load my laptop (for research purposes) and my favorite notebook (for note-taking and planning purposes) into my shoulder tote, then swipe my dad's keys from the hook by the door, leaving a note behind that I borrowed their car.

I don't have Tom's address, and since he asked me not to text him or James until I'd heard back from him, I do the next best thing.

I hit up his baby sister. I've known her as long as I've known James, and I bought a lot of Girl Scout cookies from her over the years. Surely that kind of loyalty will buy me the info I need.

Gwen: Hey, happy Spring Break week!

Bex: Hey! Ditto! What's up?

Gwen: I need a favor. Can you send me Tom's street address?

Bex: ???

Bex: <gif of a monkey with its mouth hanging open>

Gwen: What does that mean?

Bex: <gif of a girl giggling behind her hand>

Gwen: Did you have a stroke?

Bex: <gif of a woman rolling her eyes>

Gwen: Seriously. Stop sending me gifs I don't understand. Use words so I know you haven't been kidnapped or had a stroke.

Bex: Everything makes so much more sense now.

Gwen: Okay, that doesn't help.

Bex: You. My brother.

Bex: <gif of a child rubbing her hands together>

Gwen: I'm still confused. Can I have his street address or not?

Bex: You sure you're not with him now?

Gwen: If I was with him now, why would I need his address?

Bex: You're no fun

I don't know what she's talking about, but finally she shares his contact info with me.

I type it into my parents' navigation system. Austin traffic is always a mess, and clearly my years in Hillsdale have spoiled me. Even in Saturday morning traffic, it takes me nearly thirty minutes to make my way to the other side of town.

His address is on the far east side of town. I drive past the older homes that have been renovated. Past the new subdivisions that have gone in to try to accommodate Austin's recent growth. Eventually, I reach a neighborhood that's a mixture of older homes and newer construction. It's a little residential and a little industrial and far enough outside the city that the lots are multiple acres. I pass several quonset-style buildings that—based on the sculptures out in the front—are studios for artists.

When I reach the right address, it's a narrow drive sandwiched between one of the studios and a place called Honey Pot Farms.

I expected Tom to live somewhere sleek, modern, and soulless in downtown. A trendy condo with a lot of security, at the very least. View of the lake, for sure. But I passed all those kinds of places thirty minutes ago. This is practically the boondocks. There's not even a gate, just a mailbox and a long drive that winds past the artists' studios, past a parking lot full of junky, rusting cars, past a second building where I see the sparks of someone welding, before the view opens up to reveal a craftsman-style bungalow nestled between a grove of trees and an actual white picket fence of Honey Pot Farms.

The trees crowd the house in a way that makes it hard to gauge how big it is. The house has either been meticulously maintained or newly renovated, and the landscaping has a lush and overgrown look that—in Texas's heat—only comes through a lot of planning or a lot of care, and probably both.

I look around. There are a couple of cars parked in front of the house, but neither is the one Tom drove last night.

The house is quiet enough that I don't want to knock, in case whoever lives here is still asleep. But when I climb out of the car, clutching the full coffee mug in my free hand, I see an older man pushing a wheelbarrow on the other side of the white picket fence, so I call out to him.

"Excuse me!"

He glances in my direction and I wave at him.

He grunts and says nothing.

"Can you tell me if Tom Mendoza lives here?" I jerk a thumb over my shoulder toward the impossibly cute bungalow.

The old man glares at me and yells, "Fuck off!"

Surprised by his hostility, I stumble back a step into the door of my parents' car.

Alarm mixes with my confusion, so I pull my phone back out and text Bex again.

Gwen: I don't think I'm in the right place. Can you double check the address?

Bex: Did you pass a hot guy welding?

Gwen: I passed an artist's studio. I didn't notice if the guy was hot.

Bex: That's because you see the world through science goggles. Is there a farm on the other side with a mean old man who yells a lot?

Gwen: Yes.

Bex: Then you're in the right place. Have fun.

Bex: <gif of a llama prancing>

I tuck my phone back into my bag. Between the cursing old man and Bex's addiction to gifs, I'm starting to think I'm the only sane person left in the world.

Nevertheless, I persevere and head up the steps to the cottage. I ring the bell, wait a minute or two, then ring it again. This time, I hear movement on the other side of the door. Eventually, the door swings open to reveal a very tall man with a bare chest, long shaggy brown hair and a beard, and the most vivid eyes I've ever seen. He's got on low-slung cargo shorts. He's lean but despite that has the kind of chest that belongs on billboards. Between that and those startling eyes of his, I'm incapable of doing more than just staring at him.

He doesn't say anything but props a shoulder against the doorjamb and gives me a long, slow once-over as he scratches his chest. When his gaze reaches mine again, he smiles.

"Hi," I say awkwardly, my second thoughts multiplying exponentially. "I'm a friend of Tom's. Is he here?"

"A friend of Tom's?" the guy asks, giving me another once-over—a second-over?—in a way that makes me think I amuse him.

"Yeah."

The guy pushes away from the door and gestures me inside. "Come on in."

"I… um… I'll wait out here." Because this guy is giving me all kinds of sketchy vibes.

In general, I'm not a super suspicious person. I'm not petite and delicate like my sister, but I'm still a woman, and there's no way I'm walking into a strange house with a strange man—no matter how handsome he is. By all accounts, Ted Bundy was very good looking.

"Suit yourself," he says. He leaves the door open and walks back in.

Without the lean-muscled, possible serial killer blocking the door, I can see further into the house. In contrast to the quaint, old-fashioned exterior, the living room is painted a vibrant apple green. I glimpse black mid-century leather furniture and warm hardwood floors. In the far corner, there's a doorway into a hall that must lead to the bedrooms.

The potential serial killer ambles over to a galley kitchen that runs the length of the open-concept living space. Sleek modern appliances pop against white cabinetry. The guy rounds an island and crosses to a coffee maker before looking back toward me.

He gives a little head nod. "You want a coffee?"

"I'm good." I hold up my travel mug as evidence, but I step through the front door with caution, slipping my free hand into my purse and fumbling around until I find my mace. After all, it's possible he's offering me coffee just to lure me in.

The coffee maker is way fancier than anything I've ever seen. The guy slides a mug beneath a spout, hits a button, flips a switch or two, and the sound of grinding rumbles through the machine.

It's a very fancy coffee maker for a serial killer.

Not to mention, a thoughtful appliance layout.

"So," the guy says, "you're a friend of Tomás?"

He uses the Spanish pronunciation of Tom's name and emphasizes "friend" in a way that implies I'm not Tom's friend at all but… something else.

Confused, I take another step into the house.

Tom didn't start going by Tomás until his Boys of Summer days, which implies this man—okay, who might not be a serial killer—knows him from then.

"Yes," I answer his question, taking another step into the space. There's a pillow and a blanket on the sofa, as well as a small suitcase open on the floor, like maybe the guy crashed on the sofa. "I've been friends with Tom since we were teenagers."

The guy smirks as the coffee maker dings. "That's funny."

"Why is that funny?"

He picks up the mug and blows on the coffee. "Because I've known Tomás since we were teenagers and he's never mentioned a gorgeous redhead."

I roll my eyes, because… *gorgeous redhead?* Puh-lease.

"Is he here?" I ask again, because frankly, I don't have time for these shenanigans. "Because I actually have a lot to do today." I don't, but I'm not going to admit that to this guy. "So if he's not here, and you're not going to kill me, I'm going to leave."

The guy gives a chuckle and sips his coffee. "Kill you? Is that a metaphor?"

"I don't know," I admit, suddenly feeling like this whole thing was a horrible mistake. "You're giving off a very"—I wave a hand to indicate his bare chest and general demeanor—"hot, young Hannibal Lecter vibe."

The guy chokes and coffee spews out of his mouth.

He must have swallowed so much coffee wrong that he's actually drowning, because he drops the mug, which shatters on the countertop, and plants a palm on the counter to support himself as he hacks and wheezes.

And, if he is a serial killer, this will be how I die. Because I can't just watch him drown in coffee. Or maybe he's having some kind of allergic reaction? I don't know. But he's clearly distressed. So I hurry over, dropping my purse and my own coffee on the counter top. Once I reach his side, I don't know what to do. If he was actually choking, I could give him the Heimlich maneuver. Since he's not choking, I just thump him on his back.

"Can I get you a cough drop?" I ask. "Or some kind of EpiPen or something?"

That's when I realize he's not choking—at least not anymore—he's laughing.

"A hot, young Hannibal Lecter…" he says, gasping for breath. "Oh my God. That's the funniest—"

"What the hell?"

I look up to see Tom standing in the doorway from the hall.

His expression looks thunderous as he takes in the tableaux—the weird, bare-chested guy, and me, still patting him on the back.

Which is just awkward now that he's not choking.

I jerk my hand away from the guy and take a step back. "He was choking," I exclaim, sounding guilty, even though I don't know why. "Or maybe laughing at me. I'm not sure."

"Laughing," he says, straightening. "Definitely laughing. She said I was a hot, young Hannibal Lecter."

Tom's glare darkens as he crosses his arms over his chest before slowly turning to look at me. "How did you get my address? I asked you not to text James until I had a chance to talk to him."

"I didn't text James. I texted Bex. She gave it to me." I blow out an exasperated breath. "But she is very hard to communicate with. She keeps sending me gifs without explaining them. It's like she's speaking a foreign language."

The guy shifts to gape at me before looking to Tom and then back to me. "Holy shit. You really have known him since you were teenagers?"

"Yes, that's what I said."

He looks to Tom for confirmation.

Tom, still looking uncharacteristically grumpy, nods.

I swat at the guy's shoulder. "If you didn't believe I knew him, and you aren't a serial killer, why did you let me in?"

He shrugs. "If you thought I was a serial killer, why did you come in?"

I grab my bag off the counter and pull out my mace, waggling it. "I have mace. Then I thought you were drowning. Or choking. Or whatever. I thought you needed help."

"So you thought if you weren't going to mace me, you'd help?" The guy laughs again, and it's really starting to bug me that I don't know his name.

Before I can answer, Tom stomps across the living room to stand on the other side of the island from us. Looking pointedly only at me, he asks, "What are you doing here?"

"You said you would help. And I was eager to get started."

"So you just showed up at my house at the crack of dawn?"

"Hey, it's not that early. It's after—" I glance at my watch. "Okay, it's almost nine."

The guy is still looking back and forth from Tom to me. "Hey, are you going to introduce us?"

"No," Tom barks at the same time I stick out my hand.

"No?" the guy asks.

"Wait. What?" I ask.

"No." Tom shakes his head, swooping around to this side of the island, he wraps his hand around my upper arm and steers me away from his friend.

"No?" the guy repeats again. "Seriously."

Tom stops in his quest to lead me out of the kitchen. He gives his friend a glare.

The guy quirks an eyebrow, almost like he's asking a question. From the corner of my eye, I see Tom give an infinitesimal head shake.

Then the guy asks, "Phoenix?"

I swear he says it like a question.

I don't think he's using upspeak, the way I do when I'm nervous. It's a habit I'm working on, I swear.

No, this seems to be part of some bigger unspoken conversation between Tom and his friend that I don't quite understand. And frankly, it's making me more uncomfortable than when I thought he might be a serial killer.

After a second, the guy chuckles, following us around the island and holding out his hand to me.

"Dallas," he says.

I look from him to Tom and back again as I wiggle my arm free from Tom's grasp. "Will people please stop saying city names!"

Tom blows out a breath and gestures between the guy and me. "Gwen, this is my friend Dallas Boyd, one of the members of Boys of Summer. Dal, this is Gwen Mathews. We…" He trails off for a second, clearly unwilling to claim an actual friendship with me.

So I jump into rescue him as I reach for Dallas's hand. "I'm James's best friend. Or was before he got married. When we were in school together."

"Right." Dallas gives my hand a perfunctory shake. "James's best friend." He raises his eyebrows at Tom—again in a silent conversation I don't understand. "Well, that explains Phoenix."

"Fuck you," Tom growls under his breath.

Dallas just laughs. To me, he says, "I'm glad you didn't mace me."

"You could have told me who you were, then I would have known I didn't have to."

Dallas shrugs, stepping around Tom and me to grab a shirt out of the suitcase. "Usually if a woman shows up here, she recognizes me."

"And that gives you permission to be creepy?" I ask.

Dallas gives me an assessing look, like he really doesn't understand what I mean. Then he looks back at Tom. "I didn't mean to be creepy. Honest. I have no idea what she's talking about."

Feeling like I have to justify the fact that I thought one of Tom's former band mates might be a serial killer, I gesture to his previously bare chest. "He was shirtless. And being all…"

Since both of them are looking at me like they have no idea what I'm talking about, I lean against the counter, trying to look arrogant, and give Dallas an exaggerated once over.

They exchange a look.

"I didn't hit on her," Dallas protests, holding up his hands palms out. "I swear."

"You"—Tom, points to Dallas—"stay out of this. And you"—he takes my hand and starts leading me toward the hall—"come with me."

This time, I let Tom lead me away. Frankly, I'm just glad I finally know I'm in the right place. But I'm also a bit unsettled by the entire encounter.

Somehow everything about this morning seems to be a giant warning flag that I'm on the wrong track. Last night, after Tom left, I convinced myself that he could be a stand in for James.

But showing up here, meeting Dallas Boyd, not recognizing him, and mistaking him for a serial killer only highlights the truth. Tom is not James. Furthermore, Tom is not my friend.

To him, I'm just his brother's weird and inconvenient friend.

"It was nice to meet you, Dallas," I call out over my shoulder.

Dallas is still standing there with his shirt hanging open and his palms out. "I didn't hit on her. I swear to God."

CHAPTER 11

TOM

As I lead Gwen through the house and out the back toward the studio, I remind myself I have nothing to be angry about.

Not really.

Gwen didn't do anything wrong in getting my address from Bex. Dallas didn't do anything wrong by hitting on Gwen.

And, despite his protests, he *was* hitting on her. The second she mimed him looking her over, I knew it. I've known Dallas for well over a decade. He's good looking and practically oozes charisma. Back in our BoS days, we had a name for that look of his: the panty dropper.

I'm not exaggerating when I say he could have given that look to any other woman I know—other than Bex—and I wouldn't bat an eye.

Again, I'm not a jealous guy. That's not my thing. But this is Gwen.

And… Jesus, I don't even know how to handle this barrage of emotions.

I let go of her arm once we reach the backyard, where a stone path weaves through the prairie grasses to the studio at the back of the property. Just east of the studio are the two pools and a small guesthouse nestled up against the white picket fence between my property and the small farm owned by Mr. Rodgers and his daughter.

Every time I see my cantankerous neighbor, he mutters a curse. For the first time since I bought this place, I have to wonder if all instances of being cursed by him have sunk in. Maybe he's the reason for my current level of misery. I wouldn't put it past the bastard to have a voodoo doll of me buried somewhere in a pile of chicken shit.

The studio is unlocked already, because, after a shitty night of sleep, I was up at dawn working. Working through a song, playing with the reverb, mixing the tracks so all the instruments have their own space, it calms me down.

The front room of the studio is a lounge with comfortable furniture and a coffee bar. Beyond that, there are two recording studios, with my office at the back.

When I open the door to the front room and guide Gwen in, she looks around. I find myself unexpectedly nervous while she takes in the studio.

She's dressed simply in a T-shirt with a graphic of vegetables on it that reads, "Lettuce Turnip the Beet," along with worn capris and a pair of scuffed Vans. Her hair is up in a high ponytail that makes her outrageous red curls poof out even more than normal, like they're indignant about even that level of restraint. She has her glasses shoved up on top of her head. Her face is completely scrubbed clean of makeup, as it was last night at her parents' house. Despite the lack of makeup, her lips look impossibly red.

Impossibly kissable. No wonder Dallas was hitting on her. Not that she even noticed.

"This is quaint," she says with a perky smile.

"Quaint?" I try not to snarl my question.

This studio is not quaint. It's a fucking labor of love that I've worked on for over a decade, crowd sourced from nearly every musician I know, and worked my ass off to bring into being.

It's not "quaint."

It's state-of-the-art. It's a modern-day salon where artists and creatives can come together to do great work.

"Yeah. It's cute."

Fuck my life. Cute is worse than quaint.

Why I even care what she thinks, I don't know. Sure, she's one of the smartest people I know, but she's not a musician. She's not a creator.

Besides, it's not like anything I've ever done has fucking impressed her anyway.

Then she points to the words painted over the doorway to the hall. "Oh! Hive Studios. Is that hive like, 'the hive mind', or hive like bees… because you're next to Honey Pot Farms?" She gives me one of those big, toothy smiles of hers that have always had the power to gut me. "Or is it both? Because that's really clever."

Yeah, this is why, despite what I try to tell myself, I *do* care what she thinks. She's clever and smart—about some things, at least.

I should be grateful, because if she was smart about… oh, how her smiles affect me, for example… she'd have an unfair advantage over every other living creature in the world.

Resigned to knowing I'll spend the next couple hours being eviscerated by her grins, I gesture her down the hall. "I've got an office in back. Let's head down there before things get busy."

"Get busy?" she asks, heading down the hall in front of me, not bothering to hide her curiosity as she looks around. "Is someone recording later today?"

I run a hand through my hair, scratching at the back of my head. "Normally I wouldn't book time in the studio this week, but there's a band in town who really wanted me to produce their next song, so…"

She tips her head to the side, considering my words. "I guess I think of South By as one big party."

"It is a big party. For the people with wristbands. And, yeah, for some of the musicians, it is, too." I open the door to my office. She follows me in, taking in the barebones furniture. "But bands come from all over the world for South By. This might be their only chance to record with someone they only see once a year."

As I talk, Gwen sits in the seat opposite my desk. She reaches into her tote bag and pulls out a laptop, a notebook, and pencil case, stacking them into a neat pyramid on her lap.

When I wrap up my speech—okay, who am I kidding? It's a lecture—she sits there for a moment, staring down at the pencil holder, nudging it back and forth with her index fingers.

Finally, she looks up. "Can I ask a question?"

"Sure."

"Do you work at Hive Studios? Or do you own Hive Studios?"

"It's a collaborative," I hedge.

"Hmmm," she murmurs thoughtfully, looking at the wall behind me.

Suddenly I regret that I hung all those platinum albums on the walls behind my desk, because now I kind of feel like a douche.

After a second, she looks back down, rearranges the items in her pyramid, and pulls a pen out of her case, flipping open her notebook, clearly getting ready to take notes like this is some kind of class she's attending.

I have no idea what she thinks she's going to need to take notes about, but I let her go through her little ritual and try to pretend it's not just because I like watching her.

She lowers her glasses from her head to her nose, and gives her pen several clicks, like she's working herself up for whatever she's about to say.

"But you are at least a partial owner?" she asks.

The question surprises me, because I figured she'd move past that.

But she tips her head to the side as she studies me, those gray-green eyes of hers thoughtful. Then she shakes her head and chuckles. "Never mind. You don't have to answer that if you don't want to."

I have a whole suite of answers cued up, designed to redirect people to the purpose of the studio. People—media, fans, sometimes even other musicians—get distracted by me. They ask when I'm going to return to recording. Or go on tour. Or launch a solo career.

But, for the first time in a long time, maybe for the first time ever, I don't want to evade the question. I want Gwen to know the truth about Hive Studios. I want her to appreciate all the work and money I put into getting it off the ground. I want her to know what I'm trying to do here and why.

It doesn't take a genius to figure out why I want her to know.

I want to impress her. It scares me a little, how badly I want that.

What am I doing here? Really? What's my end game?

Do I really think I'm going to be able to give her advice about men or dating or romance or whatever the fuck it is she expects from me? Do I think I'll be able to do that and then just walk away? That I'll be able to give her advice and stand by while she dates another man?

Dallas is one of my best, oldest friends, and I wanted to shiv him for flirting with her.

Last night, helping her seemed like a better idea than the alternative—her getting advice from James or going on Tinder on her own. Now that she's here, I see this all in a new light. I'm screwed no matter what.

Despite all my efforts, I'm still hung up on Gwen.

Before I can decide what to do with that realization, there's a knock on my door —a loud knock—followed by some obvious door rattling and throat clearing.

"Hey," Dallas calls out. "Sorry to interrupt."

The door opens slow enough I'd have time to move a filing cabinet in front of it if I wanted to.

By the time it swings open and Dallas looks around, he almost seems disappointed to find Gwen and me seated on opposite sides of the desk.

"Oh, hey," he says, with a smile that looks almost shy. "So you're here."

"Yes. Clearly."

"Okay, well, I just wanted to let you know that… um… the musician scheduled for studio one is here a little early and is ready to get started whenever you are."

He says all this awkwardly, like he fully expects me to shoot the messenger. The "musician scheduled for studio one"—who Dallas so conveniently didn't name —is Spandex Boots, a punk-pop girl band who opened for us a couple of times. And, oh yeah, I used to date the lead singer.

Perfect.

Cassandra and I haven't been an item in years, but Dallas obviously felt like he needed to steer me around the potential pothole in the road.

I nod. "I'll be out in a minute."

Before Dallas can even close the door behind him, Gwen shoves her glasses back onto her head and stands. She's got her hand wrapped around her laptop, but everything else falls to the floor, notebooks and pens flying everywhere.

"Shit," she mutters. She tucks the laptop into her shoulder bag before bending over to pick up the rest of her stuff. Except when she bends over, her glasses fall off her head and her shoulder bag swings forward, knocking her in the head. She stands up, rubbing a spot on her forehead. "Fuck."

I don't know whether to laugh or cry.

How can one woman be so fucking smart and such an adorable hot mess all at once?

"Hey, Dal?" I call out.

Dallas ducks back in the room. "Yeah?"

"Can you walk Gwen out?" I ask as I round the desk and start picking up the things Gwen scattered. "Maybe get her some ice for her head?"

"You sure you don't want me to handle the other thing?"

"Yeah. I'm sure."

I'm fucking resigned is what I am.

Cassandra is over me, but she's always a little bit of a chore to deal with. I put up with it because Spandex Boots pays well for their studio time and deserves my full attention when they're paying for it.

Plus, now that Dallas knows who Gwen is, there's no way he'll hit on her or let anyone else hit on her. She'll be fine.

And if I'm honest with myself, I'm better off not dealing with her given where I'm at emotionally.

Yeah, I didn't tell her all about Hive Studios. I didn't show off all the platinum records—not intentionally at least. I didn't brag. I didn't boast.

But part of me wanted to. Knowing that bugs the shit out of me.

After all this time, after all these years, I'm still that fifteen-year-old kid with a crush on his brother's best friend. I'm still the eighteen-year-old willing to fly across the country on a moment's notice to make sure she's not alone at a Halloween party.

Some petty part of me is still too arrogant to accept the truth that maybe she did notice me and she just wasn't interested.

Maybe she did see me. Not the flashy, charming me everyone else saw. Maybe she was the one person who saw past the boy band glow and saw the real me.

Maybe she saw James and me with clear eyes, and she picked him.

CHAPTER 12

GWEN

I'm not a stupid person. At least, not normally.

So I have no idea why it took me as long as it did to realize that Tom would never be able to help me, but as Dallas Boyd—who I absolutely should have recognized!—guides me through the studio, I'm realizing exactly how silly my plan was. I wave Dallas back to the studio, assuring him even I can follow the trail from the studio to the house and then out to my car. I'm grateful that he leaves me alone with my thoughts.

What was I thinking?

Because Tom isn't just my best friend's brother. He's not just the annoying, arrogant braggart of my teenage years. He's not just the guy who pretended to be my friend and then blew me off. He's not just the guy who would swoop in for the occasional weekend and stir up trouble. To be honest, even back then, he was more than that.

Last night, and even this morning, I allowed myself to forget who Tom really is.

But now?

Now, I remember.

Now, I remember that he's the guy who has other famous musicians sleeping on his couch and a slew of platinum albums on his wall. He's the guy with

Grammy-winning bands showing up to record at the studio that he (probably) owns—but doesn't seem to want to admit that. What's up with that?

My point is, Tom is not the kind of guy who has time to be a stand-in best friend for his brother's socially awkward, misfit, childhood friend.

The truth is, even James doesn't have time for me right now. Tom certainly doesn't. Definitely not the week of South By.

It would be different if I had something—some skill, something—I could offer in exchange. But the truth is, I've got nothing unless he needs help creating a native landscaped garden or a compost pile. Or maybe he has a secret army of lizards he needs me to raise maggots for. Basically, unless Tom is failing tenth grade biology, I got nada.

I can't waste his time without giving him something in return, but I know this favor-imbalance isn't the only reason I'm feeling so unsettled.

Last night was weird. The whole evening was odd, from the paprikash, to the puke, to the park, to the… Okay, I've fallen into an alliterative pattern and don't know the right p words to label what happened between Tom and me in the car when he kissed me or afterward in the house.

The passion? The panty-melting? The perfection?

See? None of those are quite right. Those words and phrases are both true and incomplete.

I can't start thinking of Tom that way. Thinking about kissing Tom last night—or worse, thinking about kissing him again—is edge-of-the-map, here-be-dragons territory.

I'm still mulling over this unfortunate realization as I reach my parents' car when I see the obscenity-yelling man from the farm next door struggling to roll a wheelbarrow into a green house.

He's an older black man. It's a documented fact that people aren't good at reading the age clues to people of other races, so I have no idea if he's fifty-five or seventy-five. Regardless of how old he is, he's struggling to complete what is clearly a two-person job.

I welcome the distraction as I set my tote and purse down by the car and hurry over to the fence. Since he cursed at me earlier just for talking to him, I assume he's going to rebuff any offers of help. However, my boss at the university is of a similar grumpy nature, so I'm an expert at helping stubborn people who don't want help, without seeming like I'm helping.

There's no gate between the two properties, but the white picket fence is easy enough to clamber over. I'm only a few feet away when he glares at me.

"I could shoot you for trespassing."

Ignoring his threat, I open the door to the greenhouse for him, holding it as he guides the wheelbarrow full of trimmings inside.

"True," I say with a shrug. "But I don't see a gun on you. And I would be gone by the time you get back with it."

"Hmph," he grumbles, giving me the side-eye. "I used to have a latch to hold that door open. It pulled out the other day and I haven't had time to fix it yet."

I take in his explanation with a nod, even though I didn't ask. No one likes to need help.

"You one of those damn musicians?"

"No." I don't offer any further explanation, since I still haven't figured out what my relationship with Tom is.

"You a groupie?"

I laugh. "Absolutely not."

The man gives a grunt that indicates my answers are enough and he doesn't need me wasting his time feeding him any more information.

I follow him further into the greenhouse, allowing the door to close behind me while I look around. It's a commercial greenhouse, large enough to suit the needs of a small-scale local farm like this.

Near the entrance, there are row upon row of waist-high tables with trays of seedlings on them. He steers the wheelbarrow past all these, down the center aisle. I follow. Beyond the seedlings, there are fish tanks with raised beds above them.

I stop to gaze at them in admiration. "This is a fantastic aquaponics set up." I bend down to look at the fish more closely. "Tilapia, right?"

He lowers the wheelbarrow and props his hands on his hips to study me. "Guess you really aren't a musician then."

I grin up at him. "Nope. PhD candidate, specializing in soil microbiology."

"Sounds like a fancy way of saying you study dirt."

"Oh, not just dirt, but also the beneficial insects and bacteria that aid in the conversion of organic solids into humus, with a focus on the ratios of beneficial bacteria to pathogens."

"So you study compost?"

"Exactly. And then I dabble in the link between how our exposure to those things affects our physical and mental health."

He studies me for a bit, then nods, picking up the handles of the wheelbarrow before asking, "You gonna just stand there or are you going to get the next door for me?"

Figuring that's as close as I'm going to get to him asking for help, I trot ahead and open the door for him, inhaling the smell of dirt and compost. This is where I'm at home. Tom is platinum records. I'm potting soil.

Maybe last night in the car really was a dream sequence—a not-real experience from a moment out of time—but this is the real world. This kind of place is where I belong.

CHAPTER 13

TOM

If I had known twenty-four hours ago all the shit that taking James's phone was going to cause me, I wouldn't have done it.

Honestly, I would have walked out of his office with my own damn phone and let the chips fall where they may.

Once again, my hubris is my downfall.

I usually keep my phone off when I'm in the studio. The only reason I didn't do that during today's session with Spandex Boots is that it's not my phone. And I know as soon as James figures out he's got my phone he's going to come knocking on my door.

It's not that I expect James to be grateful that I meddled in his life, but it would be nice if he acknowledged that my heart was in the right place.

Instead, a half hour into the session with Spandex Boots, James's phone rings with The Addams Family ringtone that's reserved for my number or Bex's.

Dallas, who's in the control room with me, waves me to the door without taking off his headphones, indicating he'll take over for a while.

I answer the call as I walk through the front lounge and out the door.

"Hey," I say simply. I know it's James, and until I know what kind of mood he's going to be in, I keep it vague.

"You better fucking have my phone," he barks.

Okay. Now I know his mood isn't great.

"Obviously I have your phone. I'm talking to you on your phone."

"Don't be glib. You know what I mean. I'm pulling up to your place in five minutes. You better be there with my phone."

He doesn't give me a chance to respond before he hangs up.

I leave Dallas in the studio and head back to the main house and brew a cup of coffee. The chances that it will placate him are slim, but at least it's an offering.

His mug is ready and I'm brewing one for me when the front door slams open and James stomps in. His hair is disheveled and he looks like he didn't sleep at all.

"Do you have—"

"Right here," I say, nudging the phone across the counter toward him. Then I nudge the coffee mug his way.

"What I was going to say is, do you have any idea how much trouble you could have caused me, taking my phone like that?"

I don't bother to tell him how much trouble this damn stunt has created in my own life. Instead, I let him rant.

"I have work emails on this phone," he snaps, picking it up and shaking it at me. "Sensitive material that can't get into the wrong hands."

"You're an intellectual property lawyer, James, not a spy. And the phone never left my sight."

"If someone needed to get ahold of me—"

"No one did." I don't mention the messages from Gwen I intercepted and all that followed. Besides, I deleted all the evidence of that last night. He doesn't need to know what happened.

"It could have been an emergency."

"If it had been a true emergency, I knew how to reach you."

"Jesus, Tom." As if he doesn't know if he can really trust me, he unlocks his phone and scrolls through the texts and messages for some sign that the world nearly ended while he was unreachable. "Is everything a big joke to you?"

"Is that what you think? That I took your phone as a joke?"

"That's not why you did it?"

"No, that's not why I did it. I did it because your marriage is in trouble and if you don't get your head out of your ass, you're going to lose the only woman you've ever loved."

James points a finger at me with the hand still holding his phone. "Mind your own fucking business."

Maybe I should let it go, because I can tell he's pissed, but instead, I take a step closer. "Yeah, I could do that. Or I could help you win her back."

His gaze narrows. "Maybe you should fucking grow up instead. This is my marriage we're talking about. My life, we're talking about. It's a fucking adult relationship. This isn't the kind of problem that can be solved by showing up at a bowling alley with a bouquet of balloons."

Does he think that's a blow that's supposed to sting?

Shaking my head, I smirk. "Ouch. That's a low blow, hit me where it hurts, in the production value of a video I was in ten years ago."

He rolls his eyes. "Do you always have to be so fucking glib?"

I don't have a real answer for that, so I shrug. "Yeah. I guess I do. It's on brand. Just like you always take everything too seriously."

He opens and closes his mouth and I can't quite tell if he wants to say something else or if he wants to punch me.

Probably both.

But James has always been the mature one, so he does neither. Instead he takes a step back, and looking like he could breathe fire, he snarls, "Stay out of my business. Stay out of my marriage. And stay out of my life."

Then he turns and stomps out.

On instinct, I follow him out the front door to the porch.

Whatever else I might have said dies on my lips when I spot an unfamiliar Toyota parked in the driveway.

Obviously, a lot of cars come and go, so a single unassuming Toyota is no big deal.

But this one has Gwen's tote bag and purse sitting beside it. And, yeah, I know it's Gwen's because it has a cartoon pile of dirt and garden spade on it, along with the words "Talk dirty to me."

I don't know where Gwen is, but she obviously never left my property.

Which is just fucking perfect since James is here yelling at me about how I need to butt out of his life. If he finds out Gwen is here and about what happened between the two of us, he'll lose his shit.

So, instead of following my brother out and trying to talk reason into him, I stand on the porch and watch him drive off, praying that Gwen doesn't pop up before he leaves.

CHAPTER 14

GWEN

An hour after walking out of Hive Studios, I'm helping Newland Rodgers—my new farmer friend—turn the compost while he tells me about the history of the farm. It's not the day I expected and it certainly won't help with my dating awkwardness, but there is no place I'm happier than when I'm up to my elbows in compost.

As an added bonus, I tell Newland about my date with Derek. Newland is surprisingly easy to talk to. Yes, I suppose there's a chance he's not even listening as I babble about my graduate work and my current indecision about my future. But he does actually laugh at the story instead of being grossed out by my "maggots" before announcing that "Physicists are clearly a bunch of pussies."

"That's what I think!" I exclaim, feeling more at peace than I have since leaving Hillsdale. "Oh, sure, he may be unraveling the mysteries of the universe, but the work I'm doing has the potential to make a tangible difference in people's lives."

Newland grunts, stabbing his pitchfork into the pile and tossing the compost from one bin to the next.

"You know," I tell him. "There are some automated composters on the market that would make this job a lot easier."

He makes a scoffing noise. "Last thing I need is an expensive machine to do a job I can do myself."

"I don't think they're that expensive." I pause to look around this enclosed room at the back of the greenhouse. "But I do wonder if a few upgrades wouldn't improve your system. Maybe I could spend some time this week helping you with them."

He pauses, planting the pitchfork tines-down near his boots and propping his elbow on the handle. "Don't get me wrong, it's not that I wouldn't appreciate the help, but it sounds to me like you're looking for a distraction."

"I don't know what you mean."

He raises an eyebrow. "You didn't just wander by Honey Pot Farms. You came here after visiting that musician next door."

There's a knowing gleam in his eyes. As though Newland can somehow see straight through my defenses. As though he knows that in the past twenty-four-hours my personal universe has shifted to include this crazy, incredible possibility that I might be attracted to Tom. The only explanation is that I must look like a woman who has made a major scientific discovery that challenges everything I previously understood about the world. I'm still not sure how I'm supposed to fold this new knowledge into my understanding of the world. How can I reconcile the fact that I've been friends with James for so long and never once felt my pulse quicken when he looked at me?

I always understood that James (and by extension Tom) was a physically attractive human. They share the same strong jaw, full lips, and piercing green eyes. Yet I can't imagine lying awake at night thinking about kissing him. How can two men who look physically identical affect me in totally different ways?

Despite my feeling that Newland knows what is now my most closely guarded secret, I hastily say, "I wasn't really here to see Tom. I mean, at least not in the way you're implying."

"I didn't imply anything."

"Well, you said, 'that musician,' which does imply that when other women show up, it's because he's a musician. But that's not why I'm here."

"Mm-hmm." Newland makes a noise that sounds like he's agreeing, but also implies he doesn't buy my bullshit.

"Tom is actually an old family friend."

"Mm-hmm." He goes back to the job of turning the compost.

"He's like a brother to me. Or more to the point, he is the brother to someone who is like a brother to me. So it's not like I'm just some groupie. I didn't just show up out of the blue."

I cut myself off as soon as I realize that's not exactly true, because even though Tom agreed to help me, he didn't actually know I was coming by this morning.

"What I mean is, Tom is an old friend and he said he'd give me some advice."

"What's he giving you advice about? Because I can't imagine there's much he knows that a smart woman like you doesn't. Unless he's giving you advice about music." He pierces me with a look. "You thinking about starting a musical career?"

"No!"

Newland chuckles, as if that idea of me as a musician is the funniest thing he's ever heard. "Good. 'Cause you're too smart for that, right?"

"He's supposed to give me advice about dating," I admit, even though I'm still having doubts about this plan.

"Mm-hmm." This time, the noise sounds very suspicious.

"The truth is, I don't have a lot of experience with men. And Tom offered to help."

Newland pauses again, pinning me with a steely-eyed look. "He offered to help you get experience with men?"

It takes a beat for his meaning to sink in. Then I raise my hands up to ward off his confusion. "Oh. No! Not like that." I laugh. It sounds equal parts embarrassed and amused.

Okay, it probably sounds equal parts embarrassed and humiliated, but I try to pass it off as amusement.

"No, Tom doesn't think about me like that. I think he just meant he'd give me tips about…"

I trail off here, because I'm not sure what kind of advice Tom would be able to give me. Or, for that matter, what kind of advice James would be able to give me either. It's not like he can teach me to be less awkward. Less… well, me. It's not like he can come along on dates and throw himself in front of the conversational bus every time I bring up my research or start talking about grubs.

Newland makes another suspicious-sounding grunt.

For some reason, I feel the need to defend this plan, even as it's becoming more and more clear by the minute that the plan is poorly conceived and destined for failure.

"The point is, Tom offered to help. And it's not like I can get advice about men or dating or anything like that from anyone else. Besides, I trust Tom. I know him. I mean, not in the biblical sense. Obviously. Just…"

God. I should just stop talking. Possibly forever.

Before I can decide whether or not a vow of silence will negatively affect my career, a voice from behind me says, "Jesus, Gwen."

It's a voice that sounds suspiciously like Tom's voice.

I turn, and sure enough, there's Tom.

He's standing in the open doorway between the two parts of the greenhouse. He's got his hands propped on his hips and a scowl on his face.

I don't know how or why, but he looks even more annoyed than he did about an hour ago when I accused his bandmate of being a serial killer.

"Oh, hi," I say stupidly.

"What are you doing?" he asks, shooting suspicious glares from me to Newland and back again.

"I was just talking to Newland." When his gaze narrows further, I add on a lie, "About gardening. And composting. And the biodiversity of soil microbes."

Which I guess isn't a total lie, because we did cover some of that.

Tom blinks slowly, as though my answer has him so completely flummoxed he's stunned into silence.

"You do know Newland, right?" I gesture to the farmer.

Tom's gaze moves to Newland and he gives a slow nod. "Mr. Rodgers."

Newland grunts in return.

Weirdly, this is the moment that I remember that Newland told me to "fuck off" when I first got out of the car, and that Bex described him as "a mean old man."

It's possible that not everyone sees Newland as I do, as a sweet, old (though foul-mouthed) farmer.

"Let me get this straight," Tom asks me. "You know Mr. Rodgers?"

"Well, I didn't before this morning, but as I was leaving the studio, he needed help with the door. So I came over and helped him." The explanation falls a little flat, so I add, "He was pushing a wheelbarrow? And the latch on the door is broken? And then there was tilapia and compost?"

I stop talking when I realize I'm speaking in choppy phrases that all sound like questions.

I'm a smart woman who is about to get her PhD, and here I am, talking to the hottest man I've ever met about tilapia and compost, and I can't even do that without sounding like a moron.

Ladies and gentlemen, this is why I'm still single.

CHAPTER 15

TOM

People are always asking me, "What's the craziest thing that's ever happened to you?"

I'm not gonna lie. At the height of my BoS fame, some weird shit did happen to us. There was that time that a groupie broke into Drew's room and stole all his underwear. Or the mom who had a tattoo of all of our faces on her chest, Mount Rushmore style. Or the time fans stormed our hotel in Brazil and we had to be smuggled out in a bakery van, hiding under the bread.

But this moment right here?

No, not even just this moment. This whole morning. This past twenty-four hours.

Starting with Gwen taking her shirt off in my car, through her thinking one of the most popular musicians in the world was a serial killer, to her ending up here, amiably chatting with my neighbor who hates everyone. This may be the weirdest thing that's ever happened to me.

"Let me get this straight," I say. "You thought Dallas Boyd was creepy, but then you came over here and let this complete stranger lure you into an isolated building where he stores a wood chipper"—I point to the chipper and pile of mulch behind her—"that he could use to dispose of your body?"

She looks over her shoulder and makes a "huh" sound, like she's considering the matter, then scratches her forehead and neck, leaving behind a smear of dirt. It's like she didn't even notice the potential murder weapon he is literally holding in his hands.

"Well, when you say it like that…" She shrugs again and flashes me one of those wide, toothy grins of hers. "But it's not like an experienced composter would need a chipper." She tips her head thoughtfully. "Though I suppose that would help with the bones."

She turns to Mr. Rodgers like she's looking for a second opinion.

For the first time in the years I've known him, he's not scowling. In fact, he's laughing, clearly delighted by the macabre turn the conversation has taken.

I move closer to Gwen. Do I *really* think my neighbor has homicidal tendencies? No, but he cusses at me a lot, has threatened to shoot me more than once, throws vegetables at me, and is standing there with a pitchfork in his hand. Frankly, there are moments when Gwen makes me want to stab things, so for all I know, dealing with Gwen is the thing that will tip him over the edge.

I wrap my hand around her arm, trying my best not to notice how unbelievably soft her skin is, and guide her back a step. "Gwen, this is the man who threatens to shoot me on a weekly basis. Maybe don't give him ideas about how to dispose of my body if he ever acts on his threats."

Rodgers shoots a glare at me. "You stop playing that damn music so loud late at night, I won't have to shoot you."

I glare back.

Last night's blaring music while I swam laps was a rarity, and this bastard knows it. But I don't call him on it because the last thing I need is for Gwen to ask why I needed to swim laps in a cold pool while listening to angry, angsty music after leaving her house last night.

"Fine," I say. "I won't play loud music. You won't shoot me. Gwen and I will leave and we can all just go about our day."

Though, at this point, my day is so off the rails, I barely remember what I was supposed to be doing today.

I start to guide Gwen toward the door. "Come on, let's get out of here before he composts both of us."

"I'm sure he wouldn't—" she starts to protest.

Then Rodgers chimes in. "Now, hold up there. I was just about to offer Gwen a job."

"You were?" Gwen and I both ask at the same time.

"Sure." Rodgers scratches at his jaw again thoughtfully. "It seems to me Gwen needs something to keep her hands busy while she finishes up her dissertation, and I could certainly use her expertise with my soil amendments."

I let my eyes close in a brief moment of trying to block out this entire morning. "You're offering her a job?"

"Yep," Rodgers says blandly. "Think of it as a consulting position. Just a few hours here and there."

"Oh, wow," Gwen chimes in, sounding delighted. "That's a very interesting offer. Can I think about it and look at my schedule? I'm not exactly sure how long I'll be in Austin and I'll need to make sure I have plenty of time to prepare to defend my dissertation. But I'll definitely have more time available between defending and graduating."

"You can't be serious," I say, though I'm not sure if I'm talking to Gwen or Rodgers.

Either way, they both ignore me.

"My contact information is on the Farm's website." He picks up the pitch fork and returns his attention to the compost. "You know where to find me."

"I'll reach out to you," she assures him.

I just shake my head, muttering curses under my breath, while I guide her out of the greenhouse and across the driveway to my property.

As we approach the fence, Gwen tugs her arm free from my grasp. "Don't you think that was rude?"

"That old man is always rude. He pelted me with eggplants last night."

"I meant you. I think you were rude. To him."

"I don't really care, since he throws food at me and curses at all of my clients." When we reach the fence, I pause to jab a finger toward the greenhouse. "Plus, I'm pretty sure he offered you that job just to piss me off."

"That doesn't make sense. Why would me working for him piss you off?"

Why would it piss me off? Why does anything and everything related to Gwen irritate me? I have no answer to that question, only the unshakable awareness that it does. Everything about her gets under my skin. She's like a cactus I accidentally brushed against years ago, and a tiny spine got stuck in my skin. It was so small and insignificant, I always assumed one day it would just work its way out, the skin would heal, and eventually I'd forget about it altogether.

Instead, the spine just dug in deeper and every time anything brushes against it, I'm reminded all over again that this small, seemingly inconsequential thing is still a part of me.

"Look, I have no idea what goes on in that guy's mind. Why does he throw vegetables at me? I don't know. Maybe he doesn't like musicians. Maybe he's just mean."

"Are you okay?" Gwen asks.

"What?"

"You seem very stressed out."

"Oh, do I?"

Why would I be stressed out? Just because my brother is furious with me for meddling in his marriage. And he doesn't even know that I'm also meddling in his friendship. And hurricane Gwen has blown into town, leaving a swath of damage a mile wide. And now my malevolent neighbor is talking about fucking hiring her.

How will that work out?

She'll just… what? Spend the next several months literally right in my back yard?

Why would any of that stress me out?

"Have you considered taking up gardening as a hobby?" she asks out of the blue.

"What?"

"This is part of what my dissertation is about. How limited biodiversity in the human microbiome affects mood and stress levels and how exposure to bacteria through things like gardening and composting can have a positive impact on mood." She gives me an overly perky smile. "And stress levels. Basically, there's a biological reason why gardening reduces stress."

"I'm not stressed."

At least I wasn't twenty-four hours ago. Before Gwen came back into my life.

Before that, I had everything under control. Hive Studios was rocking along (no pun intended). I had a growing roster of musicians who wanted to work with me. Yeah, I still have the occasional panic attack or bout of anxiety, but it's better. *I'm* better. The right therapist, along with a regimen of meditation and exercise, keeps me on track and away from self-medicating with a shit ton of unhealthy habits. So, yeah, I'm good.

I'd go so far as to say I'm fucking great.

Or I was. Before Hurricane Gwen.

"I'm not stressed," I say again. Since it's starting to sound like a mantra, I repeat it a couple more times as I march back to my house.

Gwen falls in step beside me. "It's okay to be stressed."

I stop, turning to face her. "I know that." My words sound harsher than I mean them to, and she flinches at my tone. "Jesus, Gwen. I'm sorry." I scrub a hand down my face. "I didn't mean to—"

"No," she interjects quickly. "It's okay. I know I can be annoying."

Fuck.

That diffident shrug and self-deprecating smile? The combination fucking guts me, because I did not mean to hurt her.

"Jesus, Gwen. That's not what I meant."

She ducks her head, that half smile still playing at her lips. That smile that doesn't look at all like her normal wide grin. "I know what you meant."

Yeah. I'm pretty sure she doesn't.

I'm pretty sure Gwen has never known what I mean. That she's never known how she affects me. That she's never known how drawn to her I am. That it killed me imagining she and James might be more than friends. That it took me years to get over the crush I had on her. That right now, standing with her, I want to kiss her.

I want to pull her hair out of that ponytail, touch her crazy curls, and taste her again. I want to do all kinds of things with her. Filthy dirty things. Reverent, worshipful things.

The kinds of things that leave us both panting and breathless.

The kinds of things that might well obliterate my already tenuous relationship with my brother.

"Look," she says in a tone that's overly bright. "I think we can both agree that you giving me advice about men or dating or whatever isn't going to work."

Yeah. She can say that again.

None of this is going to work.

If I kiss her, I'll ruin my relationship with James.

If I don't kiss her, I'll have to basically move into my pool and spend the rest of my life endlessly swimming laps.

All of which are beside the point, because I'm pretty sure she's not even thinking about kissing me.

"It'll be best if we just both forget the past twenty-four hours ever happened." We've reached her car by now, and she turns to face me, thrusting her hand out like she wants me to shake on it. "Agreed?"

"No, I don't agree to that."

Because as crazy as Gwen makes me, am I really supposed to just let her walk away?

"What am I supposed to do? Let you go back to dating the Dereks of the world?"

"Yeah, maybe," she laughs, stepping back to lean against the driver's side door, with her legs stretched out in front of her. It's a laugh that pairs perfectly—

painfully—with her diffident shrug and self-deprecating smile. "I mean, Derek certainly wasn't a prize, but he was at least in my league."

"No guy who pukes on you is in your league."

"I mean, yeah, he was weird and socially awkward, but so am I. Obviously, Derek isn't the right guy for me, but eventually I'll find someone who is. Some scientist or engineer." She makes a thoughtful humming noise. "Maybe a doctor or a medical examiner. At least then he wouldn't be grossed out by my work, right?"

"Just stop." It's all I can do not to grab her by the arms and shake her. The temptation is so strong, I've stepped closer to her before I even realize I've done it. "You don't need to pick a boyfriend based solely on that. Besides, there's nothing gross about your work."

She arches an eyebrow. "Really?" She reaches up and scrubs at a smear of dirt on her temple. "Because I'm pretty sure I have compost on my forehead."

"And on your neck." I can't help myself. I reach out and rub my fingers along her neck, brushing at the dirt there.

"This is what I'm saying. I'm a mess. I thought Dallas Boyd was a serial killer!"

"Yeah, I'm never going to let him forget that," I say, laughing because I can't wait to tell the other guys about that. "Though, arguably, that's what he gets for flirting with someone so far out of his league."

"Oh please. He wasn't flirting with me."

She swats at my hand, which has lingered on her neck, because God help me, now that I'm touching her again, I can't seem to stop.

"Yeah, he was," I tell her seriously. "And I may have to kill him later for that," I add, only slightly less seriously.

Her brow furrows. "Because of something that happened in Phoenix?"

"Something like that."

I'm even closer to her now, my feet on either side of hers, our legs almost touching, my thumb still tracing the now clean spot on her neck. I'm staring at her lips, thinking again about how much I want to kiss her and trying to remember all the reasons why it's a horrible idea, when she swats at my hand again. This time, I let her dislodge it. I don't back away, but I plant my hand on the car window beside her head.

I'm closer to her than I have been in years, if I don't count last night when she had her tongue in my mouth. And I don't think I can count that, since she thought I was my brother at the time.

So, more to the point, I'm as close as she's ever let me get. I'm close enough to count the freckles dotting the bridge of her nose and to see the flecks of blue in her gray eyes. Close enough that when her lips part on a sigh, I feel her breath wisp over my own lips.

"The thing is…" she starts, but then lets her words trail off.

"What is the thing?" I prod after a minute of just gazing into her eyes, waiting for her to speak.

She swallows, nodding like she's working up her resolve. "The thing is, I'm a scientist."

I nod. "Yes. That may have come up once or twice."

"That means I'm too practical to pretend this is anything other than what it is."

I lean a little closer, because she's here and she's not pushing me away. So how am I supposed to resist leaning in?

"And what is this?" I ask, because I want her to say it. I want her to admit that she feels this too. This crazy pull that I feel for her. That I've always felt for her.

I need to hear her say it out loud.

Instead, she says the last thing I expect.

"This is you feeling sorry for me."

Her words literally rock me back on my heels. She might as well have planted her palms on my chest and shoved.

"Jesus, Gwen," I mutter. I take a big step back, shoving my hands through my hair.

"You say that a lot." She says it like an accusation, crossing her arms over her chest and tearing her gaze away from mine.

"Yeah, well, I tend to be frustrated a lot when I'm around you."

"Because I'm annoying?" she needles, like she's trying to get me to admit to something.

"No, Goddamn it. I'm not frustrated because you're annoying. I'm always frustrated around you because you're always putting yourself down and you're clueless about how beautiful you are. Because—"

This time, she actually does push me away. Palms right to my chest, she gives me a shove. Not hard, but surprising enough that I stumble back another step.

"What the hell, Gwen?"

"Don't do that," she says fiercely, jabbing a finger into my chest as punctuation.

"Don't do what?"

"Don't do that." She waves her hand as if trying to encompass everything about me. "That boy band thing."

"I have no idea what you're talking about," I tell her, rubbing my palm over the spot where she jabbed my chest. She has surprisingly pointy fingers.

And frankly, now I am annoyed, in addition to being frustrated, because I have literally never told a woman I thought she was beautiful only to have her shove me away and stab me in the chest.

Gwen crosses her arms over her chest and glares at me. "What I mean is don't do that charming thing where you quote lyrics to boy-band songs and tell me all the things you think I want to hear."

"I didn't quote song lyrics to you."

"'You Don't Know You're Beautiful' is literally the title of a One Direction song!" She throws up her hands in a gesture of exasperation.

"Jesus, you're suspicious." Still frustrated, still annoyed, I pace away from her and then turn back to ask, "Did it even occur to you that maybe I do think you're beautiful?"

She just blinks at me, still glaring, still distrustful. "What next? Are you going to tell me that I'm the girl you dream about? The only one you want? The one the songs are all about?"

For a second, I just blink at her, stunned. I don't know what's more shocking, the fact that she's quoting BoS lyrics back at me or the fact that she picked one of the songs that—for me, at least—was actually about her. For the first time, something like hope blossoms in my chest.

Grinning, I tease her, "You're a Boys of Summer fan."

She rolls her eyes. "Please. Everyone is a Boys of Summer fan. Your songs are catchy and contagious. The only people who don't like your music are dead inside." She narrows her gaze at me. "But that doesn't mean I'm gullible. I am far too practical to fall for"—she wiggles her hand in my direction—"your shenanigans."

"My shenanigans? You think my compliments are shenanigans?"

She frowns, her gaze moving over me, giving a surprising amount of thought to the matter. "Not malicious shenanigans. I used to think—" She cuts herself off and shakes her head. "I don't think any of this is mean-spirited, but you're charming and charismatic and you don't know how to turn it off."

There's a twinge of hurt in her voice. My spidey sense tells me I need to go back and prod a little more. To find out what she didn't say about what she used to think about me, but for now I let it go, because I'm still riding the high of learning that she's a BoS fan. Still wondering how I can leverage that into spending more time with her.

And, God help me, I'm still caught in the gravitational pull of her allure. I step closer, but resist the urge to touch her. Instead, I approximate the next line from the song, "Maybe you are the girl I looked for in the crowds."

Again, she rolls her eyes. "And maybe you're the guy who knows exactly what every plain, dorky girl wants to hear."

"Jesus, you're suspicious," I say again, but this time I'm not annoyed. I'm charmed by her attempts to push me away. Charmed by her defenses, because suddenly I get it. These road blocks she keeps throwing in my path are her way of protecting herself from me. It's not that she doesn't want me, it's that she doesn't *want* to want me. She's afraid of wanting the guy she thinks I am. If I can show her who I really am, maybe I'll have a shot.

A shot I desperately want.

Yeah. I said it.

I am man enough to admit that, after all this time, I'm still waiting for my shot with her. Because she's still the most fascinating, frustrating, brilliant woman I've ever met. And still so fucking beautiful I almost can't stand to look at her.

But I do. I catalogue everything about her, because the sun is so bright overhead, her skin practically glows. And the sunlight catches the copper strands of her curls so she seems to have a halo of pure fire.

And, honestly, I stare at her now simply because I can. That's something I haven't ever let myself do. Just look at her as much as I want to.

The few times I've seen her over the years, I've resisted the urge, because I knew if I looked at her the way I wanted to, someone—hell, maybe everyone—would know how I felt about her.

But now, since it's just the two of us, I look my fill.

Her skin is so creamy pale, I'd wonder how she's not more freckled if I didn't know she must spend most of her time in a lab. Her face is perfectly oval, her cheekbones high and sharp, her mouth a little too wide. Her eyes are alight with curiosity, except when she's glaring at me. She's tall and lean, and, yeah, a little clumsy and awkward, like she's an angel who never quite got used to living in human form. Or maybe it's just that she lives so much in her head that she's never fully aware of the world around her.

Except that right now, she's very aware of me. I can tell because her gaze hasn't left my face, and the longer I stare at her, the more rapid her breath is.

Yeah, she's just as aware of me as I am of her. Just like she was last night in the car.

Only this time, she knows it's me.

CHAPTER 16

GWEN

Part of me wants to get in the car and drive away. Just end this awkward horrible conversation right now. That's what practical Gwen would do. But isn't that part of the problem? For too long, I've done the cautious thing. The sensible thing.

What has the sensible thing gotten me so far?

A handful of mediocre boyfriends and puke on my date shirt.

And, yes, when I walk across the stage to get my doctorate, practical Gwen is the one who will get all the pats on her back. All of my planning and thoughtful decision-making has helped me kick ass professionally.

But it never got me kissed the way Tom kissed me last night.

It never made me feel the things I felt last night.

Even though a part of me wants to run away right now, a much bigger part of me wants to hear what Tom is going to say.

So when he asks if it occurred to me that he might think I'm beautiful, I answer him honestly.

I don't answer right away, mostly because the expression on his face is so intense I can't quite catch my breath.

"I don't think it's ever occurred to me that anyone would think I'm beautiful."

Some emotion flashes in his eyes. For a moment, I think it's annoyance again, because, as he already pointed out, he's always annoyed around me. Whatever it is, I'm too afraid it's pity not to jump in and defend my answer.

"It's not as pathetic as it sounds. Honest. The truth is, I barely even think about what I look like. I care about my work. About learning and solving the big problems. Figuring out the science that will allow us to heal our planet and feed people and understand our place in the universe. I know all of that is more important than physical beauty. But I also know that I'm not anyone's ideal."

Shaking his head, he gives another one of those grunts of frustration.

Before he can quote more boy-band lyrics at me, I add, "It's fine that I'm not a classic beauty. I don't—"

Before I can get the rest of the sentence out, Tom stalks over to me, cups my face in his hands, and kisses me. It's a hard, fast kiss that matches that grunt of frustration he gave earlier.

He pulls back almost instantly, his gaze roaming my face. "Just to be clear, I agree there are a thousand things about you that are more important than physical beauty. If you need me to list those off, too, I can, but I also need you to know that you are the very definition of classically beautiful. Your skin is flawless. Your smile is bewitching. In another age, artists would beg you to model for them."

His fingers brush against my hair as he pulls out the scrunchy that keeps my stupid curls off my neck. He palms the back of my head with one hand and pulls on one of my curls with the other.

"And this hair..." His gaze leaves my face and seems to trace the length of the curl. "I could write a love song about just this curl."

"I don't—" I start the sentence without really knowing what I'm going to say.

Which, it turns out, is fine, because he kisses me again.

This kiss isn't like either of the previous two kisses. It's not hard or fast or needy.

It's slow, gentle exploration. It's a question. Almost a hypothesis of a kiss.

If you let me kiss you, then you have the answers to all the questions you've never let yourself ask.

He sips at my lips. Small, intimate movements that are languid and unhurried. As if he intends to consume me, one tiny kiss at a time. Somehow I become aware that my hands have gone to his waist and my fingers are gathering the cotton of his tee, systematically pulling him closer, one millimeter at a time.

By the time his tongue brushes against my bottom lip, our bodies are pressed flush together. It shouldn't surprise me that a former pop star has mad kissing skills, but for some reason, I want to believe that's not what this is. That these aren't practiced seduction maneuvers. That this is Tom, the boy I knew before the world knew him as Tomás. And that this is the kiss he's always wanted to give me.

Eventually, when I'm weak in the knees and so breathless I'm showing symptoms of hypoxia, he pulls back just enough to meet my gaze.

His hands are still at the nape of my neck, his body still pressed against mine, as he says, "Last night you asked me if I wondered what it would be like between us. You thought you were asking James. I have no idea if he's thought about that, but I have. I've always wondered what might have happened between us if you and James weren't friends. If he hadn't met you first. Last night, when I said I would be your stand-in for James, that I would give you advice about flirting or sex or whatever, that was a mistake."

"Yeah. I think I knew that. You're obviously too busy to—"

"It wasn't a mistake because I'm too busy." He pulls back and meets my gaze, looking at me in a way that makes me believe he really means what he's saying. "It was a mistake because I can't pretend I'm just your friend. I can't give you advice about dating or other men, because I don't want you to date another man."

His words are this weird jolt to my nervous system. They're a shot of energy straight to my lizard brain, and they make me want to run for safety.

He's dipping his head, like he's going to kiss me again, when I duck under his arm and squirm out of his grasp.

I back away from him, palms outstretched like I'm trying to ward him off. "I don't understand. What are you saying? You don't want me to date another man. So are you saying you want to date me?"

Hands on his hips, he ducks his head slightly, like he's thinking it through, but when he looks up and meets my gaze, there's no indecision in his eyes. No doubt or confusion. Only that crazy confidence I find so bewildering.

"Yeah. I guess I am saying that."

I shake my head, maybe in hopes that the action will sort out my thoughts and make things fall into place.

"You and I don't make any sense together."

"You don't know that."

"Yes, I do!" I cover my face with my hands, then press my palms to my forehead, like maybe additional pressure will slow my mind enough to process this idea. "I'm a scientist and you're a rock star. It's barely conceivable that you and I live in the same world."

"Not everything has to make sense." He steps up to me, running his hands up my arms to gently pull my hands away from my face. Holding my hands in his, he gives me one of those half-smiles of his, the kind that make my heart beat faster. His eyes drop to my lips and I think he's going to kiss me again. Instead, he just whispers my name.

"Yes. It does," I argue softly, my words barely a whisper because even I'm starting to lose conviction in them. Because right now I don't understand anything. "I'm a scientist. Everything is supposed to make sense.

"All I'm asking here is for a shot. Give me one date."

"You're asking me out on a date?"

"Yes." He brings my hands up to his lips and brushes them across my knuckles. "Let me take you out on a date. Give me a chance to convince you we make sense."

Going out on a date with Tom is sheer madness. I know that.

Everything in my heart, every logical cell in my body and my brain is screaming that this will end in more humiliation and heartache than I'm prepared to endure. Despite that, I nod.

Because how can I say no?

How could I not give this man a chance?

"When?" I ask, partly hoping this date will be soon so I won't have time to chicken out. Partly hoping it will not be soon so I'll have enough time to prepare. And, let's be honest, I'll need at least a decade to prepare.

Maybe more.

"Tonight," he says quickly, clearly giving the matter way less thought than I did. He guides me back over to my car and opens the door for me. "I'll pick you up at seven."

"Maybe we should—"

But before I can voice my protest, the front door to his house swings open and Dallas Boyd steps out.

"Hey, Tomás!"

"Fuck off," Tom calls casually over his shoulder, but he's smiling as he looks down at me.

"Dude, you know I wouldn't interrupt if it wasn't a crisis. Cassandra's about five minutes away from a full-blown temper tantrum."

Tom waves a hand dismissively in Dallas's direction.

"I—" I clear my throat, because I seem to be having trouble forming words when Tom smiles at me. "It seems like you should probably go."

"Yeah, probably," he says, seemingly unconcerned about the crisis.

Walking backwards toward the house, he watches me climb into my car. Once I close the door, he turns and jogs across the lawn to the front porch, only to stop and watch as I U-turn and head up the drive.

My thoughts are a jumbled mess. And don't even get me started on my emotions. Nothing that has happened today makes sense. I try to muddle through my emotions. To figure out how I actually feel about Tom kissing me, telling me I'm beautiful, and wanting to take me on date, but trying to put names to my emotions is like trying to sequence the DNA of an Arthrobacter strain with a refracting telescope. I simply do not have the right tools for the job. So I shove aside all thoughts about my own feelings and just drive.

I make it halfway home before I pull over at a nursery I happen to pass.

It's one of the newer nurseries in town and I've never been here. Last time I drove past this spot it was a Greek restaurant. It's one of the many places that specializes in landscaping plants that are adapted to or native to central Texas. I wander around the plants for about an hour, running my fingers along their leaves and checking the moisture levels in the plants, which is really just an excuse to get my fingers in their dirt, until I feel slightly less discombobulated.

Eventually, I find a section devoted to plants that are native to the Blackland Prairie. I select a few plants and check out. Given how tight my budget is, even four plants are a splurge, but I feel more like myself as I carry them out to the car.

It's not until I'm home and in the shower, washing off the compost, dust, and sweat from my brief foray into helping out Newland, that it occurs to me that a normal woman getting ready for an actual date with an actual pop star probably would have spent her money on new clothes.

But, on the other hand, it's not like the forty bucks I spent on plants would have gone very far anyway. Which is beside the point anyway, because unless I wanted to hire a professional shopper, even hundreds of dollars at the trendiest of stores wouldn't help. As my sister is always telling me, I have the fashion sense of a colonial farmer.

The reality is nothing in my normal life or personal history has prepared me for a date with a pop star and if I think about that too much or too long, I might panic. So instead, I decide to ignore the fact that Tom is a pop star and pretend this is just a date with a guy I just met. Which isn't that far from the truth.

Whatever ideas I had about who Tom was back in school, my view of him was obviously tainted by James's perception of him. Even back in high school I knew James harbored jealousy over Tom's career. At the time, blind loyalty to my friend kept me questioning whether the things that James said about Tom were true.

Maybe I should ask those questions now, but what would be the point? It's obvious that James wasn't wholly honest about Tom. Frankly, if Tom has an excuse for his behavior, I'm not sure I want to hear it. I don't want his version of the past to muddy the waters. Instead, I'm going to go into tonight's date as if it were a date with any normal, non-famous person.

After I get out of the shower, I pop open my laptop and read through some emails from the university. I work with world renowned soil microbiologist, Max Ramsey. He's not just my faculty advisor, but also my boss. It's a huge honor that he trusts me enough to ask, but I'm still not sure I'm ready to commit to doing research in a lab.

I'm halfway through the emails when I get a text from his wife, Holly.

Holly: Just realized Max is inundating you with emails while you're on your break. Ignore him.

Gwen: Lol. It's fine.

Holly: It's not fine. He needs better boundaries. Plus, you might not be here in six months. He needs to learn to function without you.

Holly: Not that we won't miss you terribly, but you are not the *only* other competent scientist on campus, despite what he believes.

Holly: But in case you need buttering up, he is still hoping to convince you to stay.

I'm not entirely sure how to respond to this. I sense that Holly—who is genuinely one of the coolest but also most nurturing people I've ever known—is fishing for information, trying to figure out if I'm any closer to figuring out my postdoc plans. Spoiler Alert: I'm not.

I know she means well, because this is Holly. She always means well. She's like a tiny Samurai, always prepared to go into battle to defend the people she cares about. I count myself extremely lucky that I am one of those people, but even she doesn't have a Magic Eight Ball to help me figure out my future.

A few minutes later, I'm still trying to decide if her last text requires a response or if it's one of those things I can just quietly let slide into the filing cabinet of texts, when another text from Holly comes through.

Holly: <gif of crickets>

Holly: Okay, you don't have to answer that. No pressure.

Holly: Btw, didn't you have a date last night? The physicist, right? How did it go?

Holly: <gif of a man with his chin in his hands>

Gwen: <gif of SpongeBob SquarePants eating an ice cream cone>

Holly: Lol! What does that even mean?

Gwen: You know I'm not good at interpreting gifs, right?

Holly: Let's try again.

Holly: I'm waiting eagerly to hear how your date last night went.

Gwen: Horrible. He puked on me when I described my research.

Holly: Wait. Do I know what your research is about? Never mind. Not important.

Holly: The guy is a Dutch canoe.

Holly: Stupid autocorrect. I meant: douche cannoli

Holly: Duck!

Holly: <gif of a person sighing>

Holly: This is why I use gifs. My phone can't autocorrect them.

Gwen: Lol

Holly: My point is, forget that guy! Besides, no one likes physicists. They're very snobby.

Gwen: He was very snobby.

Holly: Do you want me to set you up with someone? I'm still in contact with a lot of former students.

I stare at my phone for several long minutes, completely unsure how to respond. After all, this is an actual question, so surely social protocol demands I answer.

Part of me wants to tell her no. After all, I have a date tonight and saying yes to Holly feels like cheating.

Which is ridiculous. Because I don't really believe this date with Tom will lead anywhere. At least not anywhere real. Certainly not to the kind of relationship I want long term.

Am I attracted to Tom?

Obviously.

Even though I plan on pretending he's a normal, non-pop-star for the night, he's still one of the hottest, most charismatic people I've ever known in real life. He's also surprisingly funny and thoughtful. And he's such a good kisser, I think his lips might be magical.

Despite all of that—or, let's be honest, probably because of all that—I don't actually expect this date to lead anywhere. Certainly not to the long-term, sensible relationship I want in the future. There is no way that's the kind of relationship he wants from me. After all, he basically admitted this was simple curiosity on his part. He's always wondered what things would be like if he met me first. I have absolutely no illusion that this is anything other than that. I'd be an idiot if I pretended otherwise.

If I tell Holly not to set me up with someone else, it will be like admitting to myself that I expect more from tonight. That I want more from tonight.

Wouldn't it be much better to go into tonight with my eyes open? Whatever happens tonight, it's not part of my real life. It's all part of the dream sequence that started Thursday night. As long as I remember that it's not real, I'll be okay.

In the end, I type in a quick text to Holly and resolve not to worry about it anymore. After all, I have another hour of dictation to listen to before I can start getting ready for my date.

Gwen: Sure! Sounds fun! Can't wait!

I cringe after I send the text, sure that Holly will see through my overuse of exclamation marks and realize that no one is that excited about a blind date—especially not someone who was recently puked on during one.

But Holly doesn't call me on my bullshit. Instead, in response, I get a series of confusing gifs that I guess are meant to convey she's excited and ready to tackle the challenge. Or maybe that she's training for a marathon.

At some point while I'm making notes on Max's dictation, Holly transitions to sending me pictures of the baby girls she and Max adopted. And then a video of her Flemish Giant rabbit, Tinky, hopping up to her miniature goat and scaring it so that the goat faints. Which she follows with an elaborate note about how she does know that fainting is very stressful for Bubble, the goat, and that Eli, the teenage boy she and Max adopted, is trying to train Tinky not to do it. Apparently training rabbits is hard.

Before he fell in love with Holly, Max wasn't the kind of man to have goats and rabbits in his life. Or teenagers. Or women, for that matter. He didn't know he wanted those things until suddenly they were a part of his life. Seeing how happy all that chaos has made him, I know that's what I want for myself.

Not rabbits or fainting goats, but whatever it is that will make me happy that I don't yet know I need.

CHAPTER 17

TOM

By the time I get Cranky Boots—aka Spandex Boots—out of the studio, half my day is gone.

Yes, it's work, but under the circumstances, it feels like wasted time.

Don't get me wrong, I know exactly how privileged I am to be able to do work that I love and that I'm good at. I understand that for a lot of people this would be a dream job. Any other day of the year, it's my dream job, despite how difficult Cassandra can be.

But today, she's feeling extra clingy and insecure—which is just stupid, because she sounded amazing in the studio.

When we leave the studio and head up to the small park area near the front of the property, I purposefully steer her to the path that leads around the house instead of through it.

Dallas wanders over as the other musicians load their equipment up to leave. It's a collection of local studio musicians she hired for the session as well as the other members of the band.

He's talking to one of the drummers as Cassandra slides up next to me.

"You sure that last take was good?" she asks.

Cassandra isn't the type to bat her eyelashes or simper, but I still hear the neediness in the question.

"It was amazing." I'm not even lying. Cassandra has a gritty, soulful voice that pairs perfectly with the lyrics. "Exactly how I imagined it when I wrote it."

She runs a hand up my chest. "We always were magic together, weren't we?"

Nope. Not even a little.

Even when we were dating, the only magic in our relationship was how happy the press coverage made the management company we both used at the time. Our relationship was never romantic. It was a business arrangement brokered by our managers to distract from my poor choices and her borderline abusive father. She knew that at the time, but now I can't tell if she's just bored or if her memory is tainted by all the romantic pictures of us together still out there on the internet. I'm pretty sure just the fact that we're together in the same town has already stirred up the interest of a few of the gossip websites.

But if Cassandra remembers our relationship differently than I do, who am I to disillusion her?

"Those were good times," I say. It doesn't sound the least bit convincing to me, especially since I peel her hand off my chest and put distance between us as I say it. "Speaking of good times, aren't you playing South By tonight?"

She brightens. "Yeah. You going to come listen?"

"I have plans."

"Let me know if you change your mind. I can leave your name at the door."

I already have a wristband that could get me into any of the South By events. The last time I was in a bar to listen to music, someone in the band spotted me and invited me up on stage. I looked like a dick when I wouldn't go up. I apologized later, in private, and explained about the panic attacks I get on stage sometimes—which is the real reason I haven't performed live in years.

It was a nightmare all around, because then they felt like assholes, even though they'd done nothing wrong. And everyone in the audience thought I was the jerk too arrogant to get up on stage with a local band. Yeah, that's not the kind of thing I want to repeat.

Which is beside the point, because tonight is my one shot to wow Gwen and there's no way I'm going to blow it by taking her to a bar or a concert. A) She would probably think I'm trying to impress her with my celebrity status. B) I don't want loud and crowded. I want quiet and intimate.

Of course, quiet and intimate are hard to come by in Austin this week.

Once all of the musicians—other than Dallas, obviously—are loaded into their rides and driving off, I turn to head back into the house so I can start planning a date that will knock Gwen off her feet, only to nearly impale myself on the pitch-fork Mr. Rodgers is pointing at my chest.

I jump away from the pitchfork-wielding maniac. "What the fuck?"

Rodgers jabs the pitchfork at me, making me flinch even though he's now several feet away. "What exactly do you think you're doing?"

"Fleeing for my life!" I say, continuing to back up, palms outstretched.

"Woah, woah, woah!" Dallas steps between us, waving his arms.

"What are you messing around with?" Rodgers asks.

"What are you doing?" I ask Dallas, shoving him out of the way.

"I'm protecting you," Dallas grumbles.

"You getting stabbed instead of me helps no one. You should call the police. That's what you should do."

Rodgers shifts the tines of the pitchfork back and forth between Dallas and me, like he can't decide who to stab first. He pauses on me and jabs them in my direction again. "And you should start talking."

"About what?" I ask, hands still in the air.

"About what your intentions are to the nice girl, Gwen."

"What?" both Dallas and I ask at the same time.

We exchange a look, and then I take a step forward, knocking that damn pitch fork to the side so it's not pointed directly at my chest.

"You've been cussing at me, throwing food at me, and generally being the shittiest neighbor ever for the past four years. And now you come over here and threaten to skewer me. Over Gwen?"

"Yeah." Rodgers swivels the pitchfork back in my direction. "That girl is a hell of a young woman and she deserves better than to be fucked with by the likes of you."

"Who says I'm fucking with her?"

"Two hours ago, you were kissing her up against her car. Then ten minutes ago" —He gives another jab and this time the tines of the pitch fork touch the fabric of my shirt—"you were flirting with another woman."

"I wasn't flirting with Cassandra."

Rodgers narrows his gaze at me menacingly.

I don't like to think of myself as a coward, but I'm mentally calculating whether or not I'll be able to outrun him. Sure, I work out and the guy is at least forty years older than I am, but I've seen how much he can push around in that wheelbarrow. I don't love my odds.

I glance over at Dallas. "Dude, help me out here."

Dallas gives an ambivalent shrug. "He has a point."

"Are you kidding me?" I ask. "Some best friend you are. You are officially kicked off my couch."

Dallas smirks, because he and I both know that there are dozens—if not hundreds—of other places in town he could stay.

I glare at him. "You know it's not like that with me and Cassandra. She doesn't mean anything to me. And Gwen—"

I cut myself off, because I'm not sure I'm ready to voice aloud what Gwen means to me. How tenuous this all feels.

Despite that, both men seem to lean in, waiting for me to finish.

So I shrug. "Gwen is Gwen." I look at Dallas while I say it, because I can't force myself to say these things aloud and look at the man who seems willing to skewer me if I get it wrong. "I've been writing songs about Gwen since I was sixteen. I've been in love with her since I was fifteen. She's the one who got away. Hell, she's the one I was never even close enough to touch, let alone catch. So today when I had the chance to kiss her, I took it. And tonight, I'm going to see her again, and I'm hoping like hell I don't fuck it up."

Rodgers stares at me for a moment longer before finally lowering the pitchfork and stabbing the tines into the ground so he can rest his elbow on the handle.

Thank God.

And frankly, I can't believe he held it at chest level for as long as he did. I'm pretty sure my arms would have been shaking from the effort.

He gives a grunt—I can't tell if it's a sign he's letting me off the hook or a sign he's exhausted. "So she's the one for you?"

"Hell, I don't know. I know I've never been able to forget her. And trust me, I've tried. I know the way I feel about her is different from how I feel about anyone else. But, fuck, no one meets their soulmate when they're fifteen."

Dallas reaches out and slaps me on the back of the head.

"What was that for?"

"You just called her your soulmate. If that doesn't tell you all you need to know, you deserve to get hit. You're lucky I didn't punch you."

"Yeah, I'd like to see you try."

I don't have any interest in taking on my neighbor, but Dallas and I had the same basic self-defense lessons from the BoS security team, so I'm pretty sure I could take him.

"Fuck off," Dallas says casually.

"No, you—"

"I did," Rodgers interjects quietly.

Dallas and I stop squabbling and turn to look at Rodgers, who shrugs.

"I met my girl, Doris, when I was fourteen and she was twelve. I picked a fight I couldn't win with a guy way bigger than I was, and I ran into a church in the middle of Sunday services to hide. Slipped into the back pew and she was sitting there right next to me. Changed my life." He scratches at the back of his head, staring off at the horizon. "Bugged the shit out of my mom that suddenly I wanted to go to church every Sunday when nothing she'd ever done got me there. I told her I'd found God, but I knew the truth. I'd found a reason to be a man worthy of Doris. Took me two years to get her to go out with me."

I just stare at the man, my heart suddenly pounding, unable to say anything, because that's exactly how I feel about Gwen. Everything else I do is inconsequential. I just want to be worthy of her.

Beside me, Dallas clears his throat before asking, "Did it work out? Between you and Doris?"

Rodgers nods, a smile playing at his lips. And I swear it's the first time in four years I've seen anything other than a scowl on his face.

"My Doris loved bees and farming." His half smile falls away as he shoots me a glare, before looking behind me at my house. "That house right there was her grandparents' house. She loved that house. But her asshole brother refused to sell it to me after she died. Instead, he sold it to you."

Well, shit. That explains a lot.

"Man, I'm sorry. I didn't know." Did I know there was another bidder when it went on the market? Yes. And I loved the property so much I offered over the asking price, which isn't uncommon in Austin. Still, I feel like an ass.

Rodgers gives a noncommittal grunt, which probably isn't him accepting my apology but is better than him telling me to fuck off.

"Just do right by Gwen." He clears his throat. "She reminds me a lot of my Doris. A woman like that deserves a man who treats her like a queen."

"Okay," I say, nodding. As if I know shit about how to treat a woman like a queen.

Beside me, Dallas laughs. "Dude, you are so screwed."

He's not wrong. One of the weird side effects of spending your teens and early twenties in a boy band is never having to work to get women. Dallas, the undisputed pretty boy in the group, knows this better than anyone. Fighting women off is the bigger problem. I worked hard not to treat women like a disposable commodity. I really, genuinely did. But there's a lot of space between not treating a woman like she's disposable and treating her like she's a queen.

"That's not helpful," I point out.

"Do you even know how to behave on a date?"

"I've been on plenty of dates."

"Since BoS broke up?"

"I—"

"'Cause I'm talking about a real date. A date that wasn't set up by the management company for PR? A date where you have to do more than get dressed in the outfit your stylist put out for you, walk out of the hotel, and climb into the limo?"

"Fuck off," I say, even though he's one hundred percent right. I have never been on an actual date that I had to plan. And I've never been with a woman who made me work for it.

Because being in a boy band is like growing up in a bell jar. Everything is distorted to the point you have no idea what it's like in the outside world.

Since BoS broke up, I've tried crawling out from under the bell jar. I bought a house and started a business. I have a few employees who help run things, but mostly I do it on my own. I have a therapist, but not a personal assistant. I have a financial manager, but not a house manager. If I need groceries, I buy them myself. I schedule my own appointments. I drive myself anywhere I need to go. Four years ago, I—we all—had a team of people managing every single thing about our lives. Now, I'm a semi-competent, semi-functional adult.

In every area of my life except dating.

That is the one part of my life where the bell jar just feels too heavy to lift off.

Since I'm not about to admit to Dallas that I've basically been celibate the past three years because that seemed easier than leaving my comfort zone, I stop pacing and…

Oh, shit. I've been pacing. And kneading my right bicep. And, oh yeah, my heart is pounding.

Fuck.

Damn, fucking panic attacks.

Dallas looks from my right bicep—which I'm still kneading with my left hand—up to my eyes. "You okay?"

"I'm fine. I'm fucking fine." I force myself to drop my hand, shake out my arms, and hop up and down a couple of times.

Rodgers, who's been pretty quiet for the last couple of minutes, watches me.

I try not to notice him watching me.

Because lots of people have anxiety. Lots of people have panic attacks. It's not a sign of weakness. It's not a sign I'm flawed. It's not a sign I'm not worthy of love or success or happiness.

I turn my back to him and keep bouncing on my feet and shaking out my arms, purposefully breaking the cycle of my repetitive actions, just like my therapist has trained me to do. But it's not like I can just stop moving, because that doesn't help anything.

From behind me, I hear Dallas say, "Panic attack."

He says it softly and I can tell he's not talking to me, but explaining to Rodgers, who just gives a grunt. A moment later, he asks, "We need to hit a reset button or something?"

"Nah," Dallas says with a chuckle. "Give him a minute."

After a moment, I stop, brace my hands on my knees, and draw in one deep breath and then another.

Then I turn around and ask, "How hard can it be? I make a reservation at a restaurant. I pick her up on time. We share a meal. I don't let her pay her half."

Rodgers gives another skeptical sounding grunt. Not exactly the stamp of approval I was hoping for.

Dallas is shaking his head, but I'm not sure if he's disagreeing with my plan or he thinks I'm an idiot. Maybe both.

"You can't take her to a restaurant. First off, even you can't get a reservation on this late notice. Even if you could, you really want someone recognizing you?

Gwen doesn't seem like the type who'll be impressed watching you take selfies and sign women's boobs all night."

I think back to her reaction to Mr. Dude in the park singing my lyrics at me and asking if I wanted to hang out.

Yep. I'm an idiot.

"Okay, restaurants and any public venue are out of the question. How do I take Gwen on a date that impresses the hell out of her and convinces her to give me a shot? Because you're right, Dal. Acting like a star isn't going to get me shit with her. I need the opposite of that. I need to show her that I'm just a normal guy who's really into her."

Dallas is nodding thoughtfully, so I look from him to Rodgers… only to see that Rodgers is walking away.

"Wait! Where are you going? You can't tell me that I need to plan the perfect date and treat Gwen like a queen and then just walk away."

He only half turns back to face me, scoffing as he dismisses my complaint with a wave of his hand. "I've got a compost pile that needs tending to and plants to water after that. As long as you don't act like a rich asshole who's impressed with himself, you'll be fine." He turns and keeps walking away.

"Can you be more specific?" I ask.

Dallas, ever the supportive friend, is laughing his ass off.

I punch him in the arm. "What?"

"So basically, you have to not be you." He punches my arm in return. "You fucking got this."

I rub at my arm, smiling as I realize he purposefully punched my left bicep so I wouldn't have an excuse to rub my right one.

This is why, of all the guys from BoS, Dallas is my best friend. He never makes a big deal about the panic attacks, and he somehow always knows how to move past one without making me feel like a freak.

"That's still not helpful advice," I tell him.

"Sure it is. Just be who you are when you aren't a famous pop star."

"Yeah, right. Do I know how to do that? Do you?"

"Maybe not. But you've got a couple of hours to figure it out, right? How hard can it be? Billions of people do it every day."

Okay, Dallas may be my best friend, but right now, his glib as fuck attitude is not helpful.

CHAPTER 18

GWEN

I have no idea what to wear on my date with Tom, because:

A) I don't know where we're going, and

B) My date shirt was ruined.

The good news is there aren't many places in Austin that require more than jeans. And, thanks to last night's laundry debacle, my second-best bra and matching panties are clean.

I don't have any intention of stripping down to my bra and panties tonight, but I didn't last night either and look how that turned out. The way my life is going now, I feel like it's better to plan for anything.

As an added bonus, Tom is taller than me, so I can wear my favorite pair of lace-up, pseudo-Victorian boots. They have a slight heel—which is why my sister told me I couldn't wear them last night, just in case Derek was shorter than me. I love them because they make me feel like a bad ass. Like Marie Curie!

But—obviously—without the unfortunate uranium radiation.

By the time five-thirty rolls around, I'm dressed in jeans, my Marie Curie boots, and a black T-shirt, along with my petri dish earrings.

And, yes, I do have a pair of earrings that look like a bacteria culture in a petri dish. Is that nerdy as hell? Yes, it is.

But I love them. Plus, the way I see it, even if this is an extended dream sequence, even if it is a not-real thing that is destined not to last, I refuse to pretend to be anything other than a nerd through and through.

I got teased a lot in school for being a nerd. Yes, I know, I'm a grown-ass woman who should be over and done with any lingering angst over shit that happened in high school. I know that, but what can I say? Some wounds linger. Personally, I think anyone who doesn't admit to still feeling the sting from their worst wounds has never really been hurt. My point is this: I'm long past trying to hide who I am or pretending to be cool.

Since I'm ready to go early, I help my mom load the dishwasher—because nothing screams independent adult like helping your mother with chores—and then go wait on the front porch for Tom. My parents know I have a date, but they don't know with whom.

I can't imagine the embarrassment of having to explain this situation to my parents. I'm pretty sure my dad has no idea who the Boys of Summer are—yeah, he might have a vague recollection of my friend James having a famous brother, but I wouldn't bet on it.

My mother, on the other hand, is pathologically supportive, pretty much of everyone she's ever met. So my mom has been a BoS fan since day one. I swear she even has a T-shirt that says, "All my favorite boys are Boys of Summer!"

So there's no way I'm telling her I have a date with Tom.

Instead, I described my date as "a friend of a friend," which technically isn't a lie.

I'm sitting on my front porch, reading an article on my phone, when Tom pulls up in his SUV. It's early enough that the sun hasn't set yet and in the light of day, I see that it's a Tesla.

I try not to let it bother me that he drives a state-of-the-art-electric car while my decade-old Kia is currently on life support in the shop.

He climbs out of the car, but I hurry down off the porch before he can even make it to the front path.

"You look—" he starts to say.

In the same moment, I blurt, "I bought you this," as I thrust the plant in his hands. "And three more just like it."

"Great," he finishes, looking from the plant to me and back again.

I nearly tell him that he doesn't have to compliment me. After all, I know this outfit isn't exactly magazine cover worthy. But I don't, mostly because I don't want a repeat of the "You Don't Know You're Beautiful" argument.

Instead, I nod and say a polite, "So do you." Even though I haven't really looked at him yet.

When I do look at him, I'm relieved to see he's in jeans also. He's got on a white shirt under a jacket with snaps up the front that makes me think of baseball players in the forties. He's still got that scruff on his jaw, and when I remember how delicious it felt when he kissed me, I have to stop looking at him, because if I don't, I'm afraid I'll do something stupid. Like lick his neck.

Thankfully, he doesn't notice my preoccupation with his neck, because he's still looking at the plant in his hands.

"Is this a…" He starts to ask but then trails off, seemingly unsure how to describe the plant.

"Echinacea purpurea. A purple coneflower."

His ridiculously full lips curve into a bemused smile. "Thanks."

Suddenly, my impulse purchase seems silly, so I rush to explain. "Right now, you've got daylilies planted along the fence between your property and Newland's."

Tom looks up at me, clearly confused. "I didn't think there were any flowers in my yard right now."

"They're not blooming yet, but I recognized their leaf pattern."

Tom's bemused frown deepens.

I rush to explain before he strains something trying to figure out my logic. "Daylilies are beautiful and practical. Whoever did your landscaping probably uses them all the time. But they have a very strong scent that actually drives bees away. Which is fine. Unless you live next to a small farm that's trying to raise honey. Purple coneflowers, on the other hand, are native to Texas, require very little care, and are beloved by bees."

Tom looks up at me and I'm not sure if that's amusement or pure horror on his face.

That's right. Behold the profound nerdiness.

I didn't buy him the plants for the sole purpose of driving him off, but now that we're deep in the discussion, it's occurred to me that if he can't take this level of dork, we might as well end the day now.

After a second, he grins. "So you bought this for me to help me make peace with Evil Mr. Rodgers?"

"Newland," I say pointedly, "is not evil."

"He nearly stabbed me with his pitchfork this afternoon."

"I prefer to think of him as misunderstood." I gesture to the coneflower. "And a few changes on both of your parts might heal the breach. So to speak."

Tom carefully straps the two-gallon pot into the backseat. I cringe, protesting about the damage the plant might do to the leather, but he just shrugs, so I bring him the other three plants.

Even though Tom passed the nerdiness test, I still don't know what to say to him once we're in the car and he's driving. Which is crazy, since last night I talked almost non-stop when I thought he was James.

As if the whole taking my shirt off in the car (and then later my bra) wasn't bad enough, I'm pretty sure I said a lot of stupid things.

"Where are we going?" I ask.

He slants a devastating smile my way. "It's a surprise."

"Oh. Perfect."

He slows the car down to stop at a traffic light and glances my way. "Let me guess. You hate surprises?"

"Not at all. Scientists love surprises. Every scientific discovery, basically ever, is a surprise in some way. We just like to predict the surprise and then work our way toward it slowly and methodically."

He chuckles. "Hopefully you won't hate this surprise."

"The last time I was surprised on a date, it was because my date puked on me. So you've got a pretty low bar to cross."

A moment later, before I can ask any more questions, he pulls into the parking lot of a local taco place.

It's one of the trendier taco joints in town. It started as a food truck downtown more than a decade ago. Since then, locations have sprouted all over town, and, more recently, all over the state.

This particular spot is not far from the neighborhood we grew up in and is walking distance from the high school James and I went to.

Of course, when we were in school here, it was a hot dog place that made the best Chicago-style dogs I've ever had. I try not to hold that against the current taco place. Which is doable only because the tacos here are so damn yummy.

Being a semi-famous local place, the parking lot is packed, in addition to being tiny, but Tom pulls past the restaurant, through the main parking lot to the connected parking lot of the church around the corner. He pulls into an empty slot. After cutting the engine off, he pulls out his phone and types in a text.

"Food should be out in a minute," he says. "I hope you don't mind that I ordered for both of us ahead of time. I took a guess at what you might like."

"I didn't know this place had curbside pick-up," I say, trying to sound diplomatic.

"They don't. I know the manager and begged for a favor so we wouldn't have to wait. Did you see that drive-thru line?"

I glance back and see that the drive-thru line is pretty horrible.

Before I can comment, Tom says, "Also, Dallas said I shouldn't use my influence as a local celebrity to get special treatment. He said you'd think that was douchey. So, you should know that I know this guy from grade school. James does, too."

Honestly, I'm less concerned about him using his celebrity status than I am about his high-handedness in ordering food for me. I've read my share of romance novels. As a girl, I was always confused when the hero ordered for the heroine without asking what she wanted. My mom claimed it was supposed to be romantic. I had my doubts. What if she wanted the steak instead of the salmon? What if she was allergic to shellfish? Was she just supposed to die of anaphylactic shock?

On the other hand, our food is delivered to the car in less than five minutes, so I may have to revise my opinion, because tacos in five minutes is vastly preferable to waiting in that car line.

Tom jumps out of the car when he sees the guy walking up, gesturing to me to follow him out. Part of me expects… I don't know… a confused, what-are-you-doing-with-this-chick look when he sees I'm with Tom, but the guy just nods in greeting as he hands over the food.

"Thanks," Tom says, slipping the guy cash and what looks like a business card.

"No worries, man." The guy tucks the money in his pocket, but holds the business card between his forefinger and middle finger, giving us a jaunty salute. "I'll pass this on to my cousin."

Once the guy is out of hearing range, I say, "Oh, you're right, that totally wasn't about the fact that you run a studio."

Tom ducks his head, sheepishly. "Alex has a cousin who plays the guitar and is looking for studio work. I would have listened to his demo track even if Alex hadn't hooked us up. But I don't think Alex ever would have thought to ask if I hadn't called about the tacos."

"So you're saying that by calling to ask Alex for a favor, you were doing a favor for him? That's very generous of you." When Tom doesn't laugh along with me, I ask, "Where to next?"

He gestures with his free hand toward the church. "But first, can you grab the cooler from the trunk?"

I grab the cooler bag and follow Tom across the parking lot. It takes me a couple of minutes to realize we're heading around the church to the playground in the back.

"Hey, we used to walk over here after football games," I say once I realize where we're headed.

"Yeah?"

"Yeah. Not just James and I, but a bunch of us. Okay, mostly, we'd go to the home games for a few minutes, then skip out to get hot dogs, then walk over here and hang on the playscape until the game was over."

"Sounds like fun."

There's something sweet but also a little sad in his voice, but the stretch of lawn from the parking lot to the playground isn't well-lit, so I can't read his expression.

"It was fun," I tell him. "Most of our parents assumed we were at the game the whole time, so it was hours of just hanging out. We were all too geeky to be invited to the cool kid parties and took ourselves too seriously to get into any real trouble."

"So this is where you and James formed the bonds of friendship that's lasted all these years."

"Yeah, I guess."

I don't admit that lately I've been wondering how close James and I still are. Other than exchanging the occasional text, we haven't really talked in years. Frankly, when I think about the text he sent me in January implying he was divorced before it was final, I'm a little annoyed. That text seems like a prevarication at best and it makes me wonder what other things James has prevaricated about in the past.

I can't help but remember what Tom said this morning. That he wonders what things might have been like between us if I'd been friends with him as well as James.

And I suppose it's only normal to have those thoughts, but surely he doesn't regret the path he took instead. He's a star. He's famous and talented and—I can only assume—rich enough that he'll never have to work again.

When James and I were skipping football games to eat cheap hot dogs and debate the meaning of life in a kids' park, Tom and the Boys of Summer were traveling the world and playing sold-out shows to stadiums full of fans.

It seems impossible that Tom could possibly be jealous of the life he missed out on by joining Boys of Summer, but the sense of loss I hear in his voice seems impossible to ignore. I'm tempted to dig deeper, to probe at the issue until he admits, one way or the other, if he's actually jealous of the life James led.

However, before I can, we round the corner of the church and the area where the playground used to be comes into view.

My steps slow automatically. "Oh, no. There's a fence around it now."

Tom nods but doesn't look surprised. "Insurance companies. They made the church put it up in case someone got hurt on it and sued the church."

He hasn't slowed down, so I speed up to catch up to him. I half expect Tom to scale the fence. After all, he clearly climbed the fences between our houses just last night. But instead, he finds the gate and keys in the combo on the padlock.

He holds open the gate for me and as I pass him, I say, "Let me guess, you know the manager here, too?"

He chuckles, giving me a what-do-you-think kind of shrug. "It's not like I was going to trespass on a church. That seems like asking for trouble."

He slides the gate shut behind us and leads me over to an outdoor table that's already set up with a tablecloth, glasses, and a table-top lantern that flickers like a candle.

In the otherwise mostly dark playground the scene is unexpectedly intimate and romantic. "And how many demo tapes will you have to listen to for this?"

"Zero."

"I feel like there's a *but* you're leaving out."

"But I may have agreed to record their choir's Christmas program."

Before I can comment on that, he starts laying out the meal. There are chips with guac and queso—obviously—as well as a selection of salsas, street corn, and enough tacos to feed a small army.

He points out the vegan and vegetarian options. While I'm not vegetarian, this place's fried avocado tacos are next level.

I've already got a mouth full of food when I ask, "Do you do stuff this over-the-top for all your dates?"

He shrugs noncommittally, chewing slowly before answering. "Not really."

"Not really?" I prod, teasing him. "You know that's not actually an answer, right?"

He blows out a breath. "Okay, then. No. I don't." He looks almost embarrassed, as he adds, "You know how you said you didn't have a lot of dating experience? The truth is, I don't either."

I laugh out loud, then realize he's serious and have to grab a napkin to clean up the salsa I practically spewed.

He meets my gaze. Like he's completely serious.

But all I can think of to say in response is, "I don't believe you."

"It's true."

"You're a pop star. There had to have been a ton of women."

"A ton of women isn't the same as a ton of dates. Or a ton of real relationships." He sets his taco aside and pushes to his feet before pacing in those same kinetic circles he paced last night. "I'm not going to pretend I haven't been with other women."

"I wouldn't expect you to," I say quickly, interrupting him.

He continues as if I didn't, still pacing. "I'm not going to pretend I—or any of us in the band—was a saint, but we were a tightly managed boy band. That means there wasn't much we did without management's approval. Our social media, our social lives, our appearance, all of it was managed. I mean, legally, contractually managed. Boys of Summer was together for eight years. Half of those I was under eighteen. We all knew, from the moment we signed on to the moment our contracts ended, that the success of the band and every one of the people we employed depended more on our image than it did on our music."

He's still pacing and not really looking at me as he talks.

"We knew, all of us, that one bad fuck-up could ruin it all. Not just for us, but for our families, for the crew that worked on our albums and our shows. That's what we signed up for. We knew that going in. One bad decision, one pregnant girl, one drunken outburst, one bad trip, one nasty comment to a reporter, and suddenly you aren't a boy band anymore, you're a scandal. You aren't the band moms take their thirteen-year-old daughters to see. One mistake and suddenly you're the assholes who never appreciated what they had and pissed it all away."

"That sounds like a lot of pressure," I say softly. My earlier idea that Tom is jealous of James might not be so crazy after all.

This isn't just the kinetic, restless energy of a guy with ADHD. This is more than that. This looks like full-blown anxiety, maybe even the stirrings of a panic attack.

He stops pacing and turns to me, still massaging that spot on his arm. His gaze is intense and serious. "I'm not saying I don't appreciate it. I'm not saying it wasn't worth it. You know that, right?"

"Yeah." I stand up, brushing my hands down my jeans to get the last of the taco-stickiness off them. I cross to stand in front of Tom, unsure what to do next but sure that I have to do something.

I don't know how to calm him down—how to bring him peace—I only know that something tells me I can help.

As crazy as it sounds, I feel it in my gut.

You might think that a scientific-minded girl like me is too analytical to believe in gut feelings, but you would be wrong. And all the latest research indicates that gut feelings are one hundred percent real.

So, even though I don't know what I'm doing, I go with my gut. I take his hands in mine and I do what he's now done twice to me. I bring his hands to my mouth and brush a kiss across his knuckles.

"It's okay to be grateful for something, to appreciate it, to work for it, and still recognize that it's imperfect or that it cost you something." I feel some small fraction of the tension seep out of his body, so I keep talking, moving my hands over is arms, to rub circles on the spot he was massaging on his bicep. "Marie Curie was a brilliant scientist. She discovered radiation and invented X-ray technology that saved countless lives in World War I. To this day, she's the only woman to have won the Nobel Prize twice. She also died—painfully and too young—of radiation poisoning." I blow out a breath, hoping that my rambling about Marie Curie makes sense to him. "What I'm saying is that things that are amazing gifts can also be terrible curses. Nothing is pure or perfect. It's okay to hate the things we also love."

His hands slip up to cup my jaw, but instead of kissing me, he presses his forehead to mine. We stand like that—my hands tracing circles on his arms, his thumbs brushing my cheeks, our foreheads pressed together—for a long moment.

Then he releases a wry chuckle. "I think I may need to get that on a tattoo."

"Like, that whole speech about Marie Curie? Because that was a lot of words."

His chuckle becomes a laugh, a sexy, rumbly laugh that makes my clit pulse. "Just that last bit. It's okay to hate what you love."

I laugh too, because the idea that a pop star would get something I said as a tattoo is absurd. "In really big letters." I trace a three-inch-tall arch across his chest. "Right here, where everyone can see it."

He ignores my joke and instead pushes up the sleeve of his jacket to bare his inner arm. "No. Right here, on my wrist, where I can see it whenever I need to."

I glance down at his skin, where he already has a tattoo on each wrist, before meeting his gaze.

The serious intensity in his eyes makes my breath catch in my chest. How did I ever think this man was light-hearted and easygoing?

He's not that at all. Yeah, he's a pro at making other people comfortable, but there's nothing easy about him.

He is nothing like I thought he was.

CHAPTER 19

TOM

Somehow we end up walking back to the table hand-in-hand.

The sensation of her hand in mine does things to me I can barely comprehend.

Yes, it's a turn on. Everything about her is a turn on.

This is more than just that. This is erotic and soothing and a balm to my soul like nothing ever has been.

I'm torn between wanting to kiss her and wanting to drop to my knees, declare my eternal love, and propose marriage. That's probably going a little too far, but it's not like women who just quietly accept mental health issues cropping up during a date are a dime a dozen.

Especially when that date is a former pop star. Most women I've dated—and, as I've already told her, it's not many—want their former pop stars shiny and perfect. Flawed people need not apply.

But Gwen just… accepts my jagged edges.

"Thank you for that," I say.

"For what?"

"For not treating me like I'm a freak for having a panic attack."

"Ah. That." She looks at me, then smirks. "Besides, I thought we covered this already. My standards for acceptable date behavior are incredibly low right now. You haven't puked on me yet, so you are, like, miles ahead of the last guy."

Frankly, I'm tempted to hunt this guy down. I'm not sure if I want to hunt him down and beat the shit out of him for what he did to Gwen or hunt him down and thank him for it.

We eat in silence for a few more minutes before I say, "If we're going to test out this whole compatibility thing, did you want to tell me about your research to see if it makes me vomit? You said it was something about recycling food?"

She nods, chewing her most recent bite quickly, clearly excited to talk about her work.

Even then, she asks first, "You sure? Because apparently, this is the kind of thing that ruins dates forever."

"Absolutely."

"Okay, well, I assume you know what a horrible problem food waste is in this country."

I nod, even though I've literally never thought about food waste until this second.

"Around forty percent of all the food grown or produced in the U.S. ends up in landfills. Obviously, that's a huge problem. A lot of it is perfectly edible food that never makes it onto people's plates, but that's only part of the problem. Yes, it's a big part, but it's not the part I'm trying to solve. I'm interested in the food that actually makes it into kitchens or onto plates and then doesn't get eaten. Most of that food goes into landfills."

"But it's food, right? Doesn't it just decompose there?"

"That's what most people assume, but landfills are anaerobic. Since there's no oxygen, there are fewer living creatures—fewer bacteria, no insects. That kind of thing. Think about it like this." She grabs two of the uneaten tacos and holds them up. "If I took this taco"—she waggles the one in her left hand—"and put it in a Ziploc bag and squeezed all the air out. Then I took this taco"—she waggles the second one—"and left it here on the table, what do you think would happen to both of them?"

I shrug. "I think a raccoon would probably come and eat them."

"True." She tips her head to the side. "In a raccoon-less world, what then?" She doesn't wait for me to answer. "The bagged taco will go bad and get really gross, but at a much slower rate. Even if there are no preservatives in the taco, the lack of air means it won't decompose. The taco in the open air will attract flies. They will lay eggs in it and within hours, you have—"

"Maggots," I say.

She beams at me, and I feel like I just… I don't know, discovered radiation or something.

"Exactly! Those maggots eat the taco. Black soldier fly larvae can eat their weight every twelve hours. Magically, the taco is gone, so it's not taking up space in a landfill. Not only that, but once the larvae pupate, they can be an amazing source of protein for all kind of livestock or even domesticated pets. But the really amazing thing is that their frass is a fantastic fertilizer. It's organic, obviously, but it's also way better for the soil than pure chemical fertilizers."

"And frass is…?"

She gives a cute little wince. "It's poop. Frass is insect poop. Just like our poop, it's full of bacteria. And those bacteria are actually the part of this whole process that I study, because if this is ever going to be scaled up and used commercially —to keep food out of landfills and create food for animals and fertilizer for more food—we need to understand which strains of bacteria are helpful for this process and have systems for monitoring those bacteria. If we can crack that code, we can revolutionize everything from waste disposal to food production."

I gaze at her for a few moments in absolute awe. Yeah, I knew she was smart. I knew she was beautiful. Part of me always knew she was the most amazing person I'd ever know. But this?

"So, basically, you're going to save the planet and feed all the people and generally be a superhero?"

She laughs, that genuine, goofy, joy-filled laugh that I love. "That is the idea. But, trust me, I'm not doing it alone. There are a lot of people doing a lot of science to make this happen."

"Are they all as smart as you?"

She grins, leans forward, and crooks her finger to lure me closer. Then she says, in a whisper, like she's sharing a secret, "Smarter."

She says it without jealousy or ego, like the idea delights her.

I shake my head, bemused. "You're amazing."

"Why?"

"A lot of people have too much ego to admit that there are people working in their field who are smarter or more talented or more creative than they are. But not you."

She sits back a little and waves her hand. "God, no. If I was the only smart person working on this problem, it would be way too big to solve on my own. We need all the smart people working to solve all the problems." She tips her head to the side again. "Isn't that how it is with your music?"

"What do you mean?"

"Obviously, you're a brilliant musician, right?"

I try not to preen at her words.

"But don't you think you do better work when you're working with others? You can't just create in a vacuum, right?" She once again waggles the taco she put in an imaginary Ziploc bag. "In a vacuum, the taco never becomes anything other than a taco. And if you're going to eat it right away, that's fantastic. But if you aren't, it deserves to be transformed into something bigger, don't you think?"

Then she looks down at the taco and frowns for a second before chuckling. "I guess, probably now that I've described the taco being devoured by maggots and pooped out to become fertilizer, probably no one wants to eat the taco now." She meets my gaze again. "I guess my research really isn't good dinner conversation, is it?"

I shrug. "I spent my formative years on a tour bus with adolescent boys. I've seen one of them bite his own toenails. So it's not too gross for me. But clearly—what did you say his name was?" I ask

"Derek."

"Right. Clearly, Derek has some underlying digestion issues he might need to seek help for. I'm not saying it's customary dinner conversation, but to vomit merely from you talking about it seems a bit overdone. It's not as if you brought some larvae with you like show and tell."

She points a chip at me and smiles. "That's what I thought, too."

Then we're smiling at each other and everything about this night feels right and perfect. I can't even let myself think about how she handled my near panic attack. Not so much like it was a non-issue, but it didn't freak her out and she didn't ask me if I was okay. Fuck me, I hate that question.

She wipes her hands on a napkin, then gathers all of her trash. "Do you want…" But she stops talking.

"Do I want what?"

"Nothing." She shrugs, then stands and walks to the trashcan closer to the building.

"Tell me," I prod, following her with my own trash.

"I was going to offer to come back to your place to plant your plants."

It's certainly not a man's first choice of activities when a woman suggests going back to his house. But I'll take it, because it means the night isn't over and I get more of her. And that's what I've always wanted… Just more of her.

"I'd love that."

Her head tilts and I want to kiss her again. "Really?"

"Yeah. Let's do it. I brought you some Reese's Cups for dessert, but we can eat them while I drive."

Once again, she beams. "Oh! You remembered they're my favorite from that comment I made the other night in the car."

"Absolutely," I lie.

I actually remember from that first day we met and then from that Halloween party we were both at years ago. I don't admit that to her, though.

She may be ready to share all her secrets with me, but I'm not yet willing to share mine.

CHAPTER 20

GWEN

When I stopped to buy plants for Tom, I had good intentions. Innocent intentions. Zero ulterior motives. I swear.

After all, if good fences make good neighbors, surely organically grown, bee-friendly native plants make even better neighbors.

Good intentions aside, it turns out I'm secretly a genius, because now I have an excuse to go back to Tom's house. A non-obvious, non-hey-you've-been-acting-all-night-like-you-wanted-to-kiss-me-but-you-haven't-yet excuse to go back to his house.

I don't want to be overly pushy or make assumptions, but I thought dates would include kissing.

Not that I'm complaining about the date. It's been perfect. Fantastic conversation. Amazing food. Vomit free (so far). I am just really hoping for a repeat performance of Tom's amazing, rock-star kissing skills.

And, if I'm completely honest with myself, I want more.

Yeah, you heard me right. I want more than tacos.

More than tacos.

That's how I know this is serious. I want more Tom more than I want more tacos. More than I want more Reese's Cups.

But thanks to my previously established genius, Tom agrees I should come back with him to plant the four purple coneflowers strapped into the back seat of his SUV.

We chat more as he drives back to Hive Studios—mostly about the studio itself. He describes his vision of a recording studio that's less a business and more a cooperative, one that operates on a sliding scale, making it available to new artists as well as established artists. He talks about how he crowdsourced the funding from all the successful musicians he knows and how grateful some of them were for the opportunity to give back to the community. The artists who can't afford to pay the standard rates "pay" for their studio time in other ways.

I knew some of this already, because when he didn't want to answer questions about it this morning, I Googled it at home. I read some articles in Austin American Statesman and the Austin Chronicle about Hive Studios, and though all of them skated over his involvement in the project, the coverage was glowing. So, yeah, I can put two and two together. Hive Studios is clearly Tom's love letter to the music industry. His thank you note for the success he experienced. And, now that I know about his anxiety and his panic attacks, I see that's also his way of being part of the industry, even though being in the spotlight was physically painful for him.

The love and work he's put into Hive Studios is both achingly sad and stirringly hopeful.

By the time we reach Hive Studios, I'm pretty sure there's nothing Tom could say or do to be more attractive. Except then he picks up a shovel.

Okay, yeah, I'm a weirdo.

But I am a sucker for a man who knows his way around gardening equipment. Once we've got the plants in the ground, we're both covered in dirt and sweat. I look over at Tom and he's got dirt smudged on his left cheek and down his neck. I'm tempted to brush it off, but my hands are pretty filthy.

"That's the most fun I've ever had on a date," I say. Then immediately bite down on my lip and wish it back.

Because—hello!—Tom is an actual pop star, so I'm thinking my date-bar is probably a lot lower than his.

Except when I look up at him, he's grinning. "Me, too."

I give him the side-eye. "Don't patronize me," I order, careful to keep my tone light, not wanting him to know how badly I need him to be honest with me.

He laughs. "I'm not. Honestly. Most of my dates have been carefully scheduled photo-ops. The last date I went on, the woman got mad because I refused to tag her on Instagram."

Despite his laugh, I hear the hint of bitterness buried beneath his light tone, and I kind of want to stab this woman, whoever she is. I'm pretty sure I could get Newland to help me dispose of the body.

Instead of demanding Tom give up her name and address, I meet his gaze and say seriously, "I'm pretty sure I have dirt in my hair, so whatever you do, please don't tag me on Instagram."

His lips twitch and he reaches up to tuck a strand of hair behind my ear. "You're a rising superstar in the field of soil-microbiology. I'm pretty sure the dirt in your hair is a badge of honor."

"Not if it hasn't had the genetic components of its microbiology properly cataloged and analyzed, it isn't."

For a moment, he just looks at me blankly, blinking. Then he tips back his head and laughs.

Yeah, that's right, ladies and gentlemen. I made Tom laugh. Like, bust-a-gut laugh.

I can't help but beam with pride, and as his laughter fades, I look him up and down. "You're filthy."

He gives a wry laugh, then his eyes rake over my body. His gaze is so languid, so thorough, that by the time he reaches my face again, I'm breathing heavy and my nipples are hard.

"You have no idea," he says, his voice low and full of gravel.

I bite my lip.

Yeah, I might not have any idea, but I sincerely hope I find out.

I want him to kiss me. I want him to do a lot more than that, but ever since he picked me up tonight, he's been carefully reserved. Respectful. Almost… courtly. It's both charming and frustrating.

And I have to wonder if this is part of his master plan. The previous two times he's kissed me, he made the first move. Maybe this time, he needs me to do it. After all, he said tonight was about convincing me we could make sense together. Maybe he needs me to step up and make the first move here. To show him that I think we do make sense.

As terrifying as that step feels, if I'm the one who needs to make it, I will.

I swallow, muster my courage, and say, "We should probably take a shower then."

CHAPTER 21

TOM

My cock springs to attention at the thought of wet, naked times with Gwen. Evidently, he's absorbed so much blood that I have none left to form coherent sentences, so I simply nod. I grab her hand and we walk back to the house.

She pauses and I half expect her to come to her senses and tell me to take her home. "Is Dallas still here?"

I shake my head. "No, he's out for the night." I lead her to the bathroom, then get out towels and set them on the counter. I don't want to be presumptuous. She could have meant we should each take a shower. Separately.

"Everything is in there." I point to the shower stall in the house's single bathroom. "Shampoo and soap and whatever."

Gwen tilts her head and smiles, then removes her T-shirt. Her hands are on her jeans before she frowns.

"Why are you just watching me?"

I point to the door behind me. "Did you want me to leave?"

"Oh my God." She brings her hands to her face and buries her face in the T-shirt still in her hands. "Did I read this wrong? I thought you knew 'Can I come back to your house and plant your plants?' was code for plant-your-plants-and-more." She lowers her hands and peers at me over the fabric. "Was I wrong?"

Her gray eyes are wide, and I can't tell if her pupils are so blown out from embarrassment or desire or the low lighting.

I reach out and pull her hands down. "You didn't read it wrong. I don't want to assume anything here, Gwen. Last night in the car, I shouldn't have kissed you when you didn't know who I was. I'm trying to make up for that now." Given how much I want her, how much I've always wanted her, I'm likely to assume too much. I need to hear the words. From her. "So I'm going to need you to use very specific language."

"Do you need me to sign an NDA?" she quips. Then, when I don't laugh in response, her grin falls. "Oh shit. Do I?"

I shake my head. "No, but that used to be a thing. But you know, consent and all. I don't ever want to assume."

She stands still and eyes me. "Okay, how about this? Let's get naked and get into the shower together."

My smile is probably so wide I look like a teenager seeing his first pair of tits. Then I don't wait for her to say it again, I just start taking off my clothes. Toeing off my shoes, then my socks, then stripping everything. By the time I stand back upright, she's bare except for a pair of plain cotton panties. Her legs are long and pale and seem to go on forever and all I can think about is having them wrapped around my waist. Or my head. I can't even watch as she slides those panties down her legs, because if I do, I might embarrass myself. I walk around her and turn on the water and adjust the temperature, before stepping in to the shower and pulling her with me.

I watch the water slide down her fair skin as we both wash off, and I swear I could spend hours counting and mapping each of her freckles. I allow myself to stare at her breasts now, taking note that while they're not big, they are perfectly shaped with the palest centers I've ever seen. Her pink nipples tighten under the water. I reach up to cup them, and the feel of the tight buds against my palms pulls a growl from my throat.

"You're so fucking sexy," I say. I pull her slick body to me and kiss her. It's heated and fast. Then I leave her mouth and trail my lips down her shoulder to the sensitive part of her collarbone. Her fingers play against the skin at my shoulders, alternating between squeezing me and rubbing lightly as if she can't focus. I love the idea that I'm distracting her.

I go lower still and flick my tongue against one of her nipples.

"Oh!" she says.

I caress her other breast while I continue to roll my tongue against this peak. Then I suck the turgid tip into my mouth, pulling on it until she's got her fingers threaded through my hair.

I stand and press her to the wet tiles, and I kiss her. Lips, tongue and teeth and it's carnal and hurried and so fucking hot it's a goddamn miracle I'm not coming all over her stomach.

She pulls her mouth free. "Bed. Now."

I turn off the water and help her out. I quickly dry us both off, then I pick her up and carry her into my bedroom. I gently lower her to her feet, letting her body slide down mine. The feel of her naked skin brushing against mine is sexy. Her breath catches and her wide gray eyes stare at my face as if she's seeing me for the first time.

Her palm slides against my dick and her thin fingers wrap around my shaft.

I squeeze my eyes shut, knowing I won't be able to let her play for very long. But right now, teenage me is living out a fantasy, and I want to indulge him for a few moments. I want to slow this moment down, to make it last forever. Her hand tightens around my cock and then slowly shuttles down and I know that I can't make this last.

"Goddamn, Gwen." I grab her hand and still it. "Too much more of that and this will be over before we even really get started." I turn and pull the covers back, baring the sheets on my bed. "You know you can say no at any time. There's no pressure here."

"Would you stop? I appreciate you being hyper conscious of my consent, but don't think I won't knee you in the balls if I want you to stop."

"Excellent. Then lay down on the bed so I can make you come."

She sucks in a breath but then does exactly as I ask. Her pale, lean body looks like something from a Renaissance painting all spread out on my linen sheets.

"Spread your legs for me." I grip my dick at the base of my shaft and give it a tight squeeze because just looking at her is enough to have me going off.

She opens her thighs, sliding her legs across my sheets. The tight patch of red curls covering her mound makes my heart thunder.

"So goddamn sexy," I repeat, crawling up her body and to wedge my shoulders between her thighs. "You have no idea how many times I've imagined this, getting to put my mouth on you. To taste you."

"Yes," she whispers.

I press her to the bed and don't bother to tempt or tease her. I don't have the patience right now. So I just use the flat of my tongue and lick her from slit to clit. Her tangy flavor bursts on my tongue.

"Oh shit!" she says.

Someday I want to lay back and let her sit on my face, grinding her pussy down on me while she takes her pleasure. But right now, I want to savor every lick and taste. I plunge my tongue inside her, and she's so perfect. So hot and wet. So goddamn mine.

Then I move my tongue back to her clit because I know if I don't make her come soon, I'll never last. I roll circles over the tight bundle of nerves as I slide two fingers inside her and lift them to find that rough patch at her front wall. The first press of my fingertips against that spot has her bucking against me. I press her body flat to the mattress and don't relent. I play her g-spot like a 6-string and suck her clit into my mouth.

She shrieks and then her entire body seizes and shatters. Her chorus of "yes" and "Oh Tom" is better than a standing ovation from a crowd thirty-thousand strong. I place one last kiss at the top of her mound, then crawl up her body.

She's pliant and soft against the bed, her face locked in a hazy and sated smile.

"You alright?" I ask.

"I think yes." Her eyes open and she gives me a goofy smile that sets my fucking heart on fire. "Condom?" she asks.

I reach over to my nightstand and open the top drawer. To my chagrin, I have to pull out the entire box and open it because it's been unused.

She leans up a little and eyes me. "You just had to restock?"

"Actually, I haven't been with anyone in years." I look closer at the box to check the expiration date. "These are still good though." I pull one out and tear open the foil.

"Years?" she asks.

I shrug. I roll on the latex.

"Oh," she says after noticing I've already got the condom on. "You didn't want me to, uh, reciprocate?"

"What?"

"Give you a blowjob?"

I frown. "No. I want to be inside you."

She smiles. "I want that, too."

Thank fuck. I would stop if she wanted me to, but it would be the hardest thing ever. Literally.

She loops her hands around my neck and pulls me down for a kiss. I lower my body so that I'm nestled in the cradle of her hips, and nothing has ever felt more right. At the moment, it's hard to imagine ever feeling panic again, because this, just laying skin-to-skin with her, is bliss.

Her legs part more and she wraps them around my hips. I lean back, then slowly push forward, entering her one inch at a time.

"More," she pleads.

I lean up on my forearms and pull out until I've almost completely left her body, then I press back in.

"Yes, just like that," she moans.

"So fucking good."

She smiles, looking blissed out and resplendent. "Yeah, it is."

I fuck her then, letting my body take over but staying present enough so that I can watch her every expression. She's always had such an expressive face. It's one of the things I love about her.

"Tom! Right there." Her fingernails, short and blunt though they are, dig into my shoulders. "Please don't stop."

"Never."

When she comes, her pussy squeezes my cock and I can't hold off anymore. I pour myself into her, and it feels like so much more than an orgasm. It feels like a promise and I sure as fuck hope she feels it, too.

CHAPTER 22

GWEN

I have a long and colorful history of awkward mornings-after.

It's not exactly that I've had so many different partners or even that many mornings-after—I wasn't lying to Tom when I described my recent "pun" drought—but rather that pretty much every time I've been with a man, I felt awkward the next morning.

Even with Lucas, the guy I dated for two years in undergrad, things were always awkward after sex. He always wanted me to stay the night, and I think it hurt his feelings that I never did. When we broke up, he even accused me of not liking him very much.

It was months later before I admitted to myself that he might've been right.

He never understood why I wanted to return to my own space, shower by myself, snuggle down into my own comfortable bed. I think, in some way, it was because I never really felt like myself with him. We started dating because we were both biology majors and we shared a work ethic. In retrospect, it wasn't exactly the recipe for a romantic relationship. At the time, it never occurred to me that our similarities might have created more problems than they solved.

With Tom, I feel none of those insecurities. Maybe it's his decadent king-size bed and the softest sheets I've ever felt, but when I wake up the next morning, alone in Tom's bed, I don't feel the need to bolt for the safety of my own space.

Or maybe, it's that Tom never hesitates to tell me the things he likes about me. Or maybe, I'm suffering from some kind of post-orgasm euphoria.

God knows Tom did things to my body no one else ever has. Sure, in theory, one orgasm should be pretty much like the next. In practice, that's clearly not true, because sex with Tom was nothing like sex with any of the other guys I've been with.

It's probably because he's a pop star. Yeah, last night, he downplayed his dating experiences, but he didn't deny that a lack of romantic relationships didn't equate to a lack of sexual experience.

So, obviously, all of those post-concert hook-ups he must have had turned him into some kind of sex virtuoso. He's the Mozart of orgasms.

I know I should consider the possibility that this uncharacteristic desire to burrow into Tom's bed and live here from now on might be a purely emotional reaction. Maybe I'm developing real feelings for Tom. Something beyond post-orgasm bliss.

But that seems unlikely.

After all, even though I've known Tom for years, he's been back in my life for less than forty-eight hours. Surely emotions deeper than lust take longer than that to form. Is my sudden attachment to Tom rooted in my friendship with James? Have I just shifted my feelings from one brother to the other?

No. I immediately dismiss the idea, because I've never felt even an inkling of sexual attraction to James. I've certainly never felt this kind of emotion for him.

For that matter, lust isn't an emotion at all. It's a purely physical reaction.

It's a good thing that this is post-orgasm bliss and not me falling in love with Tom. There's a whole host of reasons, starting with his career as a pop star and ending with the fact that my career may land me halfway across the country soon.

We are systematically ill-suited for a relationship. Our personalities, our lives, and our goals just don't fit. Besides all of that, this isn't real! All of this—the tacos, the shower, the sex, the snuggle—are all part of a not-real, dream-sequence-esque event in my life. A time apart from reality.

So, it's a very good thing that I am a practical, sensible woman with very few romantic expectations. Sure, I like the idea of romance and everlasting love. And, obviously, as a scientist, I can appreciate the evolutionary importance of pair bonding and the body's hormonal response to fantastic sex.

Therefore, as a practical, sensible woman, it only makes… well, sense… that I should sleep with Tom while I can. As often as I can. It's just good science!

With that goal in mind, I roll out of bed, find my clothes, get dressed, and go in search of Tom.

I find a bathroom before I find him, so I pee, rinse the sleep out of my eyes, and run a dab of toothpaste over my teeth with my finger to get rid of the morning breath. My hair is a wreck, as it always is in the morning, but in the absence of some curl cream and a wide-tooth comb, there's little to be done. I finger-comb it a bit and head out.

I look first in the room Tom said was his office. There's enough computer equipment to launch a shuttle—or produce an album, I guess—but no Tom. I'm a little nervous to head into the living room in case Dallas is back this morning, but he's not.

Instead, I find Tom sitting at the bar, a cup of coffee in front of him, a laptop open and running software that I don't recognize. He's wearing headphones and is tapping his foot on the rung on the barstool.

My steps slow and I hesitate, unsure what to do or say.

I am struck all over again by how undeniably cool Tom is. Not to mention smoking hot. I mean just the breadth of his shoulders makes my skin start to tingle.

Last night, in the low lighting of the park, and the car, and then his bedroom, he seemed more approachable. More like an ordinary human, and less like the star he is. Now, in the full light of day, he's ridiculously handsome, with the scruffy half-beard and silky tousle of hair.

I remind myself that last night he admitted to having anxiety and panic attacks and how heavy the weight of stardom feels.

Knowing these things somehow makes him more approachable and more attractive at the same time.

Before I can let any more of my doubts creep in, I walk up behind him and wrap my arms around him to rest my chin on his shoulder.

He twists on the stool and pulls me onto his lap, kissing me even before he greets me.

He pulls off his headphones and lays them on the counter. "Are you a coffee person?" he asks, trailing kisses from my lips to my jaw and down my neck. "And if you are, is this a coffee emergency, or can I take you back to bed before I caffeinate you?"

I laugh because his beard—which is so much softer than it looks—is ticklish. And because I don't know how else to respond to this overt—and rather adorable—affection.

No man has ever been like this before with me. No man has ever acted like he can't get enough of me. Or like I'm a woman to be played with.

Most of my previous partners have been serious, academic sorts who are frankly just as serious and academic in bed. Which meant there wasn't a lot of flirting or canoodling. That's what this feels like, canoodling.

It's intense and unsettling, delicious and addictive.

"Coffee," I gasp as his teeth nip at my neck, sending spirals of heat pulsing through my body. Moisture floods my core and I want more. It's almost alarming how quickly my body responds to him. Desperate to regain some control of the situation, I add, "Yes, coffee first would be good."

"Of course," he murmurs against my skin. "Coffee first." He swivels the stool back toward the counter, then stands, effortlessly picking me up as he does, before setting me on the counter.

He steps in between my legs, his hands sliding up the denim to slip under my shirt.

His mouth still teasing my neck, he says, "Coffee is a great idea." He makes no move to stop kissing me and I'm starting not to care.

"Yes. Coffee is good."

Of course, lots of things are good. Tom is good. Orgasms are good.

Truth be told, Tom and orgasms are fantastic. Compared to that, coffee can't hold a candle.

"On the other hand," I say, finding the buttons of his shirt and working them free. "Coffee is probably overrated. And it's not like anyone has ever died from caffeine withdrawal."

"Hmm," he murmurs. Then stills. Then inches back to look at me. "But I did offer. And you did say coffee first." He steps back, letting his hands trail to my knees.

He gives them a squeeze before stepping away, leaving me wishing I'd never heard of coffee.

Before I can beg him to come back, he's on the other side of the counter, repeating the complicated procedure Dallas used on the machine the other day.

"Cream or sugar?" he asks over his shoulder.

"Black." I scoot off the counter and sit on the stool he vacated a moment ago. Watching him as he moves around the kitchen. "So, Dallas isn't sleeping on the couch anymore?"

"I banished Dallas to the sofa in the studio, and warned him that if he showed up here before noon I would slice off his favorite tattoo and sell it on eBay to the highest bidder."

"That wasn't very nice of you."

"Maybe. But it was fair. Dallas is lucky I let him sleep on the sofa here as long as I did. There's a reason why I bought a two-bedroom house and immediately turned one of them into an office."

"Oh, do you disdain all guests, or just Dallas?"

"All guests. During our BoS days, we all practically lived on top of one another. There was always someone around. I used to hide in the bathroom just to have a minute alone. At one point, my handler thought I was doing lines of coke in there."

"You weren't?" I ask the question before I think it through. "Sorry. Scratch that. It's not my business."

He meets my gaze in that solemn way he does when he wants me to believe what he's saying. "Never. One of the other guys dabbled in drugs. We all drank, probably more than we should have. But I never did drugs. I know it's hard to believe, given that drugs, sex, and rock 'n' roll is practically part of American mythology, but it's true."

"You don't have to explain yourself to me," I say.

I don't want to be that person who questions everything her partner tells her. I wouldn't know how to be that person anyway. And I don't like the idea of assuming that I have any say in what Tom did in his past life or will do in his future life.

But Tom is shaking his head. "I may not have to explain myself to you, but I want you to be able to trust me."

"I do."

It's a bit surprising to realize I mean it. Forty-eight hours ago, I probably would have described Tom as impulsive and feckless, not someone you can rely on. But everything has changed since then. And somehow, inexplicably, I do trust him. I was wrong about Tom. I made judgments without having all—or really any—of the facts.

"Did you know I was the youngest member in the band?" he asks as he pours my now finished coffee.

"I didn't."

Before I can ask why, he answers the question for me. "Boys of Summer was always a five-boy band." He crosses to stand on the other side of the counter, just opposite me, before sliding the mug across the counter. "Clark, the manager, envisioned it that way from the beginning. Five boys, different backgrounds, different ethnicities. The modern American boy band, representing the modern American experience. There was a different Latino guy in the band before me, Matías. He was from L.A. They were still in rehearsals when Matías got caught doing drugs. Clark fired him. His contract was so tight, in the end he owed them money."

"How did you feel about that? About replacing Matías?" I ask.

He shakes his head and gives a wry smile. "You don't need to psychoanalyze me. I've been through a lot of therapy."

I roll my eyes. "That's not what I was doing. Also, *so* not my field of research. I just genuinely wondered how you feel about it." I parse my new words carefully, because conversations about race and ethnicity are never easy. But I guess the most important conversations never are. "I know how James felt about being Latino in Texas, because he talked about it a lot when we were close. I remember once, in college, some TA made a comment about 'the immigrant experience' and looked right at James while he said it. I thought James was going to punch the guy."

Tom laughs. "Yeah, I can see that. James was always a little prickly about being considered an immigrant since our mom had family living in Texas back when Texas was still part of Spain. It always pissed Mom off, too. 'Latino's are not interchangeable,' she would say. 'We're people, not animal crackers.'"

I laugh along with him because I've heard her say that, too. "Why was it animal crackers? I've always wondered that."

He shrugs. "I have no idea." He pins me with a look. "It wasn't because she didn't want to be thought of as an immigrant. She wasn't ashamed to be Latina, she just—"

"Yeah, I know." I cut him off, putting my hand on his arm. "I know your mom. Besides, no one wants to be defined by the color of their skin."

"Exactly."

"I guess that's why I asked, though. I'd heard your mom make that animal cracker comment. It must have been… awkward, at the very least, to have your band managers treat you exactly like that. Like one Latino could be just subbed out for another one and no one would even notice."

He gives me a long look and nods slowly before turning away, propping his hip against the counter, and staring out the window. The way he doesn't answer right away makes me think that either he's collecting his thoughts or collecting his composure.

Finally, he says, "By the time I figured out I was hired to replace Matías, we'd already signed the contract. Dad didn't care as long as we were getting paid, and Mom…"

I see him swallow visibly.

"Well, they got divorced a year later, and that was it."

His words are like a vise around my heart because I hear what he doesn't say out loud. That he blames himself for his parents' divorce. That he's afraid his position in the band, and the fact that his dad let him be treated like an animal cracker, created a rift in their marriage.

"You know your mom is proud of you, right?" I say gently.

He smiles, his gaze darting to mine and then away. "Yeah, I do." He chuckles. "A lot of other people's moms, too. That's the thing I didn't expect about being the Latino boy in Boys of Summer. At first I was so worried about whether or not I was Latino enough or in the right way, whatever the hell that meant, but it turned out there were a lot of people who were just excited there was a Latino kid in this all-American boy band. I didn't understand going into it how much representation matters, how important it was for people to see someone like themselves on stage."

"Representation is so important." I've seen that in my own career as a scientist. The stories of the women who have blazed this path before me keep me focused and determined. Still… "That sounds like a lot of pressure."

"It was. It is. How does one guy represent the experience of… what is it? Sixty million Americans? The short answer is, you can't. You don't. But you keep trying. You try to be honest and grateful. You try to be respectful of the chance you've been given. You try to be worthy of it."

"Is that why you have anxiety?" I ask carefully, hoping he understands that this is mere curiosity on my part. Usually, I don't give a lot of deep thought to what's going on inside other people. If they want me to know, they'll tell me. If they need my help, they'll ask. But it's different with Tom, this need to peel back his layers and see inside his head.

Maybe it's because he looks so much like James on the surface but is such a wholly different person inside.

If you'd asked me back in high school which of them had more depth, which of them was more interesting, I automatically would have said James. James seemed like the smart one. The ambitious one. The one determined to pursue justice and incrementally improve the world. Hell, if you'd asked me that last week, that's how I would have answered.

Tom, on the other hand, seemed like the guy who was only interested in fame and money. The guy who let that fame go to his head and forgot who his real friends were. The guy who got sucked into the vacuum of fame and no longer had time for Monty Python marathons or Stonehenge jokes.

But right now, I feel like I'm seeing the real Tom for the first time in years. It's like I had on glasses that distorted my view of each of them. I had on rose-colored glasses when it came to James and jerk-colored glasses when it came to Tom.

I couldn't see past the fact that I thought we were friends and then he cut me out when he became famous—except for that one stupid Halloween party, which was part of some kind of joke or dare on his part. But so what if he didn't have time for me after Boys of Summer hit it big? He's making time for me now.

There's a slight stirring of apprehension in the back of my mind because this—whatever *this* is—isn't friendship, and it's still not likely to last more than a few days because I'm leaving town soon and… well, Tom is a pop star. It's not like I'll hold his interest for longer than that anyway. But I push those fears aside.

Tom hurt my feelings when we were teenagers because I didn't see it coming, but I'm an adult now. I know this can't last. I don't expect it to. Which means it won't hurt when he leaves.

But I shove all those thoughts aside, because I'm more concerned about him than I am about my own fragile heart.

Since he still hasn't answered me about the anxiety, I gently prod, "Let me guess, this is why you started having panic attacks?"

"That probably didn't help," he says with a shrug, planting his hands on the counter between us, palms down. Once again, the simple, geometric design on the inside of his wrists catches my eye. "But a lot of people with ADHD also have anxiety. It goes with the territory. I don't know if they just coexist, or if it comes from having extra energy and always being told you can't move. Sit still. Stop fidgeting. Why can't you listen?"

"That must've been so hard on you," I say, thinking about what my friend Holly has told me about how empathetic most people with ADHD are and how deeply they feel everything. How, for some people with ADHD, rejection or criticism is deeply, almost physically painful. And how the physical, scientifically-documented differences in the brains of people with ADHD mean they don't uptake serotonin and dopamine hormones the same way the rest of us do. Those are—literally—the hormones that make us feel happy and loved. Which basically means the brains of people with ADHD are starving for approval and joy.

When I think it through like that, it nearly breaks my heart. The idea that this amazing guy, this incredible, funny, caring, guy is starving for love makes me want to slice open my own heart and pour love directly into his.

But, that sounds creepy, so I don't say it out loud.

Instead, I ask, "Is that why you have serotonin and dopamine molecules tattooed on the inside of your wrists?"

He looks down, turning his hands palm up to bare the tattoos. With a smile, he says, "Caught that, did you?"

"Well, I am a molecular biologist. I wouldn't be a very good one if I didn't recognize molecules." I don't admit to the deep dive research I've been doing on ADHD. My need to have a complete picture of all the elements and angles of Tom Mendoza feels a little stalker-ish to admit aloud.

"You have no idea how many people think they're constellations."

I roll my eyes. "Why doesn't that surprise me?"

"Probably because you know more geniuses than I do," he says, coming over to my side of the counter.

"Maybe. But I've also known a lot of stupid geniuses, too."

"If we're talking tattoos…" He swivels my stool so that I'm facing him then reaches for the hem of my shirt and pulls it over my head.

I let him because he clearly wants to change the subject to something less intense, and… well, also because I want to feel his hands on my skin. I love the way my skin practically burns beneath his touch.

He runs his forefinger over the crest of my breast, just to the left of my sternum, where my one single tattoo lives. "I didn't have you pegged as a tattoo kind of girl."

I glance down and am unintentionally bewitched by the sight of his fingers against my skin. I love seeing his darker, more bronze skin move along my pale and freckled skin. So different, but perfect. His fingers stop at the quarter-sized tattoo of a rounded diamond with a hashed X in the middle. He traces the X, ever so gently, with a fingertip before looking up at me. "On anyone else, I would guess it's a botched X-Men tattoo."

I give a breathy laugh. "It's Photo 51."

"You say that like I'm supposed to know what Photo 51 is."

"It's the first clear picture of DNA ever taken. Rosalind Franklin used X-ray diffraction to take the picture. The ringed X shape is—essentially—the shadow cast by the double helix. The photo provided the inspiration for the model developed by Watson and Crick that won them the Nobel Prize."

"Why haven't I ever heard of her? Was she their assistant or something?"

"No. She was doing post-doc work in a totally different lab." I struggle to contain my secondhand frustration on her behalf. "If the stories are true, not one but two different male colleagues handed parts of her research over to Watson and Crick without her permission. Apparently, she was difficult to work with."

Still tracing the shape with his thumb, he cups my check with his other hand. "That's a pretty grim story."

"It is," I agree. When you're a woman working in a field dominated by men, stories like hers abound. I actively work not to let them get me down. "And it also isn't. You can't control how other people treat you. You can only control how you respond. She faced tremendous sexism but did brilliant work despite that. Sexism didn't keep her from doing the work she wanted to do. It only kept the world from acknowledging it at the time."

"That is an extraordinary attitude." He presses a gentle kiss on my lips. "Which shouldn't surprise me at all, since you are pretty damn extraordinary. And extraordinarily pretty."

Once again, he picks me up like I weigh nothing and sets me on the counter. My shirt is off, and it takes him only a moment to slip off my bra.

"I thought you were going to let me drink my coffee first," I say on a sigh as he sucks my nipple into his mouth.

"You had your chance and wasted it talking. Now I'm too turned on by listening to you be inspirational and nerdy."

I laugh because I can't help myself. But my giggle turns into a moan when his teeth scrape against my sensitive tip.

"Why are you wearing so many clothes?" he murmurs against my skin.

"Take them off," I say.

He steps away from me, moves his laptop and other things, and puts them on one of the other stools. Then he unfastens my jeans and manages to pull them and my panties off without any assistance from me. I'm naked and spread open on his kitchen counter before I can even contemplate how much Lysol it will take to disinfect the kitchen when we're done.

"Now who's wearing too many clothes?" I ask.

He pulls his T-shirt off and tosses it on the floor behind him before reaching into his back pocket and pulls out a condom.

I struggle not to drool at the sight of his muscles. He's got the lean, sculpted chest of a swimmer and I send up a silent prayer to whoever designed the first lap pool. I want to spend hours just staring at his chest. Maybe years. I'll have to see if there are any universities offering PhD's in the analysis of Tom's chest.

But I try to play it cool and raise a brow at him. "Pretty confident of how this was going to go this morning?"

He unfastens his jeans but doesn't take them off. "Not confident, merely hopeful. With you, Gwen, it's always hope." He closes the distance between us again and cradles my face.

His kiss is gentle and romantic, and I do not have time for that right now. I'm so hot and wet and needy for him that I just want him inside me. I slant my mouth against his and swipe my tongue into his mouth as I wrap my legs around his waist and pull him tighter to me, fumbling on the countertop with my hand for the condom.

He breaks the kiss and swipes a thumb through my slick folds. I hiss in response at the electric pulse that shoots through me at his touch. I'm already close to coming. I should ask him later if there's like a school rock stars go to where they learn some kind of ancient Kama Sutra magic, because I'm never this close to climaxing with so little foreplay. I've also never wanted a man the way I want Tom. I don't allow myself to examine that notion too closely because right now it's about our bodies connecting. Nothing more.

I reach down between us and free his dick from his boxers. There's something so crude and titillating about being completely naked and just having his cock free.

"I really need you inside me right now," I say.

He swallows visibly, then he tears open the condom wrapper and rolls it on. He once again swipes his thumb through my folds, then positions himself. In one swift movement, he's seated to the hilt, and I cry out from the pleasure of it.

He grips my hips, pulls back, then thrusts again.

"Goddamn, you feel good," he growls. There's something in that growl that's reminiscent of his singing voice. I'd never admit that to him, that I know his music. But I'm reminded of who he is when he does that. While I never pegged myself as being the kind of girl who had a rock star fantasy, evidently I do.

I trace the single tattoo on his chest—the Boys of Summer logo—but then his fingers are tightening on my hips, his hands so big they nearly cover my entire ass.

"So good," I moan.

"Touch your clit, Gwen. Make yourself come," he says.

I'm certainly not a stranger to bringing myself pleasure, but the commanding of it is surprisingly sexy. I trace my hand down my breast, then my belly, and finally reach my clit. I don't know what's sexier, the demanding tone of his voice or the gleam of satisfaction in his gaze when I follow his orders. He's fucking me hard so I'm trying to work with a moving target here, but I manage to get my finger on that hard nub. I frantically rub circles against it and everything in my body tightens. My body is so primed, so on the edge of exploding, that I'm breathless as I wait.

When my climax finally hits, it's earth-shattering. My own personal big bang as I'm pretty sure my molecules are rearranging themselves as I convulse around him.

"Fuck!" he roars, then he's coming too.

We sorta collapse against each other, our labored breath mingling. That was dirty and carnal and fast.

But it was more than that, too. It was deep and emotional and suddenly I feel laid bare by all the things he makes me feel. All the sexy, tingly, orgasmic things that are unlike anything else I've ever felt, and also—alarmingly—all the tender, vulnerable, and gentle things. Yeah, all the physical stuff… I expected that. Because a) Tom is so frickin' hot and also an actual rock star (and, as per my previous observations, has been blessed with rock star superpowers in the kissing-and-more arena), but also b) every time he's touched me since that first kiss in the car two nights ago, he's left me wanting more, which just isn't how my body normally reacts with anyone.

So, yeah, I was prepared for sex with Tom to blow the walls off my box of previously held expectations for sex.

What I didn't expect was this emotional cataclysm. This sudden need to hold him close and stroke his hair. To burrow into him. To pours parts of myself into his soul. To greedily accept parts of his soul in return.

All of this feels horribly, terrifyingly too big for me.

Before now, my deepest emotional relationship was with Reese's Cups and my beloved compost pile and all the tiny larvae living there. All of my emotional relationships with actual humans—yes, even James—have been so shallow compared to what I'm feeling now.

I don't even know if I'm built to care for something bigger than tacos, larvae, and Reese's Cups combined. The very idea that I might feel that way about anyone is scary—overwhelming. And this isn't just anyone. It's Tomás Mendoza.

My chest tightens and it suddenly feels as if I'm under water and can't find my way to the top.

I push at him, as gently as I can, and he leaves my body, taking care of the condom.

"Bathroom," I manage to say over my shoulder as I jump off the counter and flee like the damn coward I am.

CHAPTER 23

TOM

When Boys of Summer broke up, the first things I did were sublet my apartment in LA, put my stuff in storage, and buy a car. It was the first car I'd ever owned, ironically, since by the time I was old enough to drive, BoS was hitting stardom status and I had a driver and personal security team that went everywhere with me.

So, I bought a used Subaru and left LA. I didn't stop driving until I felt like I could breathe again. I found an Airbnb I loved in the mountains of New Mexico, so I rented it and didn't talk to another person for four months.

I hired the teenage daughter of a nearby neighbor to shop for me and gas up the Subaru. I communicated with her—and everyone else for that matter—solely via text. I didn't talk to my manager or my agent. I didn't talk to Bex or my mom. I didn't even talk to James.

My therapist insisted we at least communicate via Skype. Once I convinced her I hadn't gone completely off the rails on her like Syd Barret—the former songwriter from Pink Floyd—she talked to my mom and got her to back off. I literally got a note from my doctor so I wouldn't have to talk to anyone.

At one point, an ancient stray cat showed up. I started feeding it out of sheer pity, and once I was ready to interact with people again, I talked to the cat.

I hiked. I slept. A lot. I listened to all the music I hadn't had time to listen to when I was a pop star.

When you're a teenage superstar, people are always saying you don't have enough knowledge or education to appreciate "real" music. They weren't wrong. I started with the boy bands who had paved the way for Boys of Summer, then moved on to other modern pop and worked my way back. I practiced the guitar for hours a day. Taught myself how to play the piano. Taught myself to cook—something I'd never had to learn.

Everyone who knew me well enough to know about my anxiety left me alone. Everyone who didn't, didn't matter and couldn't reach me anyway.

Four months. I went four months without talking to another soul.

My first morning with Gwen, I don't get her alone for more than forty minutes before the castle walls crumble and fall.

Right after Gwen gets in the shower, I get a string of messages from my mom. The first several play it cool, like she's texting out of the blue. "Just wanted to check in on you," she says. But it goes downhill quickly from there.

Ten minutes after that, I get a text from Dallas that simply reads, "I'm sorry. Really."

Three minutes after that, I start getting alerts from the text chain I have labeled, "The SoBs of BoS." That's when I know why Dallas apologized.

Drew: Heard you finally landed that plane in Phoenix. <High five emoji>

Drew: Hope you had a good flight.

Drew: <eggplant emoji peach emoji>

Drew: <gif of a woman slapping her own ass>

Drew: <gif of moist macaroni being stirred>

Drew: <gif of Cardi B dancing>

Josh: Jesus, Drew. You text your mother with that phone?

Drew: No. But I text yours

Luther: Drew, grow the fuck up

Drew: What? Our boy finally gets laid and I'm not supposed to comment?

Luther: Show a little fucking respect is all I'm saying. Not our business.

Luther: Ever. But especially if it's Phoenix.

Drew: <gif of school teacher shaking her finger>

Drew: Disagree. We're a team. It's totally our business. Especially if it's Phoenix.

Luther: Move on, dude. We're grown men. Some of us have jobs and don't want to be texting about this shit during the workday.

Drew: <gif of pouting child>

Drew: When did you become such an old man?

Luther: When I became a father, asshole

Drew: <gif of a woman blowing kisses>

Drew: You know you love it.

Luther: No. I really don't. My kid plays games on this phone. You think I want her seeing the shit you send?

Josh: <gif of a referee separating boxers>

Fuck my life.

I answer my mom's texts first because I'm a good son.

Mom: How are you, mijo?

Mom: Just wanted to check in on you.

Mom: Don't be mad at Bex, but I heard you had a date last night.

Mom: And you know I try to respect your boundaries, but if you're actually dating someone and it's serious, I'd love to meet her.

Mom: Bex is rolling her eyes at me. But is it really too much to ask?

Mom: Bex says it's none of my business. I just want the best for you. And I hope she's a nice girl.

Mom: Bex says that's sexist and judgmental of me and that I shouldn't hold your future girlfriend to unrealistic expectations imposed by the patriarchy. But when I said, "nice," I meant I hope she's a kind and loving person, because that's what you deserve. I didn't mean to imply "pure" or "virginal" or anything like that.

Mom: Bex says I should stop texting you before you move back to New Mexico and stop talking to us again. I love you.

Mom: Come to dinner soon.

Tom: I will come to dinner soon. And, yes, you can meet her when the time is right.

Tom: Love you

My friends may suck balls, but my family is the best.

I love how my mom texts like she's talking to me on the phone, in complete sentences, with punctuation. It's fucking hysterical. Misguided and weird, but hysterical.

Bex hasn't texted me since the other night, but I text her next anyway.

Tom: WTH? You fucking told on me?

Tom: You're dead to me now.

Bex: Sorry! You know what she's like! It was like the Spanish Inquisition over here.

Bex: <gif of Monty Python Spanish Inquisition scene>

Bex: I have no idea how she knew something was up, but she def knew

Bex: Do you think she has the sight?

Bex: <gif of woman shuddering>

Tom: Just stay on damage control, okay?

Tom: I'm trying not to fuck this up

Bex: Does she know about Phoenix yet?

Tom: Why can't people stop talking about that?

Bex: <gif of girl blinking innocently>

Bex: Because we love you and want you to be happy

Tom: <gif of man shooting the bird>

Bex: <blowing kisses emoji>

Next, I shoot a single text to Dallas.

Tom: You're dead to me.

Dallas: Again. I'm sorry.

I don't bother to reply. By then, there's another string of texts from the SoB chain.

Josh: 4 real, tho

Josh: Did u land PHX?

Josh: Because if you did, it's time to settle up!

Josh: <gif of raining money>

Tom: This chain ends

Tom: Right

Tom: Fucking

Tom: Now

Tom: Or I'm killing this number and none of you will ever hear from me again.

Josh: So it's official? Who had 2022?

Tom: I'm serious.

Drew: <gif of person laughing on the floor>

Drew: <gif of woman cracking a whip>

Drew: <gif of a tennis ball in a vise>

Drew: Somebody want to call time of death on Tom's balls?

I'm turning off my phone when Gwen comes out wearing a pair of my sweatpants and shirt and looking so fucking adorable I can't decide if I want to take her back to bed and fuck her until we've both gone blind or just stare at her for hours while I write sappy songs about her.

Which is, in fact, something I've spent entirely too much time doing.

The songwriting, I mean. Not the staring at her. That would be creepy.

"Something up?" she asks when she notices the phone in my hand.

I set the phone on the counter and walk over to her, burying my face in her neck, inhaling the scent of her. She didn't wash her hair, so it still smells like her, and I love the combination of my soap on her skin and whatever minty-fruity product she uses on her curls.

"Just questioning all my life choices," I murmur.

"That doesn't sound good." She runs her hands up my arms, pausing to rub the spot on my bicep.

The fact that she does that, that she clearly noticed that tic I have of rubbing at my bicep when I'm spiraling, and now she does it too… gah. That kills me.

I think of that stupid gif Drew sent implying my balls are in a vise and that I'm whipped.

The crazy thing is, I don't even care.

I don't care if the guys think I'm whipped. I don't care if I am whipped.

I only care that this amazing, thoughtful, brilliant woman cares enough about me to have noticed something like that.

My anxiety doesn't freak her out. She doesn't think I'm weak for not being able to handle the pressure of fame. She doesn't think I'm ungrateful. She just accepts it. Accepts me.

I have no idea what I did to deserve having this woman in my life—and am under no illusion that I actually do deserve her—but I'm definitely greedy enough that I'm going to do everything in my power to keep her here.

I don't want her just while she's on break. I don't want her just for now. I want her forever.

Keeping my hands buried in her hair, I pull back enough to look at her. "How do you feel about New Mexico?"

She gives a startled laugh. "I don't know that I have any feelings about New Mexico. Or really any of the states."

"Let me rephrase that." I glance down at my watch. "Starting in about an hour, the studio is booked. So let's get out of here. I know about this great Airbnb in the mountains of New Mexico where we could be alone. It's doesn't even have internet. We can drive out and be there by tonight."

She pulls my hands from her hair and steps back. "But if people have booked studio time, don't you need to be here?"

"I'll make Dallas do it. He owes me."

"But you're the producer, right? I mean, when people book studio time, isn't it because they want to work with you? Or is that not how it works?" She laughs again. "I have no idea how your industry works. Like, at all."

"Come with me to New Mexico, and I'll answer all your questions on the way."

"I can't come with you to New Mexico."

"Why not? I thought you said you're done with your classes and you're just finishing up your dissertation."

She turns, pacing away from me, fiddling with the hem of the T-shirt as she walks. For once, I'm not the one pacing. I'm standing perfectly still, watching her pace.

"I don't. But that doesn't mean I can just run away to New Mexico with you. I certainly can't if there isn't any internet there. I can't just disappear. I still have work to do on my dissertation. And my boss has to be able to reach me by email."

Watching her pace is almost like having an out-of-body-experience. Seeing the physical manifestations of someone's anxiety, instead of experiencing it myself.

It's unsettling watching her, because I know what she's feeling. At least I think I know.

I don't know what she's thinking, I don't know what her thought process is right now, but I can take a pretty good guess about the physical sensations in her body. The burst of adrenaline brought on by fight-or-flight. The need to move. The pounding heart. The thoughts moving so fast you can't pin any of them down.

"Hey," I say.

She stops moving and looks at me.

"It's okay," I tell her. "If you don't wanna go to New Mexico, we won't go to New Mexico. We'll just be together here. That's what matters to me. That we're together."

She throws up her hand in an expression of obvious frustration. "This is just happening really fast."

"No, it isn't. We've known each other for years."

"No. I've known James for years. I've known you for a matter of hours."

"Wow." I give a wry chuckle. "That's a low blow, don't you think?"

"I didn't mean it that way. But it's the truth if you think about it. If you counted up all the hours we've spent together, over the course of our lives, it's not that many."

"You're going to blame me for that?"

"I'm not blaming anyone. I'm just saying that this is moving really fast. We hadn't seen each other in years, then all of a sudden we're sleeping together and now you want to go to New Mexico."

"This isn't sudden," I tell her. "I thought I made that clear yesterday. I've always had a thing for you. I've wanted you since the moment we met."

"You really expect me to believe that?" she laughs. "You were, what, fifteen? There's no way that you've 'had a thing for me' since then." She even uses air quotes for emphasis.

"It's the truth. You need me to prove it to you?"

She shakes her head. "No. I—"

But I tell her anyway.

"You asked what happened in Phoenix. Nothing happened in Phoenix. Dallas giving me hell about Phoenix isn't about something that happened when we were on tour there. Hell, I don't even know if we ever played in Phoenix. Phoenix is the name of a song about you."

I walk over to my laptop and wake it up. It only takes a minute to pull up the demo tape I made years ago, when I first pitched the song to Clark.

I fucking hate listening to myself sing.

I have a good voice, near perfect pitch, decent range. I'm good. Not brilliant. Not really worthy of the fame and success I've had, but I'm good enough. That doesn't matter because I still hate to hear myself sing.

This is worse, because it's my raw, sixteen-year-old voice, still relatively untrained, and paired with my awkward guitar playing.

Nevertheless, I hit play.

I can't watch her listen. I've never been able to watch people listen to my music. Not the stuff from Boys of Summer, not anything since then. Not even the stuff I've produced for other people. It's physically painful to me, anticipating their reaction, analyzing every flicker of expression, trying to guess if they think it's any good. So, I keep my back to her.

By the time teenage me reaches the chorus, I'm the one pacing, kneading my bicep so much I'll probably have bruises.

She's like a Phoenix
Every time she leaves,
My heart bursts into flames.

I try to tell myself,
that I don't need her,
but when she smiles,
My love comes back to life.

It gets better when the vocals end and it's just the godawful guitar playing the last of the melody. I finally manage to pry my fingers off my arm and stop pacing. I squat, forcing a few deep breaths as the last notes drift through the room.

Then I stand and turn to face Gwen and find her sitting on the sofa, her head in her hands as she listens.

"I wrote that. For you. I have the first draft of it in a notebook from when I was fifteen. I recorded that version when I was sixteen. We wanted to write our own songs, play our own instruments. We each wrote a song and pitched it to our manager."

She finally looks up, a frown on her face. "I don't understand. That sounds familiar, but I've heard all the Boys of Summer songs. That's not one of them."

I jam a hand through my hair. "No, it's not. Clark pretty much laughed his ass off. Then he reminded us he was in charge and threatened to sue us for breach of contract if we tried that shit again. So, we all kept playing the songs he bought for us."

"Then why have I heard it before?"

"Two years after the band broke up, I reworked it and eventually sold it to country musician Larinda Scott."

For a long moment, Gwen just sits there, thinking. Then, abruptly, she pushes to her feet and heads for the door.

"I have to go," she blurts.

And just like, she's gone.

I think again about that gif Drew sent of my balls in a vise.

He could not have been more wrong.

It's not my balls she's crushing. It's my heart.

CHAPTER 24

GWEN

I make it about ten feet beyond Tom's front door before I realize I don't have a car. Tom drove us here last night so I'm trapped here.

I know what I should do. What the logical, adult thing to do is. I should go back inside and ask him to drive me home. Or call a rideshare. Or something!

But I can't go back inside. I can't face Tom again, not after bolting like that. I can't face him any more than I can face how I'm feeling right now. So instead of acting like a reasonable, intelligent adult, I walk over to the fence between his and Newland's property and clamber over. The greenhouse is down the path to my left. This time of day, I suspect Newland is in there taking care of the seedlings. I really don't want to see him though. I really don't want to see anyone right now.

I don't know exactly what I do want to do, but trying to explain my actions to someone else when I barely understand them myself seems like an impossible task. I'm sure if I explained the situation to Newland, he would listen sympathetically and then offer me a ride home. Or he verbally kick my ass and tell me to act like a grown up. I feel too emotionally fragile for either option.

Instead of heading to the greenhouse, I follow the path to the right, through the fields, to the small farmhouse close to the road. There's a single rocking chair on the front porch, and I hope Newland won't mind if I make use of it while I stew over my options.

I have my phone in my pocket, thank goodness, since I keep my driver's license and a credit card in my phone case, but I left my purse and my clothes at Tom's.

Obviously, at some point, I'll have to go back for them.

Or maybe I can send someone else to retrieve them for me, repo-man style.

I pull out my phone and open the same rideshare app that failed me so spectacularly two nights ago.

It's a Sunday morning so there aren't any surge fees; however, I am out in the boondocks. It says a lot about my state of mind that I don't hesitate to accept the exorbitant price it will take to have someone drive out here to pick me up.

By the time the car arrives, I've changed my mind about where I want to go. Thankfully, it's easy to convince the guy to drop me at the car rental place by the airport since it's much closer than my parents' house.

The guy, an older, grandfatherly type, gives me a stern look as he drops me off and asks, "You sure you're alright?"

I guess he doesn't get many Sunday morning walk-of-shame pick-ups that need to go straight to the airport.

I assure him I am.

By the time I rent a car, I have officially blown through what little savings I had.

Which is fine. I'm sure it's fine.

Lots of people leave grad school with credit card debt, right?

Besides, I've been running the science building's food-waste composting program for two years now. I know that at least a third of the food that gets dropped off is still edible. Surely, I can live off that until I graduate. It's not like I'll need to be mentally sharp to defend my dissertation.

I'm making a mental list of all the people who contribute to the compost, trying to remember whose food is the most edible, when I admit to myself that my thoughts are veering away from eccentric weirdo and dangerously close to crazed weirdo.

But by this point, I'm halfway to Hillsdale and there's no way I'm going to turn around and drive home so I can explain my irrational behavior to my parents, let alone my sister.

I am not the emotional one in the family. All through high school, my sister had regular bouts of overwrought drama. She sobbed for three hours on the living room sofa when she accidentally left her sneakers in her gym locker and she thought she'd "lost them forever!"

On the other hand, I cried silently in my room for eight minutes when I got my waitlist email from Stanford, the school I'd wanted to attend since I was eleven. Then I made a PowerPoint presentation about why UT, the local school I'd been accepted to, was actually a better fit for my long-term goals.

My sister sobbed the whole time I presented my PowerPoint to the family. "You're just giving up on your dream!" she'd wailed.

I've never wailed in my life.

I'm just not the wailing type. Marie Curie never wailed. Neither did Rosalind Franklin.

Obviously, I don't know that for a fact, but I think we can safely assume they were not wailers either.

As I drive to Hillsdale, I feel like wailing. Just a little.

Instead, I stop at the gas station I always stop at that's about halfway between my parents' house and Hillsdale. I buy the biggest cup of coffee they sell (because I never did get coffee this morning) and a family-sized bag of Peanut M&M's. It's a sign of how bad things are that I feel too soul-sick to buy Reese's.

Thinking about Reese's Cups just reminds me of Tom, of the hurt in his eyes as I left. Yes, eating the whole bag of M&M's will probably make me sick, but I need something I can crunch on to get out my anger.

Yeah, maybe I'm not the one who should be angry. I'm the one who left. That was my choice. That's on me.

So if I'm feeling hurt, if I'm feeling heartbroken, it's my own damn fault. I recognize that, but it doesn't make me any less angry.

Yeah, I was the one who walked out, but how did he expect me to react?

Did he honestly think that hearing that song about me—that beautiful, heart-wrenching song—would convince me that he's really loved me since he was fifteen?

Hearing that song convinced me of exactly one thing: Tom doesn't know me at all.

He has some romantic fantasy of me that he's built up in his mind, sure, some ideal based on… I have no idea what… Maybe it's about the fantasy of what his life would have been like if he hadn't joined Boys of Summer.

Obviously, there are details I don't know, might never know, about his years in the band, but from what he said, the experience was obviously hard on him. The pressure, the panic attacks, all of it no doubt exacerbated by the fact that his parents got a divorce a year after he joined the band. He makes such a point of saying over and over again that he knows how lucky he was, that he appreciates all that being in the band did for him, that he's grateful. He says it all with the kind of stoic desperation that convinces me how hard it must've actually been.

I'm sure there were fun times, and I'm sure he's glad he gets to do the work he does now, but I'm equally sure those years scarred him in ways he doesn't yet grasp.

And somehow, he fixated all of that pain and emotion on me.

More specifically, on this idealized version of me he has in his mind. The phoenix who haunts him, who always flies away, only to come back again and break his heart over and over.

It's beautiful, haunting, and tragic.

It also has absolutely nothing to do with the person I actually am.

He doesn't want to go to New Mexico with me. He wants to go to New Mexico with the phoenix. The girl he could never have.

CHAPTER 25

GWEN

I spend the next four days mostly alone, in the lab, grateful that my years of nerdy reclusiveness have convinced people I'm the kind of person who would have time off and choose to spend it at work.

I still haven't figured out how to get my purse and clothes back from Tom, but after a string of texts convincing my parents I haven't been kidnapped or gone mad, they agree to bring me the stuff I left at their house as soon as my car is out of the shop. They'll drive up to Hillsdale in my Kia, then return the rental back in Austin.

It's pretty obvious they know that me leaving Austin so suddenly was the result of some big emotional trauma, but I think the idea of me having emotions at all makes all of us so uncomfortable we make a tacit agreement to pretend otherwise.

Priya and Jax, the other two grad students who work in the lab, are on vacation, so I don't have to deal with questions from them. On my fourth day back in the lab, Max shows up. When he sees me, he just grunts noncommittally and gets started on his own work.

Thirty minutes later, Holly shows up with a pricey latte, a bag of Reese's Eggs, and a hug so tight I nearly burst into tears. She doesn't stay or ask questions, just tells me she knew it was bad if Max noticed I was upset and texted her about it.

I have to agree.

When she leaves, he goes with her, leaving me alone in the lab with the Reese's Eggs and the latte. I drink the latte, leaving the eggs untouched until my normal lunch break. Then I bring them down to the faculty compost, carefully unwrap each one and toss them in.

I know it's sacrilege, but I can't bring myself to eat them, and I don't want to hurt Holly's feelings.

Back in the lab, after composting the Reese's Eggs, I download Larinda Scott's song, "The Phoenix", and listen to it on repeat. I can't find the version Tom played for me of him singing it anywhere on the internet. In a world where everything eventually gets leaked somewhere, that says something.

The pronouns are switched in the Larinda Scott version, so she's singing about the guy she can't have. A few of the other lyrics are switched up as well, but the bones of the song are the same.

On my fifth day back in the lab, Tom shows up.

Which should not be possible, but there's a knock on the door, and when I open it, he's on the other side.

"How did you get in?" I demand, after a long second of staring and catching my breath.

Ignoring me, he enters the room.

"You can't be here," I protest, but this time it sounds weaker, because he looks so damn good it hurts. I'm still holding the door open and I gesture with my free hand. "You need to leave."

"Did you really think I was going to let you run away from this? From us?"

He pins me with one of those intense looks of his, the kind that feels like he's reaching right into my body and touching my very soul. I feel myself leaning into him, wishing he would kiss me.

Yeah, I can't let that happen. That's the kind of thing that got me into this mess to begin with, so I scoot past him, letting the door close.

"You shouldn't have been able to get into the building without a student or faculty ID, let alone onto the floor."

He leans back against the closed door and crosses his arms over his chest. "I ran into a fan while I was sitting on the steps outside waiting for you to come out. He let me in."

"What did you offer him? Are you going to listen to his demo tape? Record his a cappella group's next album?"

"Tickets for his daughter's birthday to Drew's upcoming concert in Houston and a meet and greet after. As an added bonus, it will piss Drew off because the guy's daughter is twelve. Drew likes to think his fans are cooler than twelve-year-old girls. I did warn the guy that Drew is a total ass."

"I don't even want to know who it is, because he could get fired for letting you in!"

Tom just shrugs, like it's not his problem.

"How did you even know where to find me?"

"I follow you on Instagram. And LinkedIn."

"No, you don't."

"Yeah, I do."

"I have less than two hundred followers, and I know all of them. I think I would have noticed if any of them were Tomás Mendoza Official."

He puts his hand over his heart and cocks his head to the side. "Aww, you follow me. That's sweet." He blows me a little kiss, but there's something hard in his eyes. "But you're right. Tomás Mendoza doesn't follow you. But you haven't vetted your list as carefully as you think you have, because Thomas Mendel has followed you for three years. Though, I should probably admit he's not actually a grad student in Oxford. Also, I'm kind of disappointed you didn't realize it was me. I thought picking a pseudonym named after the father of genetics was a little on the nose, but you never even questioned it."

I don't even know what to do with that information. I don't know what to do with the fact that Tom went to the trouble of creating a fake persona just so he could follow me or that he knows who Mendel is. I throw up my hands. "Do you realize you sound like a crazed stalker right now?"

"Yeah, I do realize it." He laughs, shaking his head as he starts pacing the cramped confines of the lab. "I am painfully aware of exactly how crazy I sound. If I sound crazy, it's because that's how I feel. You make me feel crazy."

"I don't know what I'm supposed to say to that," I admit.

"Well, you could start by telling me how you feel," he says.

He stops massaging his arm. I can tell he has to physically stop himself from doing it by the way he flexes his fingers and fists his hands before he continues talking.

"Because I gotta be honest here, I feel like I'm flying blind. Four days ago, I laid it out. And you walked away." He stops his pacing and turns to look at me. "I love you, Gwen. I always have."

That stare of his. Those crazy green eyes that seem to look right into my soul. Right into my heart. I know he's waiting for me to respond, to tell him that I feel it, too.

And I can't.

Not because I don't feel something for him. I do. I feel so much it terrifies me.

I have no experience with these big emotions. No way to regulate them or keep them from overwhelming me.

Right now, I can hardly hear over the pounding of my heart. I can hardly stand still, because my hands want to reach for him so badly they're shaking.

And I'm terrified that if I admit any of that to him, he'll realize how few defenses I have against him.

So, I fall back on my scientific training.

"Confirmation bias," I say abruptly.

Tom just blinks in surprise. "What?"

"It's the human tendency to look for evidence that supports what you already believe."

"I know what confirmation bias is." He scrubs a hand through his hair and then down his face, before bringing it to his arm to massage his bicep. "Jesus, Gwen,

I just told you I love you and that's your response? You want to talk about confirmation bias?"

"Yes, I do. Because you also just told me that I make you feel crazy. And that you've 'always loved' me." I put air quotes around the phrase *always loved*, because I want him to hear how crazy that sounds.

Over the past week, every time I haven't been able to handle my emotions, I've acted on instinct. I've done mindless tasks instead of figuring out how I actually feel. I've done laundry and shopped for plants and driven back to Hillsdale. I did all those things to keep myself from examining my emotions. I can't do that anymore. I can't keep running from how Tom makes me feel. I can't pretend he's not a pop star. I can't pretend this will all work out. I have to be honest and logical.

"I want to talk about confirmation bias," I tell him. "Because someone here has to be logical and it clearly can't be you. So it needs to be me. I need it to be me."

"I don't even understand what you're talking about."

"Your stint in Boys of Summer was clearly hard on you. You suffer from anxiety and panic attacks. And all of that sucks. You've mentioned working with a therapist, which is awesome. I commend your hard work to get emotionally healthy. I really do."

"So that's the problem?" he asks, suddenly pale. He says his next words softly, like he's confirming something he always believed was true but never voiced. "You don't want to be with me because you think I'm crazy?"

"No. Of course not." Oh, God. I'm doing this all wrong. "It's not that at all."

"Then what is it? Give me one reason why we can't be together."

"Whatever you went through, you used the idea of me to get you through it. And that's what the song is about, right? 'The Phoenix'? It's all about the unattainable love that kept you going through the hard times. The idea of loving me was a coping mechanism, but it was just a fantasy. It wasn't really me."

"Fine." He grinds out the word, stalking across the room to stand in front of me. "You think I didn't fall in love with you when I was fifteen. Or think my feelings couldn't last this long. Whatever." He wraps his hands around my arms, yanking me closer to him. He's not rough or in a way that scares me, but there's desperation in his touch. "None of that explains what I feel for you now. Because I love you now. Today. In this moment. You might be able to explain away what I felt for you when I was teenager, but you can't logic your way out of what I'm feeling now."

God, he's breaking my heart. He's breaking me. How many times am I supposed to stoically listen to him declare his love and be strong enough to be the logical one?

"That's where the confirmation bias comes in," I tell him gently. "You want to believe you love me. You need to keep believing it. A week ago, when we met again after not seeing each other for years, you already believed you loved me. The more you believe it, the harder it is to admit you're wrong."

I watch him thinking it through, trying to poke holes in my logic.

I almost wish he was less smart. That he wouldn't eventually see I'm right.

Or maybe I wish I was less smart, that I could have just blissfully believed him when he said he loved me.

But then what? I would fall hopelessly in love with him, only to have him realize he doesn't really love me? That he was infatuated by some fantasy version of me that exists only in his mind?

Because someday, he's going to wake up and see me. Really see me, the woman I am. He's going to realize I spend my days analyzing maggot poop and culturing the bacterial content in compost. He thinks I'm some exotic phoenix, but the truth is, I'm less magical creature and more Beaker from the Muppets.

When he sees me for who I really am, he will leave me.

No. Who am I kidding? He's a good man. He'll try to stay. He'll try to stick with it. And, honestly, that might be worse.

I can't wait around for that to happen.

Even the bravest version of myself can't imagine that ending well for me.

After a long hard minute of staring at me, he shakes his head. "I'm not wrong. I know what I feel."

He tries to pull me closer, but I put my hands up between us to stop him.

I can't let him kiss me again. I'm strong, but I know I'm not that strong.

"I know you think that." I push a little harder, so that he steps back. "But you're wrong. And I need you to leave."

His gaze turns hard as he looks at me. "So that's it, huh? You won't believe me and there's nothing I can say to convince you. So, what? We just pretend this didn't happen? Go back to the previously scheduled programming?"

"I think that's best."

He gives a tight nod, then turns to leave.

I stand there for several long minutes, just breathing in the lingering scent of him. Then I quietly log out of my computer before crossing to the clean room we have at the back of the lab. I follow all the normal protocols, change out of my shoes into booties, scrape my hair back into a knot that's as tight as I can get it, and change into a clean lab coat, before using my badge to let myself into the foyer between the clean room and the rest of the lab. In the foyer, I set the timer and scrub my hands for the full three minutes, but I don't make it into the clean room.

None of the rituals that I hoped would calm me down worked. I'm still fighting back tears. Here, in the foyer to the clean room, in this tiny space that only four people in the world have access to, I am completely alone. It's just me. Me and these terrifying emotions. This crushing grief. This love that is threatening to overwhelm me.

This love that is overwhelming my body, my heart, and my better judgement.

Instead of going into the clean room, I lean against the door and slide down to sit on the floor. That's when the tears come. The tears that I've kept in check my whole life. The emotions I thought I was somehow above or immune to.

I cry over Tom's broken teenage years and over the anguish he went through trying so hard to be perfect so that he wouldn't waste his chance. I cry over not being able to be that fantasy phoenix he thinks he loves. I cry over my own wasted heart.

Tom may not understand confirmation bias, but I do.

I understand it all too well.

I understand that I can never live up to the fantasy version of me he has in his head.

And I also understand that I had a fantasy version of him in my mind, too. I thought he was shallow and self-centered. I thought he was just some famous person with no depth who happened to look exactly like my best friend.

He came into this expecting to fall in love with me. He expected me to be his dream girl, therefore human nature and confirmation bias have convinced him I really am that person.

I came into it expecting the worst of him, and I was proven completely wrong. Tom is amazing enough to overcome all my bias against him. And now I'm hopelessly in love with a man who could never love the real me.

CHAPTER 26

TOM

I'd like to think it's a sign of my emotional growth of the past three years that when I walk out of Gwen's lab, after practically begging her to give me a fucking chance, I don't climb into my car and drive aimlessly until I find a place I can disappear.

I don't drive off and get lost in New Mexico, and not only because too many people know the location of the cabin now.

I did not spend three years in therapy so I could run away just because I can't have Gwen. Before this past week, I never even considered having her was a legitimate option. So, I got a taste, and I pled my case. She rejected me, and there's not a damn thing I can do about it.

Instead, I get back in my car and drive home to Austin. I act like the fucking adult I am. I head into the studio and I do my fucking job.

For one straight week, I do everything I'm supposed to be doing. I show up at the studio every time someone has a slot scheduled. I follow up on emails and paperwork I'm behind on. I eat three healthy meals a day. I swim for hours. I even hire a landscaper to pull up the last of the daylilies and put in plants that are bee friendly.

The only thing I do to acknowledge the havoc Gwen wreaked on my life is to send Dallas a single text telling him it's over between Gwen and me and asking him to get the other SoBs to back off.

This time around, the ashes are just ashes. I'm all out of magic.

Whatever he says, it works, and I don't hear anything from them about her.

Dallas must have reached out to Bex also because an hour after I send the text to Dallas, Bex stops asking me about Gwen. Even my mom stops texting about it. As much as I hate the idea of Dallas and Bex talking about me behind my back, I'm thankful I don't have to field questions from her, too.

Then, one day, about a week after my trip out to Hillsdale to see Gwen, I wake up to find Drew Walters asleep next to me on my bed in the pre-dawn light.

At thirty, Drew is the oldest member of Boys of Summer. He's also the least mature, the biggest asshole, biggest fuck up, and an all-around harbinger of doom.

Waking up to find him in my house—let alone asleep on my bed—nearly gives me a heart attack. At least he's not spooning me, but that offers little comfort.

As soon as I'm fully awake, I realize what his presence means. If he's here, the rest of the SoB's are, too.

There's no way Drew would show up on his own. It would never occur to Drew to worry about anyone else, let alone bother to check on them. No, if Drew's here, every one of those assholes is here.

I roll onto my side to face Drew, pull my knees to my chest and kick him, gently but firmly enough to roll him off my bed to the floor.

There's a loud thud followed by curses as he wakes up.

"What the fuck, man?" he scrambles to his feet and glares down at me.

He's balls-out naked. Because of course he is.

Someone else stumbles in and flips the switch by the door. I sit up, blinking in the sudden light. Because, yeah, Drew's dick in bright light is exactly what I needed.

I see Josh over by the door, scrubbing a hand over his short, spiky hair. "Are we getting up? Because I just fucking fell asleep." He points an accusing finger at me. "You need to get a more comfortable couch. And a damn guest bed."

I throw a pillow at his head. "I don't have a guest bed or a comfortable couch because I don't want you dickholes crashing at my place."

"Daddy, what's a dickhole?" asks a voice that is too young and too feminine to belong to one of the SoBs.

The second we hear that voice—the voice of Luther's four-year-old daughter—we all snap to action. Josh tosses the pillow at Drew, who clutches it to his crotch. I throw a blanket at Drew at the same time, which leaves me dressed in boxer briefs, because I don't sleep naked like a fucking Neanderthal.

Josh turns and squats in front of Lola, the most adorable kid in the universe, and says with total confidence, "He said 'brick hole.'"

She looks up doubtfully at her dad, who is standing behind her. She purses her lips. "I think he's lying."

Luther clamps a hand down on her shoulder and starts to steer her out. "Don't worry, baby girl. You just didn't get enough sleep. Let's get you back to bed."

I scramble off the bed and grab a pair of jeans from the chair in the corner. "Hey, Lola, why don't you try to fall back to sleep in my bed? We'll clear out of here and let you have it all to yourself."

By now, Drew has wrapped the blanket around himself like a toga, except he still has my pillow covering his crotch under the blanket. I give him a shove toward the door as I walk past him, stepping into my jeans.

I'm definitely going to have to burn my pillow now that he's rubbed his junk all over it.

Probably all of my bedding.

Or maybe I could auction it all off for charity. It would serve Drew right to have his dick pillow out in the world.

As I pass Luther, it's obvious he's torn between glaring at me for cussing in front of Lola and being grateful I'm giving up the bed for her. I ruffle Lola's curls as I walk past.

Like the spitfire she is, she punches me in the thigh. “Don’t touch my hair. It’s not a petting zoo.”

“Got it.” I blow her a kiss. “See you on the other side, sweet pea.”

She glares back, clutching the ratty Cookie Monster stuffed animal she carries with her everywhere.

Over her head, I mouth to Josh, “Brick hole?”

He shrugs and follows me out of the bedroom.

Once the three of us are out, Luther shuts the door behind us, staying in my room to get Lola back to sleep. A moment later, the sound of rainfall drifts through the closed door. Clearly he found my white-noise machine.

I head into the kitchen and turn on the coffee maker so it will start warming the water while I pour the beans in. I run the grinder, sending up a silent prayer that it’s not louder than the white noise.

Dallas stumbles in the back door, scratching his bare chest. “Hey, what are y’all doing up so early?”

“The real question,” I say, fighting the urge to coldcock Dallas, “is what they’re doing here at all.”

“Dude,” Drew says, hopping up to sit on my damn counter. “You needed us. So we came.”

“Get your bare ass off my counter before I have to burn down my entire house.”

He shrugs but doesn’t move. “My bare ass is on your blanket, not your counter.”

“Then get your bare ass dressed and get the fuck out of my house. Who sleeps naked in another man’s bed? Who does that?”

Josh—ever the peacemaker—wanders over and claps a hand on my shoulder. “You needed us, so we came. That’s the important part.”

“I don’t need you. What I need is this asshole”—I point at Drew—“to get dressed.”

“Why don’t you stop trying to distract us by complaining about Drew? Tell us what happened.”

"Nothing happened. I'm fucking fine."

"You're not fine," Dallas says softly.

"I'm fine," I grind out.

"We're worried about you," Josh says.

"Well don't be. I'm fine."

Yeah. It's the third time I've said I'm fine. Obviously I need to stop saying that before it becomes obvious how not fine I am.

I blow out a breath. "I'm here, aren't I? I didn't go off the map. I didn't disappear. I'm right where I'm supposed to be. I'm showing up to therapy. I'm getting work done. I'm as steady and stable as Luther. I couldn't be more fine if I was one of Josh's five-thousand-dollar bottles of wine."

Drew chuckles. "Dude, five k on a bottle of wine? If you need to throw away money, you can just give it to me."

"What? I like good wine." Josh shrugs and then points at me again. "And you're deflecting again. You may be keeping up appearances, but you are clearly hanging on by a thread, or Dal wouldn't have called us in."

Before I can throw any more roadblocks up on this intervention, my bedroom door opens, and Luther comes out. He shuts the door softly behind him, but if the glare he hits us all with is any indication, he wishes he could slam it.

"Y'all are a bunch of grown-ass men, bickering like children." He levels his glare at me. "You're lucky Lola fell back asleep as easily as she did."

I hold up my hands, palms out. "Hey, I didn't ask you to come."

"No, you didn't." He crosses the room to plant his palms on the counter. "Because you're too fucking stubborn to ask for help, but that shit needs to stop now. Was I too stubborn to ask for help when Mikala died and left me with a ten-month-old I didn't know I had? No, I wasn't. I needed help, and y'all set aside your bullshit and helped. Because that's what family does. Some of you guys have family; I don't. So, for me, you're it." The steady, no-nonsense gaze of his pans back to me. "If you need me and Lola, we're here for you, but I don't have time to waste listening to you claim to be fine when you clearly aren't."

I don't know what to say to that because he's right.

Luther has always been the glue that held us together. Josh always kept us talking and pulled us apart when someone threw a punch, but it was always Luther who brought us back together when we were all ready to walk away forever.

Maybe it's because his mom was like a mother to all of us, and when she died of breast cancer, it was like we all mourned as one. Or maybe it's because he was the one who called it from the first day I joined. The first time the five us were alone, he told us we couldn't let them treat us the way they'd treated Matías. He said if we stuck together and watched out for one another, we'd have more power. But we couldn't waver and we couldn't fight amongst ourselves. The bond between us was forged by him.

So when he pins me with a look and says, "Start talking," I do.

Dallas quietly makes coffee for all of us. Josh pulls up chairs. Luther listens stoically. Hell, Drew even puts on pants.

And I tell them all of it.

The parts they didn't know, at least.

Obviously, they knew some of it already, because they knew I'd been in love with her since about the time the band formed. And they also knew things were never great between James and me, not since then either.

I don't have to tell them that as much as I love the band and the music we made and the life it's allowed me to have, I also resent it. I don't have to say any of that out loud, because I know they feel it, too. We all have the same crazy love/hate relationship with BoS and Clark and our fame.

But I do tell them about my more recent attempts to fix my relationship with James and how they all keep failing. I tell them about his friendship with Gwen and how it kept me from pursuing her, and about the crazy way she came back into my life and the crazier way she left it.

About her stubborn refusal to believe I actually love her.

By the time I finish, the coffee is gone and everyone is silent, processing.

Yeah, I feel better, having said it all out loud, but I don't have any illusions that they'll be able to fix this.

It isn't like with Lola, where we all came together and learned how to change diapers and took shifts living with Luther while he figured out how to be a dad. Yeah, that was hard as fuck on all of us—him most of all, obviously—but at least we had a path forward. There were physical things we could do, one step at a time.

Sitting there in the quiet kitchen, the early morning sunlight finally shining through the windows, I can't help but think we're all worried about the same thing: that this isn't fixable, that there is not a damn thing I can do to convince Gwen I love her.

And then there's the worse alternative. Maybe she does believe I love her, and it doesn't matter. Maybe it's just that she knows she doesn't love me in return. Maybe she knows she can never love me. Maybe everything that happened between us was just her stretching her wings.

I know she's not the kind of woman who would sleep with a pop star just because she could, but she might be the kind of woman to have a no-strings affair just because she could.

Which means maybe this thing—this life-altering thing that happened to me—was only a fling for her.

After all, a week ago, she honestly thought she didn't like me. It's entirely possible she still doesn't.

And I wonder if that's why I didn't call in the troops to begin with. Maybe I knew all along there was nothing anyone could do.

It's Drew who breaks the silence first. "I have to ask, man. Are you sure she's not right?"

Josh reaches out and hits Drew on the side of the head. "What the fuck kind of question is that?"

Drew yelps and rubs his head. "I'm serious. Dal says she's gorgeous, so I'm sure she is."

Dallas interrupts, hands up, palms out. "I didn't hit on her."

"And clearly she's brilliant," Drew continues, as if Dallas hadn't said anything, "if she's getting her PhD in worm guts or whatever. But how well do you know her? Really? You admitted you only spent the past couple of days together and that you barely knew her before that. Maybe this really is all in your head."

For a long moment, all I can do is stare blankly at Drew, and I'm not sure if he's stunned me into silence because he might be right, or just because it's Drew who floats this idea. On most days, Drew has the emotional sensitivity of that gif of a dog taking a shit.

But he's the one who pulls this?

If it had come from any of the other guys, I probably would have scoffed and not even considered my answer, but since the question comes from the world's biggest a-hole, I actually think about it.

"I don't know how to answer that. My gut says that sometimes you just know. You know when something is right. That's how I've always felt about her. Being with her only confirmed it. She settles me, eases something inside me."

I start pacing automatically, and for maybe the first time in my life, I don't feel like I'm pacing to get away from my thoughts. I feel like I'm chasing them, as though if I just move fast enough, I'll catch up to them and have the answer.

"But if you need more than that to believe I love her, yeah, there's more. I love that she's crazy smart about science but stupid about people. I love that she cares passionately about weird things like compost and the health of maggots but doesn't give a fuck what she looks like. I love that her Instagram feed is a total disaster. She has no social media game. It's all dirt and bugs and blurry pictures of the dogs she walks at the pound to help socialize them. I love that she smells like strawberries and mint and sometimes just a little bit like dirt. I love that she saw my tattoo of a semicolon and didn't ask about it. I love that she saw my serotonin and dopamine tattoos and knew exactly what they were." I pause, finally catching up to my thoughts, and I turn to look at the SoBs. "I love the way she eats a Reese's Cup. It's like she peels them, eating all the chocolate from the outside first, and then eating the peanut butter. Who does that? Frankly, it's a little gross. But I love it."

The guys all exchange looks, nodding—even Drew—so I guess I convinced them.

"'My mistress's eyes are nothing like the sun,'" Drew says quietly.

Again, we all turn to stare a Drew, but it's Luther who asks, "Did you just quote Shakespeare?"

Drew might actually be blushing as he rubs a hand over the back of his neck. "Yeah."

"Shakespeare?" Dallas repeats the question. "Like the playwright, poet guy?"

"What?" Drew shrugs. "Luther gets a full-time job for the health insurance and shit and everyone's okay with that, but I go to college to get my degree and y'all fall out of your chairs in shock?"

"Um..." I clear my throat, because clearly our surprise is crossing a line. "No. That seems..." Okay, I can't pretend like I'm not shocked, but at least I can be supportive. "That seems great. What are you getting your degree in? Shakespeare?"

"No, dude. Nobody gets their undergraduate degree in Shakespeare. I took a class. That's all. And we read some of his sonnets."

"Sonnet 130," Luther chimes in, because his mother was an English teacher so of course he knows this shit.

"Right!" Drew exclaims, snapping his fingers and pointing at Luther. "It's great because it's not the same old romantic shit everyone else was writing. Instead of talking about how beautiful his mistress was, he talked about how ordinary she was. Her eyes didn't shine like the sun. Her lips weren't red as flowers or whatever. Her skin didn't glow. But he loved her. He didn't care how she looked. He loved her too much to waste his time talking about how physically perfect she was—or wasn't—because that's not what he loved about her. He just loved her."

I shoot Luther a look, not entirely sure I can trust Drew's interpretation of a sonnet when the guy usually communicates in gifs. Really gross ones.

But Luther is nodding, and when he sees the question in my eyes, he says, "Yeah. I think that about sums it up."

"Okay," I say slowly, still not sure how this is supposed to apply to Gwen. "So, what are you saying? I need to quote Shakespeare to her?"

"No," Dallas says, nodding. "You need to write her another song. I mean, that's the problem, right? She thinks you're in love with the Phoenix, not with her. You need a song that shows her you love her. The person she is now. All of the parts of her that she's clearly worried you don't see and won't like."

"Great. Just to sum up here, you all think I need to write her a song that's as good as one of Shakespeare's sonnets and that's better than the Grammy-winning song I already wrote about her."

"Exactly." Drew beams.

"But first," Luther interrupts, "you need to make shit right with James."

Yeah, somehow, I think that might be even harder than writing this new song, but I know Luther is right. If I'm not man enough to own how I feel to James, then I don't deserve Gwen.

CHAPTER 27

TOM

Even though the crowds from South By are gone, parking downtown is still a nightmare, so I make Dallas drive so I don't have to park and then hike for a mile to reach the building where James's law firm is situated.

I don't have an appointment, but I'm able to charm my way past the receptionist because her daughter is a fan of The Vamps, which she obviously thinks is the band I was a part of. I'm too amused by her mistake to tell her that I'm not in The Vamps. And they're a British band, to boot. Still, I promise to get her daughter a signed vinyl album. No idea how I'm going to pull that off, since I don't know any of them, but I'll figure that out later.

I find James in his office, on the phone with a client. He glares at me like he's trying through sheer will alone to develop the mutant power to vaporize his enemies with a single look. Still talking to his client, he tries to wave me out of his office.

I shake my head and mime that we need to talk.

He gives a confused shrug, so I guess what they say about twins having their own language is bullshit.

Not that I didn't know that already.

I try sitting in one of the expensive leather chairs opposite his desk, but I'm jangling my knee so much the chair is squeaking. When James shushes me, I get up and pace for a bit. I don't know why the hell I didn't take a fucking lorazepam before coming here. Probably because I haven't needed one in over a year.

Finally, he gets off the phone. His tone, which was slick but polite with the client, changes the second he hangs up.

"What do you want?" he asks, sounding both tired and annoyed

"We need to talk," I tell him.

"I'm at work."

"Yeah, well, you haven't returned any of my texts in more than a week, so you didn't leave me a lot of options."

His gaze narrows. "Come back tonight. After eight." Then he looks at the calendar on his phone. "Make that nine."

"I'm here now."

"Again," he grinds out. "I'm at work, and the firm expects me to be earning them money during business hours. My rate is five hundred dollars an hour. I can't just take the afternoon off to chat with my brother."

"Fine. Bill me. Do you need me to sign a contract and put you on retainer?"

He glares at me like he's actually thinking about it. That asshole.

Then he gives an imperious shake of his head. "That won't be necessary."

"That's very generous of you."

His sigh, which seems to imply that I'm a burden and that I'm the asshole here, says everything about our relationship. "What do you need?"

I open my mouth. Then, for the life of me, I can't think of what to say. Where to start. How to cover the vast acreage of discontent that's been sown between us.

So, I sit and bury my head in my hands while I try to sort it out. People always think that ADHD is just an abundance of nervous energy. That's just the tip of the fucking iceberg. It's not just too much physical energy. It's too much emotional energy, too. It's the inability to regulate the big emotions. And it's too much mental energy. It's the inability to order your thoughts. The inability to say what you mean in a way that makes sense to other people.

And, yeah, every once in a while, it's even the opposite of all of that. It's intense stillness and focus. It's the perfect words, laid out in the perfect order to convey exactly the right message.

I'm not the kind of guy who prays much. Yeah, I grew up going to church, so I do a lot of asking for forgiveness, but I don't pray for things I want or need. I have too much to ever ask for more. But right now, I pray for the right words with James. I pray I don't make this worse.

I'm still sitting there, head in my hands, when I hear James push his chair back and go to the door. A moment later, I look up when he returns. He's holding out a tumbler of amber liquid and taking a sip out of a second tumbler.

"Jesus, Tom. Have a drink."

"I don't drink," I tell him.

He just shrugs and sets the drink on the table beside my chair. "Your choice."

He leans back against the desk, stretching his legs towards me as he sips his drink—probably Scotch.

Eventually, he says, "You wanted to talk. So are you going to talk, like, ever?"

I look up at him. "Could you at least try to be less of an asshole?"

"You're obviously having a panic attack. This is me trying to be less of an asshole."

I don't bother correcting him. This isn't a full-blown panic attack. This is just massive anxiety.

Even though I still have no idea what to say, I push myself to my feet—because I can't have this conversation with him looking down on me—and I blurt, "I'm in love with Gwen."

Confusion flickers across his face. "Who?"

"Gwen. Gwen Mathews. Your best friend. I'm in love with her."

His confusion blurs into something else. Not anger, which is what I expected.

I was so ready to defend myself against his anger—to argue with him about it or justify my feelings—that it takes me several beats to recognize the surprise on his face.

After a second, shaking his head, he asks, "Still?"

"What do you mean still?"

He sips his drink. "Well, you clearly had a thing for her when we were in school. I just figured you were over it by now."

"You knew?" I ask. And then, just so there's no confusion, I clarify, "You knew I was in love with Gwen in high school?"

"Yeah. I didn't know it was supposed to be a secret."

I start pacing again. "Did she know?"

He laughs with a snort. "God, no. Because she's Gwen. That kind of thing never occurred to her. I probably knew four different guys who were in love with her, and she never noticed. Sometimes I think the only reason she was friends with me was because I was the one guy who could talk to her without acting like a moron. Well, that, and she was never good at being friends with girls."

"You knew I was in love with her?" I have to say it again, because it's such a seismic shift in my world view. "And you never said anything to me?"

"You didn't exactly hide it. Remember that year she wanted to wear matching costumes for Halloween? She made those stupid double helix costumes for her and me to wear to Davis's Halloween party. And when you found out I wasn't going to wear mine, you flew home from—" He snaps his fingers like he's trying to pull up the memory. "Where were you on tour?"

"Pittsburgh."

"Right. You flew down from Pittsburgh to wear the stupid costume instead of me?"

"Yeah. I remember that."

We were eighteen at the time. BoS was on tour in the northeast. We didn't have a concert that night, thank God, but I missed out on the one night off that week to attend that party and dress as the other half of Gwen's double helix.

When Bex called and told me how excited Gwen was about the costumes and how upset she thought Gwen would be when James showed up dressed as a zombie instead, I talked Drew into flying with me back to Texas. Clark fined us ten grand a piece for going missing in the middle of a tour.

I wore the stupid costume and showed up at the party for her. For two straight hours, she thought I was James and we hung out, dressed up in these horrible costumes she'd made out of painted dowel rods and Styrofoam balls. We couldn't sit down in them, and they were so clumsy, Davis's mom banished us to the back patio after Gwen's adenine molecules fell in the punch bowl.

It was the most fun I'd had in years, until James showed up, dressed as a zombie, and Gwen realized I wasn't him. Things went to hell after that. And, yeah, that was the last time I ever pretended to be James, until this thing with the phone.

Now, I'm sitting in his office, all these years later, and he's still laughing at the memory. "Yeah, I knew then you had it bad for her, but I figured you outgrew it." He gives me an assessing look. "Have you been holding back all this time because you thought I would be mad at you if you hit on her?"

"Wouldn't you have been?"

He thinks about it, taking another sip. "At the time? Yeah, I probably would have. Because I had this idea that you were off living the dream while I was stuck in pre-calc." He sets his glass down with a sigh, then rubs at his forehead. "The truth is, I was kind of a dick. To you, I mean. It seemed like you had everything I'd ever wanted. It didn't seem fair to me that you should get to have her, too."

"I didn't want to take her away from you," I try to protest.

"You wouldn't have meant to, but it would have happened. You know what women are like around you. You're the good looking one."

"Dude, we're identical twins," I point out, baffled by this statement.

"You know what I mean. You're the charismatic one. The charming one. The one all the women fall for. Even Gwen, who is so clueless about her own emotions. I think she was half in love with you after that one day."

I give a bitter laugh, thinking of all the times I offered her tickets or whatever only to be shot down. "That's not the way I remember it."

"Look, about that—" He clears his throat. "I never told her you wanted to see her again."

"What?" I shake my head, trying to make sense of his words.

"I just didn't tell her. Every time you asked about her, every time she asked about you, I just blew it off."

"You blew it off? What does that even mean?"

"You'd offer tickets to her and I just wouldn't pass along the message, that kind of thing." He's still leaning against his desk, still sipping that damn drink of his like he hasn't just admitted to screwing me over.

"Are you fucking kidding me? You knew I liked her. You just admitted to that. You knew she was important to me and… what? You just let her think I'd forgotten all about her?"

He just shrugs, his gaze drifting from mine like he's fucking bored by the conversation.

But I see it. The flicker of guilt in his gaze. That's how I know he didn't just let her think I'd forgotten about her. He actively bad mouthed me. "This is why she's never liked me," I mutter as the realization hits me. "You purposefully made me look like an asshole. And that's why she hated me all this time."

"Look, I already apologized. I admitted to being a dick about it, what more do you want?"

What did I want? I want details. I want to know exactly what he said to her and when. I want to know what he told her about me. I want to know exactly how much damage he did.

But even more than that, I want it to just not be true. Which makes me feel even more like a pathetic loser.

"I want you to be better than this," I tell him. "Jesus, James. You're my brother. My twin. I thought you had my back no matter what. And now I find out you were talking shit about me to the girl I was in love with. The girl you knew I was in love with."

"She was my friend first."

"That's bullshit and you know it. You're my brother and you're supposed to have my back, but instead, you fucked me over."

He pushes away from his desk and gets in my face. "Don't even pull that brother bullshit with me."

Surprise rocks me back a step. "What?"

"All that bullshit about how I should have had your back because I'm your brother. That shit would be a lot more convincing if you hadn't forgotten you had a brother as soon as you joined Boys of Summer."

"What are you even talking about?"

"All those interviews with the band. All the times you described them as your brothers. They were your family. Your closest friends. How do you think that made me feel?"

I've never heard this kind of bitterness and anger in his voice before. I'd gotten used to the disdain, to the icy distance between us, but this visceral anger is like a kick in the teeth.

"That was all an act," I protest. "All of that was scripted for us by the band's PR."

He gives a bitter laugh. "Well, it didn't sound scripted."

"Of course it didn't. Because we had hours of coaching. We had actual acting lessons on how to look like we were having fun."

But James is just shaking his head. "Yeah. Sounds tough."

"I don't care how it sounds. It was work. It was a job that I was contractually obligated to do."

"You didn't even come to my wedding," he says, almost like it's not a big deal anymore. Like he's so bitter about it, he's stopped caring.

"If there'd been any way for me to be there, I would have." It's all can I say, because the reason I missed his wedding isn't my story to tell.

It was a bad time for all of us in Boys of Summer, but even if I could explain it, even if I could make him understand the pressure we were under, it might not matter. And maybe he's right, anyway. I missed his wedding because I sitting in the hospital with Luther, Dallas, and Drew, waiting to see if Josh was going to make it. We took turns sitting with him. We didn't leave him alone for months. We went through fucking group therapy together. And then we all got semicolon tattoos on our biceps. It was the hardest weekend of my life.

Because it's not my story to tell, I don't tell James. But importantly, I don't want to tell him. This guy? This asshole who shares my face and my blood? He doesn't deserve to know the truth.

"Sure you would have," he says, scoffing. "Just do me a favor and stop pretending you're the victim in this story. Maybe I was a dick back in high school about the Gwen thing, but she was my best friend and she was there for me when my own brother wasn't."

"Until you fell in love with Maggie and pretty much cut her out of your life."

"Are you here to bitch at me about how I treat Gwen or about my relationship with Maggie? Because I don't think I have the patience to listen to both today."

I just stare at him. My brother. My twin. The man who's supposed to be my ride or die. A man I feel like I don't even know anymore.

Shaking my head, I walk for the door. "I don't know," I tell him on the way out. "I don't know why I'm here anymore."

I came here thinking I wanted or maybe even needed his permission to be with Gwen, but I couldn't have been more wrong. After finding out that he screwed me over with Gwen, I don't care what he thinks about the idea of us being together.

CHAPTER 28

GWEN

It's a documented fact that babies need micro-exposure to a variety of viruses and bacteria during their first few months of life in order to properly train their immune systems.

Despite that, I'm still nervous about meeting Holly and Max's new twins for the first time, so I put on a clean shirt and scrub my hands like I'm getting ready to go into surgery.

And, yes, I know that's ridiculous. They aren't newborns anymore by the time I finally accept Holly's invitation to come over, but babies—with all their fragility—make me nervous.

I figure this is a good time to visit, since it's been several days since Tom visited me at the lab and I'm already a nervous wreck. This way, if I burst into tears, I can blame it on infant-induced hysteria or something.

Max and Holly adopted the twins, Luna and Bella, almost as soon as they were born. They are the half-siblings to the two older kids they are still in the process of adopting, Rosa and Eli. I've met Rosa and Eli numerous times already. Rosa, who is quiet and nerdy—like me—is fantastic. Eli, who is all teenage boy bravado reminds me of Tom.

When I show up for dinner Friday night at their house, I realize instantly that washing my hands was unnecessary, because the Ramsey-Dolinsky household is a study in chaos. Between the two teenagers, the two babies, and the numerous pets, these kids are going to have the immune systems of medieval milkmaids.

Things are extra crazy right now, because Max just got in from being out of town giving a lecture in New York.

As soon as Holly opens the door, she says, "Hold this," and hands me a baby. "I need to clean up some bunny shit before the goat tracks it on the carpet."

I stand there in the doorway, holding one of the girls out in front of me like she's covered in toxic waste.

She looks up at me with huge brown eyes and smiles with drool-moistened lips.

Holly is already on her knees with a damp paper towel. "Thank God you got here. Sometimes the goat tracks it all over and then faints and lands on it. Then it's in her fur."

I look from Holly to the baby and back again. "Um… which one is this?"

"That's Luna." Having cleaned up the mess, Holly pops back to her feet and heads for the kitchen, presumably to throw away the rabbit poop and wash her hands, so I follow as she explains, "Max developed a system to help us tell them apart. Luna only wears cool tones—blue, green, and purple. Bella wears only warm tones—red, orange, and yellow."

Sure enough, the baby in my arms is wearing a purple, ruffled onesie.

We make it to the kitchen where Rosa and Eli are both sitting at the table with books open in front of them.

Rosa hears the last part of the description and shakes her head. "That's Bella." She points at the baby who is in a bounce seat up on the table, cheerfully kicking her legs, also wearing a purple onesie. "This is Luna."

Holly looks from one baby to the next and frowns. "Well, snickerdoodle. How did that happen?"

Eli looks up, holding up his hands in a gesture of innocence. "There was an exploding diaper, and all the warm-toned onesies were dirty. I did what I could."

Holly laughs. "Fair enough." She smiles at me as she washes her hands. "If there's any chance once you graduate you want to step away from your future in academia and become a full-time laundress, let me know, because we would totally hire you."

Holly walks over to me. I think she's going to take Bella from me, but instead she just shifts my hold on the baby. "Try it like this. Tucked close to your body."

As soon as the baby is tucked close, she reaches up and yanks on my hair.

I look from the baby to Holly and ask, "What is a socially acceptable amount of time to hold a baby and will it offend you if I hand her back?"

Holly just laughs and ignores my questions. "Sit," she says. "Relax. Let me get you a drink. I know you're out of your comfort zone, but it will be good for you."

All of which I interpret as, I should do what she says, because Holly is a force of nature. Since she is also the woman who taught me—at twenty-six—how to style my hair so I didn't look like I'd been electrocuted and that I really can't get away with wearing purple, I follow her instructions.

I have to shift things around a bit because my phone is in my back pocket and no one likes to sit on their phone. Also, the gifts that I brought for the girls are in a tote bag, so I set that on the table as well.

Max shows up, and I have to look away because Max and Holly are so adorable together, I can't stand looking at them. I will never get used to seeing my big, gruff, genius of a boss turn into a puffball every time he's around Holly.

At some point, Holly brings a glass of wine and a tiny dish of almonds, my favorite snack. She slides the frozen lasagna into the oven before coming over to sit at the table too and opens the gifts. She oohs and ahhs over the mobiles I bought to hang over the babies' cribs, but Rosa has to tell her that the shapes are molecules.

Then she laughs almost to the point of tears, giving a big sloppy kiss to Max. "Oh, I bet you love these!"

Which is why I bought them.

I knew Max and Holly had gotten a lot of presents for the babies that were cute, delicate clothes and adorable toys, things Holly could appreciate. Max never said it out loud, but I sensed he might be feeling lost on the baby-present front.

He nods approvingly at the mobile, and I can see him studying and identifying each of the molecules.

And, yes, Holly is right; eventually I do calm down about holding the baby. I might even marvel a little at how soft her skin is and how good she smells.

We're partway through dinner when I get a couple of texts. Since my phone is out, I glance at them. I'm surprised to see they're from James.

I haven't heard from James in months, not since long before the spring break puking debacle. I think we exchanged texts in January about his divorce, but that was it.

Based on what Tom had said, I knew he wanted to handle the talking-to-James-about-the-switched-phone thing. If James is texting me now, I assume it's because Tom told him.

I don't read the messages as they come in, because, even though I'm holding a baby, I'm too soul-sick to think about Tom, or even James. It used to annoy me that Tom looked so much like my best friend. Now, it's the opposite. I'm annoyed that James looks so much like the man I'm in love with.

Then James texts me a picture. I barely glance at it, but I instantly know what it is.

But Eli—being a nosy teenage boy—picks up my phone. "What the hell is that a picture of?"

"Language," Max growls.

Eli rolls his eyes and picks up my phone. "What was that a picture of?"

I sigh. "Just a picture of me from Halloween a long time ago."

"What'd you go as? Some kind of porcupine?"

"No."

He waggles my phone to make the picture appear on the lock screen again.

"Don't be nosy," Rosa says, reaching for the phone.

"No, it's okay," I say, not wanting to get Eli in trouble. I unlock my phone and hand it back to Eli so he can see the picture of me from Halloween when I was seventeen.

Technically, it's a picture of me and Tom.

We are in matching costumes that I made. I'd spent a month carefully cutting the wooden dowel rods to the right lengths, painting them, and hot gluing them to the matching white sweat suits I'd bought, and then studding each dowel rod with painted Styrofoam balls.

Looking at the picture now, I wince. We did not look as good as I had remembered.

Eli picks up the phone and stares at the picture. "Okay, if you're not a porcupine, then what were you supposed to be?"

"Matching strands of a double helix," I say.

I made the costumes for me and James, but James refused to wear his—though he didn't tell me that at the time. So, Tom wore it instead. I always assumed he wore it as a prank to make me look stupid. Of course, now I know that can't possibly be true.

"Cool!" Rosa says. "Let me see."

She takes the phone from her brother and zooms in on the picture. She's laughing with delight. "This is awesome! But…" She trails off. Pinches her fingers on the phone to zoom in even more. "Who is this with you?"

I glance at the picture even though I know what it shows. Davis's mom took the picture and forwarded it to me and James later.

When she took it, I thought it was a picture of me and James… along with some random guy dressed in a pirate costume I didn't know.

Tom and I are standing next to one another, showing off the way our pair bonds align, my sequence of adenine and guanine molecules perfectly lining up to match his thymine and cytosine molecules.

Rosa squints at the phone. "Is this Tomás Mendoza? And is that Drew Walters dressed up like a pirate?"

She looks up at me, surprise on her features.

"Who?" Max asks.

"Two guys from Boys of Summer, one of the most popular boy bands ever, that's who."

"Oh, I remember them," Holly says, then hums a bit from one of their songs.

Eli and Max exchange confused looks.

"I can't believe you know Tomás Mendoza and Drew Walters! I had a poster of Boys of Summer over my bed for years. What are they like?"

"I…" All I can do is shrug. "I barely remember meeting Drew. I don't think I recognized him at the time. But, yeah, I've known Tom for a while."

"And…"

"And he's a great guy."

I take the phone back from Rosa and look at the messages from James.

James: Tom stopped by my office today and told me what happened between you.

James: I don't think I ever told you this, but that Halloween, he and his friend flew in from Pittsburgh to be at the party because I was too much of a jerk to wear the costume you made and he didn't want you to be half of a double helix by yourself.

James: The band manager fined them both ten grand apiece.

Gwen: Why are you telling me this now?

James: I acted like an ass. I'm sorry.

James: I still think you deserve better than him, but you should know the truth.

James: He's always been the other half of your double helix. You should at least give him a chance to prove it.

By the time I get to the picture James sent, I'm in tears.

And before Holly can even prompt me, I'm telling the story. Eli bails immediately. Max stands in the corner, awkwardly rocking the baby he's taken from me. It's his listening that's awkward, not the rocking of the baby. Somehow, he's a pro at that already.

Rosa and Holly listen sympathetically, Holly occasionally refilling my glass.

When I get to the part about why I sent Tom away, Max hands off the baby to Holly and plants both of his hands on the table in front of me.

"When I hired you, I didn't think you were this fucking stupid."

I flinch from his words, stammering a response, but he doesn't give me a chance to finish.

"If you don't love this man, that's one thing, but you are too brilliant a scientist to get away with using scientific principles to excuse cowardly behavior."

"But… confirmation bias."

"That's bullshit and I think you know it. You don't give up on an experiment because you're worried about confirmation bias. You design the experiment around it, and it's a moot argument, because human relationships aren't scientific research anyway."

"But—"

He leans down, meeting my gaze in a way he usually doesn't. In the three years I've worked with him, I don't think he's ever looked me square in the eye like he is right now. For the life of me, I can't tell if what he sees in my eyes disappoints him.

I think of all the times he's yelled at me. All the times when I first started working in his lab that he lost his temper and berated me for simple mistakes. Dr. Ramsey is a self-proclaimed asshole and a nightmare to work with, but I don't think I've ever felt the sting of anything he's said to me the way I feel these words.

"People like us," he says sternly, "don't get chances like this. We don't expect love. Fuck, maybe we don't even deserve it. But if we're lucky enough to stumble upon it, we better fucking be smart enough to grab it with both hands and not let go."

He straightens, meeting Holly's gaze across the table. "If you're lucky enough to find someone who loves you, you do anything you can to keep them."

Seeing the way Max looks at Holly, seeing the way she returns his gaze… it doesn't help. By all normal standards, they're mismatched. He's a world-renowned genius, but she's a lecturer. She's witty and loving and everyone's favorite person, but he's reclusive with minimal social skills. They don't make sense, until you see them together.

Even though I've spent the past three years working with Max, I don't think I've ever argued with him. Until now. "But you and Holly are perfect together. You match. Even if Tom thinks he loves me, we don't make sense together. He's this amazing, talented pop star, and I'm just this ordinary, dorky girl."

Max glares at me. "That's the stupidest thing I've ever heard. You're not ordinary. You're brilliant."

"No, I'm—"

Before I can protest, Max cuts me off again, this time with an inarticulate grumble, but it's Holly who steps forward, putting her hand on Max's arm, saying, "Let me try."

He seems to relax some the moment she touches him. They exchange a look and then he steps aside.

"Gwen, you're a woman in academia," she says gently. "There will always be people willing to tell you that you aren't smart enough or good enough. Your job isn't to agree with them. It's to prove them wrong. Do you honestly think that if you weren't exceptional, Max would have hired you in the first place? Do you think he'd have kept you working for him all this time?"

Max gives a grunt of agreement. "Exactly." His gaze swivels back to mine. "You better be as smart as I think you are."

I decide not to argue with them on this, because I know how stubborn Max is. Instead, I pace for a few minutes and then I ask the next, terrifying question. "What if I do give him a chance? What if I just fall more and more in love with him and he just realizes that I'm not really that special?"

Holly just looks at me, her expression a little sad and a lot hopeful. "You just have to be brave. No one ever thinks they're worthy of the person they love. Falling in love is all about taking risks. The only way to prove you're not worthy of love is to give up."

By the time I leave their house a few hours later, I'm exhausted, but I'm still thinking about what Holly said as I settle into my bed in my tiny, shitty apartment near the university. I've lived here for four years now. All this time I've been telling myself I've lived here because it's cheap. Just like I've been telling myself my Kia is fine, even though I've nearly driven the wheels off it. Just like I've been telling myself I can't make a decision about my future until I finish my dissertation.

All of those things are true, but they are also excuses.

I don't like change. It's scary and risky. It's easier to keep moving forward on a path than it is to ask yourself if you're on the right path.

I haven't needed to question my path in life very often, because I've loved being a student and I love my field of research. But I don't love being alone. And I hate the idea that I'm being a coward.

Maybe Tom isn't really in love with me. Maybe he won't stay in love with me once he realizes how boring I really am. But Holly is right. There's only one guaranteed outcome here. If I do nothing, I lose Tom. If I don't fight for him, if I don't fight for the possibility of us, then I really don't deserve him.

That's what it comes down to.

At the end of the day, I want to deserve him.

CHAPTER 29

TOM

I've been working on my Sonnet 130 song for nearly a week, and it sucks.

I keep going back to the original sonnet, reading and re-reading it. And, yeah, that probably doesn't help, because any fool will tell you that the fastest way to feel like a hack is to read the greatest writer of the English language.

Every time I read it, I wonder if Drew's interpretation is right. Was Shakespeare really writing about how much he loved his mistress, despite the fact she wasn't perfect? Or maybe he was just pissed off. Maybe good ol' Will, like me, had done everything right and his girl still broke his heart. Maybe Sonnet 130 isn't about how much he loves her, but instead about how much he wishes he didn't love her.

Maybe that's why the song doesn't work.

All I know is, I've been working my ass off, and it's falling flat. I even called in reinforcements, and it still sucks.

It's been a week since my trip to Hillsdale, and not only are all of the SoBs still here, but I called in a favor with Larinda Scott. Larinda is a great vocalist, but only a fair songwriter. Fortunately, she's good friends with MC Nash, who is a fantastic songwriter, and she talked him into pitching in. If even he can't fix it, it's a lost cause.

It's bad enough that we've stopped working in the studio. Nash headed off into town to grab food, while Larinda's entourage is shopping at the vintage stores on South Congress. Now, it's mid-afternoon, and it's just me and Larinda sitting out by the firepit in a pair of Adirondack chairs. Her multi-colored streaked hair is up in a sloppy bun. She's got her guitar on her lap as she plays around with chords, a notebook open on her knee, and her phone on the arm of the chair so she can do a quick recording of anything she likes.

My own guitar is on the ground at my feet because I've given up trying to write in favor of just staring morosely at Larinda.

Her face is bare of makeup. Even messy and tired, she's beautiful.

She looks up at me, catches me looking at her, and frowns. "What are you thinking?"

I sigh. "How much easier it would be if I could fall in love with you."

She laughs and sticks her tongue out at me. "God. In love with a musician? Been there, done that. Don't kid yourself. It sucks just as much as loving anyone else. Maybe more because you have to hear them sing songs about how they stopped loving you."

I let my head drop back to the chair and stair up at the sky. "When I was fifteen and loved her from afar, she barely acknowledged I existed. I thought that sucked. I was famous and everyone I met wanted a piece of me, but not her. When the band broke up and everything in my life sucked, I thought, okay, this is why it didn't happen then. I was too young anyway. I didn't have my shit together. So, it was okay that she still didn't even know how I felt about her." I tip my head up to look at Larinda. "You know?"

She nods. "Yeah, I do. Sometimes having the right person at the wrong time is harder than not having them at all."

"I think, in some way, everything I've done since the band broke up, all that time I spent in New Mexico getting my head straight. Moving back to Austin and starting Hive Studios. All the planning. All the work. I think somewhere, in the back of my mind, I thought if I could just get my shit together, she'd see I was worth it. That I was worth her."

But now, Larinda is shaking her head. "Nah. That's not how love works. You can't make yourself worthy of love. Love happens regardless of whether or not you're ready for it. The love comes first, then you spend the rest of your life earning it."

I chuckle. "You're pretty damn smart about love for someone who still hasn't had her happy ending."

She waves her hand. "Hi, I'm Larinda Scott, and I'm a romance addict."

We both laugh, but the truth is, I wish I was a romance addict, but I'm not. No, I'm a Gwen addict. And hits of Gwen are a lot rarer.

Before I can say anything else, Larinda gets a text. She reads it, frowning a little, and then stands.

"You know what I think you need? You need to go swim some laps. Clear your head." She waggles her phone. "And I need to call my agent. I'm going to head inside and do that. Give me an hour. Maybe an hour and half? Then we'll try again, okay?"

She grabs my guitar and her own then heads up the path back to the studio. Right before she rounds the bend, she turns back to wave me in the direction of the pool.

I don't have anything better to do than follow her advice, so I head back to the pool house, change into one of the pair of board shorts I keep there, and swim laps. I don't even blast music while I swim. That's how fucking mopey and pathetic I feel. I swim in silence, with only my thoughts to keep me company.

By the time I pull myself out of the pool, shower, and change, my muscles are aching. I'm exhausted but don't feel any better about anything.

I head back up to the studio, my steps slowing when I see some unfamiliar cars in the small lot in front. I don't remember having anyone scheduled in the studio today, but my head is obviously not in the game.

I almost walk past and head up to the house, but Dallas steps out and waves to me.

"Hey, I think you need to see this."

I follow him through the lobby into the control room of studio one. Through the soundproof, plate-glass window separating the two rooms, I see that Larinda and the rest of the guys in the band are all set up with their instruments. Larinda's on guitar. Drew is at his drum kit. Luther has his bass. Josh is at the keyboard. Even little Lola is standing beside her dad, a tambourine in her hand. Dallas is usually lead vocals, but he's here in the control room with me.

I look from him to the vocals booth.

And that's where I find Gwen.

Her hair is up in a ponytail, a mad poof of curls haloing her head. She's got on headphones, her hands holding them over her ears. She's dressed in jeans and a T-shirt with the periodic table on it. It reads, "I'm smart, but only periodically."

When she sees me, she gives me a huge smile and waves, then gives Dallas a thumbs up.

He leans over and hits the mic to talk to her. "Okay, Gwen, you got this."

Luther counts out a beat and the band all starts playing.

The theme to The Brady Bunch.

It takes a few notes to recognize it, but, yeah, that's definitely the theme to The Brady Bunch.

They play a verse as intro before Gwen starts singing. Her voice fills the control room, and she is truly horrible.

Her rhythm is off, and she barely hits any of the notes. But the song lyrics?

The song lyrics are everything.

It's the story of a girl named Wendy,
Who has always been something of a dork.
She was smart, and she knew all the science
From viruses to quarks.

It's the story of a guy named Thomas,
Who had always been too cool for school.
He joined a band, and became even cooler.
Made all the women drool.

Well, then one day, Wendy needed to be rescued

And he got there and saved her just in time.
She's a dork, but even she can see it.
He's the thymine to her adenine.

I can't write songs
So this song sucks
Still it's a way I can say I love you, too.

By the time she finishes, Larinda is wincing and Dallas has his face buried in his hands, he's laughing so hard. Even little Lola has stopped shaking her tambourine to stare in horror at Gwen's singing. Only Drew, jamming away on the drums, seems not to have noticed how bad her singing is.

Well, Drew and Gwen.

She is pumping her fists in the air and jumping up and down like she just won a Grammy.

Then she meets my gaze. Hers is full of questions and hope as she asks, "What do you think?"

I lean forward to the mic. "I think that's the worst, best song I've ever heard."

Through the two sets of soundproof glass, I see her sigh in relief. There's a moment when she seems to be blinking back tears. Then she rips off her headphones and runs out of the booth, through the live room—nearly knocking Luther off his feet—and into the control room, where she throws herself into my arms.

I catch her, picking her up so she wraps her legs around me as she plants a kiss.

It's not a long or sexy kiss, but just the press of her lips, the feel of our breath mingling fills me with a sense of rightness. She grabs my face in her hands and holds me back before I can deepen the kiss.

In the background, I'm vaguely aware of the band and Larinda cheering, but most of my attention is focused on Gwen as she says, "I'm sorry I'm such an idiot. Please tell me I'm not too late."

I let her slide down my body to the ground. “You are right on time.” I duck my head and give her another, slower kiss. “Even if your rhythm is horrible.”

She grins. “Have I never warned you about my horrible singing voice?”

“No. It didn’t come up.”

I kiss her again, because it feels like it’s been a decade since I’ve had my lips on hers. Like I need to learn every nook and cranny of her mouth all over again.

But I’m also aware I have an audience, so I dig deep and find some restraint.

Still in the live room, Larinda steps up to the microphone and asks, “Does this mean you and I can stop working on your song?”

“Yes, please!” I call back, barely looking at her, because I only have eyes for my girl.

My other half.

The rhythm to my harmony.

The peanut butter to my chocolate.

The adenine to my thymine.

CHAPTER 30

GWEN

Needless to say, I feel more comfortable once all the famous people leave me and Tom alone.

For starters, he's the only person I want to be with right now.

For finishers, while torturing some very musically talented people was fun in theory, it is not an experience I want to repeat anytime soon. At least not until I've had the chance to die of embarrassment.

Tom is still kissing me as the band leaves the studio. Drew is the last one out and he makes a lewd gesture that Tom doesn't see but has me cracking up.

Tom pulls back and meets my gaze. "Can I assume you're laughing at something gross that Drew did?"

I nod. "I don't even know what that gesture was supposed to mean, and I don't think I want to either."

Tom dips his head to kiss my jaw. "That sounds like Drew."

"Is he ever serious?"

"Rarely. But you know what, talking about him is not exactly what I want to be doing right now."

My whole body goes on red alert, partly from all the adrenaline pumping through my veins from making my recording debut, but mostly from having Tom's lips on my skin and his hands working their way up under my shirt.

It takes a lot of willpower to plant my hands on his shoulders and say, "Wait. Can we hold on?"

He stills but doesn't pull away. He keeps his mouth on my skin as he asks, "Why? Because if you're going to change your mind, you've picked a really shitty time to do it."

I cup his jaw and nudge him until he looks at me. "I will never change my mind about loving you."

He gives a tiny nod, his eyes closing in obvious relief.

And that about kills me.

It also convinces me that stopping now so we can talk is the right thing to do.

"But I think we need to talk first."

"Nah," he says, starting to pull my shirt off.

I swat at his hands. "Yeah. We do. Or rather, I do." I finally get his hands off me, which at least gives me the strength to step away from him. "You might not need this, but there are things I need to say. Things I need to admit."

He blows out a breath and runs a hand through his hair before nodding.

"I was an idiot and—"

"You don't need to do this. You don't need to grovel."

"I do!" I step back to him and cup his face again. "I was just so afraid. You are this amazing, talented guy, and I didn't know how to believe you could ever love me."

"But I do love you," he says.

I ignore him. "And then I heard that song about the phoenix, and it confirmed everything I feared. Phoenixes are magical creatures. They're not real. They exist only in our imagination."

Now it's his turn to pull my hands away from him. He paces for a minute and then turns to look at me. "You see the irony, right?"

I shake my head. "I don't know that I do."

"Pop stars aren't real either. They're just as magical, just as much an illusion. And if the guy you think you're in love with is Tomás Mendoza, then we still have a problem, because he doesn't exist any more than that phoenix does."

"I know that," I tell him simply. "I was never confused about the difference between Tom and Tomás. I know you're not the slick and glossy pop star. I see you. I know who you are. You're charming and personable and funny, but all that hides anxiety and survivor's guilt. You never ask for anything from anyone without finding a way to pay them back in spades. It's obvious that you and the other guys from the band went through heaven and hell together, and you're somehow still friends. That alone says everything about the kind of person you are. It was never that I didn't see the difference between you and Tomás. It's just that Tom is such a great guy, I still had trouble believing I could deserve him."

"You can't—"

I press a finger to his lips. "Let me explain, okay?"

He nods, pressing a kiss to that finger.

"I didn't know how to trust that you love me. But you know what I do trust? I trust the laws of nature. I trust that when nature leaves a gap in one thing, it creates something else to fill it. There's a reason why the double helix is shaped the way it is. Why thymine and adenine are always paired up. Why cytosine always pairs with guanine. They fit together. They match on a molecular level. They fit together for millennia before we understood how or why. And I think you and I are the same. I think we just fit."

He drops his forehead to my collarbone and breaths deeply. Slowly, in and out. Eventually, I feel him nod. Then he angles his mouth and gives me a soul-stealing kiss.

When he lifts his head, his eyes are gleaming with mischief. "Okay, now can I show you in practical terms all the other ways we fit?"

I laugh. "Yes, but—"

"No buts."

"But we still have so many things to work out. Your home is here, and I have no idea where I'm even going to be living in six months or what I want to do or—"

He gives me another one of those kisses. This time when he lifts his head, his gaze is serious. "We will figure all of that out. If you can't find a job in Austin, or don't want to live here, I'll follow you wherever you go."

"But your studio! You can't leave Hive Studios!"

He smiles. "Hive Studios can be here no matter where I am. It was never meant to be only for me anyway. I've been waiting half my life for you to notice me. I don't ever want to be apart from you again."

That's a pretty hard argument to dispute. So, I don't.

Instead, I let him show me all the ways we fit together.

ABOUT THE AUTHOR

I write the kinds of books I want to read. Fast-paced books with lots of world-building, snarky heroines, and swoony heroes. I love story, pop culture, gossip, and baked goods. I'm a modern-day hippy and certified LEGO nerd.

I live in the Austin, Texas hill country, with my geeky husband and two extremely geeky kids. We have dogs, chickens, cats, and more LEGOs than should be allowed by law. Oh, and I stress bake. So if my characters talk about food a lot, that's why.

Emma Lee Jayne also writes as Rita award winning author Emily McKay.

Find Emma Lee Jayne online:
Facebook: http://bit.ly/3aYlucC
Instagram: https://bit.ly/3523Y3x
Goodreads: http://bit.ly/3aWXAhO
Pinterest: http://bit.ly/3866I1W
Website: http://emmaleejayne.com/

Find Smartypants Romance online:
Website: www.smartypantsromance.com
Facebook: www.facebook.com/smartypantsromance/
Goodreads: www.goodreads.com/smartypantsromance
Twitter: @smartypantsrom
Instagram: @smartypantsromance
Newsletter: https://smartypantsromance.com/newsletter/

Read on for:
1. Sneak Peek of *Not Fooling Anyone series* by Allie Winters, book #2 in the Lessons Learned series

2. Sneak Peek of *Street Smart* by Aly Stiles, book #1 in the Work For It series
3. Emma Lee Jayne's Booklist
4. Smartypants Romance's Booklist

ALSO BY EMMA LEE JAYNE

Love Letters to Tabitha

Tabitha Talbot has too many secrets…

One, she's pregnant. Two, she's been dumped by her long-time boyfriend. Three, suddenly single, she finds herself attracted to one man she can't have—her radio show co-host and confirmed bachelor, Sam Stevens.

Turns out, pregnancy hormones really do make you stupid.

Sam Stevens knows too many secrets…

His life is supposed to be easy and commitment free. The only thing he's supposed to care about his work. But when he finds out Tabitha is pregnant and single, he realizes the one woman he can't have might just be the one he wants.

Too bad he's spent years convincing their listeners—and her—that he never takes anything seriously.

Secrets never stay secret for long…

When their show manager finds out Tabitha was dumped—and she refuses to tell him about her pregnancy—he devices a sure fire way to boost their ratings: the station hosts a contest where listeners write her love letters to win a date with her. When Sam agrees to help his geeky neighbor write a letter to Tabitha, he finds himself telling her how he actually feels about her.

After years of teasing and taunting Tabitha on air, can he convince her he's ready to settle down?

ALSO BY SMARTYPANTS ROMANCE

Green Valley Chronicles

The Love at First Sight Series

Baking Me Crazy by Karla Sorensen (#1)

Batter of Wits by Karla Sorensen (#2)

Steal My Magnolia by Karla Sorensen(#3)

Fighting For Love Series

Stud Muffin by Jiffy Kate (#1)

Beef Cake by Jiffy Kate (#2)

Eye Candy by Jiffy Kate (#3)

The Donner Bakery Series

No Whisk, No Reward by Ellie Kay (#1)

The Green Valley Library Series

Love in Due Time by L.B. Dunbar (#1)

Crime and Periodicals by Nora Everly (#2)

Prose Before Bros by Cathy Yardley (#3)

Shelf Awareness by Katie Ashley (#4)

Carpentry and Cocktails by Nora Everly (#5)

Love in Deed by L.B. Dunbar (#6)

Dewey Belong Together by Ann Whynot (#7)

Hotshot and Hospitality by Nora Everly (#8)

Love in a Pickle by L.B. Dunbar (#9)

Checking You Out by Ann Whynot (#10)

Scorned Women's Society Series

My Bare Lady by Piper Sheldon (#1)

The Treble with Men by Piper Sheldon (#2)

The One That I Want by Piper Sheldon (#3)

Hopelessly Devoted by Piper Sheldon (#3.5)

It Takes a Woman by Piper Sheldon (#4)

Park Ranger Series

Happy Trail by Daisy Prescott (#1)

Stranger Ranger by Daisy Prescott (#2)

The Leffersbee Series

Been There Done That by Hope Ellis (#1)

Before and After You by Hope Ellis (#2)

The Higher Learning Series

Upsy Daisy by Chelsie Edwards (#1)

Green Valley Heroes Series

Forrest for the Trees by Kilby Blades (#1)

Parks and Provocation by Juliette Cross (#2)

Story of Us Collection

My Story of Us: Zach by Chris Brinkley (#1)

Seduction in the City

Cipher Security Series

Code of Conduct by April White (#1)

Code of Honor by April White (#2)

Code of Matrimony by April White (#2.5)

Code of Ethics by April White (#3)

Cipher Office Series

Weight Expectations by M.E. Carter (#1)

Sticking to the Script by Stella Weaver (#2)

Cutie and the Beast by M.E. Carter (#3)

Weights of Wrath by M.E. Carter (#4)

Common Threads Series

Mad About Ewe by Susannah Nix (#1)

Give Love a Chai by Nanxi Wen (#2)

Key Change by Heidi Hutchinson (#3)

Educated Romance

Work For It Series

Street Smart by Aly Stiles (#1)

Heart Smart by Emma Lee Jayne (#2)

Book Smart by Amanda Pennington (#3)

Smart Mouth by Emma Lee Jayne (#4)

Lessons Learned Series

Under Pressure by Allie Winters (#1)

Not Fooling Anyone by Allie Winters (#2)

Out of this World

London Ladies Embroidery Series

Neanderthal Seeks Duchess (#1)

www.ingramcontent.com/pod-product-compliance
Lightning Source LLC
Chambersburg PA
CBHW030620310726
48979CB00003B/807
* 9 7 8 1 9 5 9 0 9 7 4 9 5 *